THE NINTH LIFE

THE NINTH LIFE

A Blackie and Care Mystery

Clea Simon

This first world edition published 2015
in Great Britain and 2016 in the USA by
SEVERN HOUSE PUBLISHERS LTD of
19 Cedar Road, Sutton, Surrey, England, SM2 5DA.
Trade paperback edition first published
in Great Britain and the USA 2016 by
SEVERN HOUSE PUBLISHERS LTD

British Library Cataloguing in Publication Data

Simon, Clea author.
  The ninth life.
  1. Cats–Fiction. 2. Detective and mystery stories.
  I. Title
  813.6-dc23

ISBN-13: 978-0-7278-8571-5 (cased)
ISBN-13: 978-1-84751-679-4 (trade paper)
ISBN-13: 978-1-78010-737-0 (e-book)

All Severn House titles are printed on acid-free paper.

Severn House Publishers support the Forest Stewardship Council™ [FSC™],
the leading international forest certification organisation.
All our titles that are printed on FSC certified paper carry the FSC logo.

Typeset by Palimpsest Book Production Ltd.,
Falkirk, Stirlingshire, Scotland.
Printed and bound in Great Britain by
TJ International, Padstow, Cornwall.

For Jon

ACKNOWLEDGMENTS

Trying something new is always a bit scary, and this book might not have reached completion if it weren't for the encouragement of early readers like Jeanne Powers, Lisa Susser, Naomi Yang, Brett Milano, Chris Mesarch and, of course, Jon S. Garelick. Thanks as well to Vicki Croke, Caroline Leavitt, Lisa Jones, Frank Garelick and Sophie Garelick for all their support and love, and to Ann Porter, who gave me the key to unlocking this story. My agent Colleen Mohyde of the Doe Coover Agency has been unwaveringly supportive, and the wonderful Severn House team of Emma Sudderick, Kate Lyall Grant, Charlotte Loftus, Sara Porter and Michelle Duff have been with me all the way, for which I am exceedingly grateful.

ONE

*A*t first, they were shadows. Bars before the sun, dark against the light. I could make out three: two brown, or mostly, and – in between – a taller figure, black and narrow. Three vertical lines against a dull white sky. But as I watch, they begin to waver, their outlines rippling and losing shape as the light around them dulls into the dusk. Into the mud. Receding from me as I go under. As I, too, begin to fade . . .

No! I gasp, choking, and begin to cough, breaking the surface with a desperate effort. Water in my mouth. My nose. Burning my throat as I gag and spit. I can't see, can't hear anything but my own ragged breath. I have broken through, but I cannot last. The cold is weighing on me, dragging me down . . .

No! I cry in protest, my voice a wordless howl as I fight to stay afloat. Flailing, I gulp in air and swallow water, my last breath exploding from me in another cough. I am going numb. Losing the fight. My own sodden limbs conspiring to drag me down.

No! Hands grab me from behind. Pulling at me, hauling me backward – ducking me. I kick and flail. Find purchase beneath my feet and twist, lashing out. The loose gravel beneath me gives way to dirt, and I scrabble for balance as I turn, ripping myself loose from those hands to glare at the person now before me.

'Whoa.' He steps back. She – I shake the water from my eyes. Her body slim as a boy's, but with the hint of curves. Her hair ragged and short. Dripping, a strange shade of pink. 'Calm down, why don't you?'

I hiss, my throat too raw for words. I don't know this person – this girl – but I have felt the awful strength of those hands. Hands that reach for me now. I jump back without thinking – too exhausted for anything but pure instinct – and feel one foot slide back into the icy flood.

On all fours like a beast, I pull myself out and shake off what water I can, all the while keeping my eyes on the stranger. This girl who now stares back is pale, her face as bloodless as I feel my own to be. Her cheeks wet from the rain, her eyes red. Who is she, and how did she – how did I – get here?

I am panting and I catch myself. Make myself regulate my breathing, needing to jumpstart my frozen brain. I'd been sinking. Drowning in some kind of torrent. A river or whirl-pool. Caught by a sudden flood? Or had I been sabotaged? A victim of . . . No, it is all blank. All I have is what I can now see.

This girl – the pink-haired one – has pulled me from the water. Had she also pushed me in? Children could be evil, though how I could have been so vulnerable stymies me. I struggle to remember. Those figures. Three against the light. None of them had pink on them.

A snort, then a gasp. I look up to see the girl covering her face with fingers bitten to the quick. A moment later, I see why as she makes a fist to wipe those red eyes. She's crying, the rain alone insufficient to camouflage her tears, and for the briefest of moments I regret my wordless anger. Have I hurt her, as I shoved her off? Have I been ungracious to the person who may have saved my life?

I watch her, silent, as she wipes her face on a sleeve too wet to offer much utility. Fourteen, I decide. Fifteen tops. Signs of acne around her nose and the last of her baby fat still rounding out her cheeks, the only place where childhood's softness lingers. It was that hair that had thrown me. Ridiculous color.

'You'd think . . .' She's muttering, more to herself than to me. Her voice is soft. She's self-comforting, rather than addressing me, but the cadence reveals some education. Enough to be at odds with the worn clothing and ragged hair.

I strain forward to catch more. There's something here, but then she's crying again. And one hand shows an angry red welt, where, I fear, I must have scratched her in my frenzy.

I have hurt this girl, this young woman. And all the evidence tells me that she may have saved my life. It was uncivil of me, and I am ashamed. She has sunk to the ground now and is sitting in the mud. The rain has let up, and her sobs are clearly audible over the rush of water. Behind me, I hear the current, the flood, and shiver at the memory of its crushing cold. I look up at my companion. She has wiped her cheek with the back of her hand and a faint smear of blood has been transferred, like warpaint under the pink thatch. She's a child, for all her age, and shivering.

My own body heat has begun to return to normal, and so I drag myself close beside her. She sniffs and turns to me. Puts out one hand gingerly and waits. I lean in, the worn denim of her jeans soft over her skinny leg, and she wraps an arm around me. Shared warmth makes for mutual comfort and a rising tide of contentment begins to rumble through me. Who this girl is, I do not know. How I got here, I cannot yet answer. But as exhaustion takes me, and my eyes grow heavy, I am struck by the oddest of thoughts.

I have begun to purr.

I am a cat.

TWO

wake with a start from a vicious dream. Three figures, their eyes cold, watching me as I sink. No more than that, not that I can recall, and I struggle to make sense of the scene before it fades; of the three figures – men, I am sure – who stand above me. They make no move to help, which does not surprise me. There's malice in their eyes, and I know they are the reason I am sinking. The reason I am . . .

'Hey, you want some?'

I am torn from my reverie by that voice. The girl is extending a dirty hand to me, holding out – can it be? – a chicken wing. The aroma reaches me even as I register what it is, and I realize I am starving. I have never smelled anything more enticing. More *meaty*. I grab the wing from her and, holding it still against the ground, tear at the flesh. It's cold. A day old, I gather, and spotted with what tastes like coffee grounds, sour and dark. I do not care, and make quick work of the morsel, bones and all, growling as I eat. I am too hungry to be embarrassed and find myself licking my paws when I am done, as much to lap up every bit of savory fat as to clean my black fur.

'Hungry, weren't you?'

Famished, I want to say. Instead, I blink up at her. She's still eating her piece: a breast that, unless I miss my guess, had already been bitten into before it was discarded. Something about the tearing of the skin. It doesn't match her mouth, which has a slight overbite. This chicken was discarded. This girl, this child, must be as desperate as I to eat it, and yet she has shared her foraged meal. With me, a cat.

I want to thank her. To ask her name and how she came to be here, alone and hungry as I am. But the limitations of my species hold me back. I push my head against her, a purr once more rising deep within my chest, and catch the hint of a smile. She understands.

'You're welcome, Blackie.' That's not my name, but never mind. 'We're good luck for each other. Don't you think?'

I blink up at her and wait. My silence, I know, will bring forth more of an answer than any question I could have formed. She looks around, a furrow forming between her shadowed eyes, and I take in the bank we are sheltered against: a half-formed cave up a small, steep slope from where the water now lies still and muddy. The rain must have stopped while I slept, protected by the overhang. She peers up, blinking as the sun grows brighter, and my curiosity is piqued. The ledge above us sparkles. Asphalt, drying in the sun. We have sheltered by a road, the cause of my near demise its drainage ditch.

With a leap, I make the ledge. I am warm and dry and have eaten enough, and I'm feeling my strength. But as I raise my head to explore further, hands grab me, pulling me down. It's the girl, and so I sheathe my claws, waiting for an explanation.

'Let me make sure they're gone. OK?'

I flick my tail, annoyed. My senses are more acute than hers, I have no doubt. But since I have no way of asserting this, I simply stare. No, I do not want to meet my attackers again. Those three dead-eyed men. Although the idea that they would lie in wait seems illogical. I was clearly overpowered, overwhelmed by the raging water. Without this girl . . .

She is nervous. I should have noticed. The way she has explained herself to me alone may not say much, but now I see how she has bitten her lip raw. Her tongue darts out to wet it, and I do not think it is hunger that makes her salivate, makes her swallow. She may in truth be looking out for me, but she is concerned about her own safety as well.

Would those three men . . .? No. Whatever their cruel reasons, they were focused on me. She did not figure in that scene, in my dream. Someone else is hunting her. Someone or something has threatened this odd-looking girl who dragged me from the flood and shared her paltry meal. I lack the means to inquire, but one thing I know: I will protect this girl, if I can. With tooth and claw and whatever instincts I possess.

With this resolve, I find myself tensing as she stands to

peek over the ledge. She grips the asphalt, pulling herself up just so, her worn sneakers finding purchase in the dirt. She may think her actions are covert, but that shocking pink crop gives her away. It has dried while I – while we? – slept, to be lighter, brighter and more elevated than before. If anyone is waiting, it announces her before she would choose to make herself known. I am struck by her lack of awareness. Did nobody ever school this child in self-protection? She has courage, of a sort, but if I were training her . . .

'All clear.' She jumps down and turns toward me, reaching out, and I skitter back. She's hurt; her emotions clear on her pale, young face, and for a moment I am concerned that those big eyes, as green as I sense mine to be, will fill once more with tears. But I am no pet to be hauled about by a human. Not even one that I – yes, I realize it's true – trust. She stands, letting her hands fall to her side, as if to deny her original intentions. I know somehow that she sees me as cool, my gaze judgmental. I know, just as surely, that I cannot be influenced by her emotions. What matters is that she learns to mask these lapses. That she learns to survive. Turning from her, I leap up to the ledge and wait while she scrambles up beside me.

'OK, then.' She's licking her lips again. Anxious, now, rather than sad, and from the way her eyes are darting, not entirely sure of her surroundings. Despite the dirt, the water, the cave that sheltered us overnight, we are in the city. Down by the docks, my nose tells me. The smell of fish and rot would be overpowering if I weren't used to it. I know this place, though I do not trust it. There will be prey here, and food to scavenge. But I am not the only predator in this stone and asphalt wasteland. Not the only one to haunt the piers.

We set out, walking along an overpass, a stretch of pitted pavement that bridges the marshy land below. The culvert beside us is now a trickle that runs into a drainage pipe, but the sides of the ditch are steep and worn. Even if I had survived my dunking, I now see I would have been swept out to the harbor. It bothers me that I do not remember how I became immersed, though that memory suggests something other than a hard rain and poor footing.

No matter. I am not one to dwell on what could have

happened but did not. I store away my impressions of the culvert – the pipe, the water. The way erosion has recreated something almost natural here in this urban setting. I look around. A cluster of buildings lie ahead, but I can sense which one the girl is leading me to. It looks empty, its windows dark where the glass has shattered. Somehow, I know it isn't.

A car whizzes by, as large as a tank. The spray of gravel it kicks up catches my hindquarters. I'm stiff, despite that jump. Of course. In retrospect, it seems obvious. I am older. If I were in my prime I would not have been caught last night. Trapped and nearly drowned in the storm drain.

The girl's pace has accelerated, and I trot to catch up in a fashion I realize must seem a tad dog-like. Well, so it is. Despite a certain feline pride, I am not vain. I need to keep an eye on her, my erstwhile savior. There's an edge to her that I do not understand, and I fear for her until it is resolved.

She heads toward the building, clambering over a pile of rubble in her way. I leap to its summit to appraise the situation before following. There's more in the dark than the simple vermin of the waterside locale. Stirring bodies of various sizes announce themselves, to my ears at least. Even in the dim light I see several, the sounds of perhaps a dozen more in rooms beyond. Her entrance as much as the dim sunlight has woken them. With her human senses, she cannot make out all that I do, but she proceeds without fear.

A pale figure rises to her right. He is tall. Big, but not, I think, one of the three I recall. There is something about him that suggests youth, despite his worn face, the grit that accentuates the lines around his mouth. He is less bulky, less stiff than those three – though how I know this, when I only saw them in silhouette, I cannot say. Outlined against the window, he stretches. I suspect we are supposed to find him cat-like, but his movements are exaggerated. He is hiding something in his assumed nonchalance.

'You're back.' I see the question rather than hear it. The boy – young man – who has spoken thrusts his jaw out. He's been hurt. Rejected, I'd say, and I glance at my companion to gauge her response. 'Sorry about . . .' His voice softens. 'About what happened.'

She shrugs, unaffected. Or, no, sad. 'Thanks.' Her voice has flattened from its natural cadences. She is pretending at something with this boy. 'AD around?'

He nods toward the back and she passes him. I follow, keeping my distance, all too mindful of his unclean body. My whiskers bristle, aware of his eyes on me as I pick my way through the broken wall. Aware, too, of the others who have woken with less fanfare and who gather now in our wake.

'Care.' One word, but she looks up. We've entered a back room, she stepping over a pile of bricks, me through a smaller hole in the stove-in wall. The figure addressing her is squatting by an open flame. Like the others, he is rank, stinking of sweat and this close, river mud. Of something else as well. Bitter and sharp, it emanates from the fire and I sink back into the shadows. It's not the flame – although I distrust that blue sprite – it's the odor that offends. The wall behind me is open, the wooden frame holds more worms than plaster, and I leap up to a crossbar for the cleaner air and a better view.

'Want some?' The fire-keeper looks up, shadows playing across his angular face. He's older than the others, his eyes sunken and dark.

Care – could that be a name? – shakes her head, dismissive. This is a conversation they've had before, the details understood. 'I'm here for my things. I'm heading out.' Despite her anger, her tone is tentative, explanatory. This man has some kind of power over her. 'Moving on,' she adds, for emphasis.

'Moving on?' He stirs the fire and the shadows shift. Something else does as well. Care can hear it, too. He's smiling. Mocking her. She holds her silence, though I can feel her tense from here. He wants more. 'You still sore about your old man, darling?'

Your old man? Darling? I recoil. The greasy lout's endearment reeks of possession and entitlement, and my feline sense of propriety is offended at the idea of a creature such as this being the child's love interest. But no, the girl – Care – is shaking him off.

'It's not like he's going to need you.' He tries again. 'He's not going to need anyone to do his dirty work anymore.'

I didn't require the repetition to get his drift, but the speed with which she reacts sets us both straight.

'It wasn't like that.' She snaps, anger doing more than comfort could to rouse her. 'He was teaching me how to be an investigator. I helped him on his cases.'

'Suit yourself.' He turns back to his fire. She has passed some kind of test, the rules of which I do not understand, but she does.

She crosses over to a pile of cinder block and shoves one aside.

'You might want to talk to Tick.'

'Tick?' The girl whirls around. This means something to her. To the others in the space, too. From my vantage point, I sense a shift. 'He's here?'

'Hey, Care.' The watchers part as a small figure comes forward, skinny as a rat with a mop of dark hair that nearly covers his eyes. He nods at her, pushing that hair back, then turns toward me, his hand outstretched. 'Check out the cat.'

I hiss. He stops, mid-reach. He's small, for a human, but I'm not taking chances. Any closer and I'll jump.

'Whoa, kitty. OK!' He backs up, hands raised, but the sparse crowd that has gathered has converged behind him and he must stop. He's watching me, and I him. There's something wrong here.

'Tick, what are you doing here?' Care is talking to the boy – a mere slip of a child, skinny as a wraith – but he keeps staring at me, his dark eyes huge in his thin face. I don't like that direct stare. Never have. My back begins to arch. People. You can't trust them, and this boy is making too much of a fuss. 'Tick?'

'Care!' A girl butts between them, dragging a young man behind her. They're stumbling, impaired. I smell that burning again and draw back, the wet of my nose stinging. The gang leader nods at her, approving. 'She's back,' he says.

'Where you've been?' Now that AD has given his approval, everyone starts crowding around the girl. Everyone except that one boy, Tick. He stands as still as stone, his eyes on me. He must see my fangs. But – no – his dark eyes dart. He is watching the girl beneath his lashes. Watching in silence as his colleagues mill about her.

I will make an experiment. Jumping down, I pick my way through the debris. I saunter past him, over to her. Sure enough, he looks but does not follow. Although his head remains bent, as if he were watching the ground, his eyes follow the girl's actions. Meanwhile, as quickly as it arose, the hubbub has subsided, bodies readjusting in the half light. The couple, giggling, retire to a shadowed corner, while that first boy – young man – looks on. The others gather round the fire, blue flame reflecting off their wide and anxious eyes. The boy stands now in shadow, watching.

The girl has turned her back on all of them. Turned back toward that pile of rubble. She has taken a book, its cover bent and broken, from beneath a brick. Wiping it on her pants, she shoves it into a denim bag. Some clothing follows, as colorless in this dim light as her faded blouse, those worn-out jeans. She pulls the bag up on her shoulder and looks around one final time.

'Tick, what happened?' Her voice is so soft, I wonder if he hears her, alone among the shadows. He's staring at the ground as if willing it to open for him. A child's wish. He can't be more than ten or eleven. 'I thought, since we found your mom . . .?'

He shrugs and seems to shrink, making himself smaller even than he's been. I wrap my tail around myself. No need for further clawing here. Her bag packed, she steps toward him, curious rather than angry. It doesn't matter. He has no fight left in him.

'Talk to me, Tick.' The words sound wrong in her mouth. She's aping someone else. Not AD, though. Someone who stood back, who taught her not to suggest the answers.

Hands in pockets, he turns toward the glassless window. In the weak spring light, his face looks strangely aged for one so young. Gaunt where it should be round, and as hungry as a kitten. Hungry for attention, too, I see. But whoever has instructed Care did so well. She waits, and sure enough, he turns again. Not to face her, but to stare at the ground by her feet.

'Tick?' Her voice is soft. 'Is it the scat?'

He starts to nod then shrugs again, and the movement of his narrow shoulders conveys something to the girl.

'I'm sorry,' she says and reaches for him.

He flinches and she stops herself. 'It didn't work, Care. She tried . . .' He glances up to where the man has gone back to his cooking. Something went wrong there, that much is clear. 'He was looking for you, the old man was. The day before it happened. You know.'

'The old man?' Her voice has tightened. I sense the others listening.

'He had a message. I was supposed to find you. Only—' He breaks off. Kicks at the dirt.

'Tick?' Again, I hear it. A tone that isn't natural to her. She's holding herself back. Thinking of someone else.

He hears it, too. Stands a bit straighter. 'The balance is off,' he says, the words foreign in his mouth. 'The balance, or maybe the scale.'

'Yes?' She's waiting. She must be aware that every creature in the room is watching her now. Everyone except me. I use the moment to survey the wan, rapt faces. Even AD looks up from the burner, his eyes slits.

Tick sighs, and the last of his resistance seems to dissolve as he exhales. 'He said someone is weighing down the scale. That you'd know what to do. That Fat Peter wasn't on the level.'

'Fat Peter?' She's leaning in. 'He said that?'

'Uh huh.' The boy nods. 'He said it was urgent, that I should find you. I figured it was a job. You know, like we used to do, helping him figure out who done what. And since I was back, since my mom – I figured I could do it. I mean, I'm sorry you won't get the coin—'

'The coin?' She explodes, spitting the word out. 'I'm not thinking of the coin. This was a message, Tick. A message. If you had found me, if you'd told me this before, maybe I could've saved him.'

THREE

The response is immediate, and not what I would have anticipated. The girl is angry. Red spots appear high on her pale cheeks. She's gotten loud, her arms up in the air. These signs all communicate that if she had fur, it would be on end. So I brace for an attack. A counter to her accusation.

What I don't expect is the roar of sound. Ears flattened, I wheel to see heads thrown back, their mouths open, exposing black teeth and gaping jaws. Foul breath joins the miasma. They are laughing, all of them – even the couple, who have emerged from the darkness by the rotted stairs. All except the boy.

AD silences them, standing to raise one dirty hand. 'That's good, darling,' he says. He's tall and rangy, his voice too soft for his size. 'I like to see some spunk in you.'

My fur rises, even if hers can't, and I prepare for a leap. I do not know this man but I do not trust him.

'But you should be thanking Tick.' He's moving closer. I gauge the distance. Focus on his eyes. 'If it weren't for him coming back to us, him sticking by us, you might have been there when the old man was offed. You might've gotten it too. Accessory and all that.'

Care had frozen from the noise. Now she shrugs, her shoulders still stiff with rage. I pick up the movement even as I watch the man. She's readying for a fight, too.

'That's not what accessory means, AD.' Her voice is quiet but her jaw is clenched. She cannot help herself, I think. I will her to be silent. To have caution.

'Care and her books. Getting above herself with the old man's investigations.' He turns to the others and gets another laugh. He is showing teeth. His version of a smile. 'Don't know everything, though, do you?'

'Guess not.' She looks down, then over at the boy, and the

moment passes. The softness of her voice and the downcast gaze have appeased AD. I keep my eyes on him. Those teeth. But I sense Tick digging through his clothes – a pocket, a fold. 'Tick?' She senses it too.

'Here.' Whatever he has retrieved, it's heavy for its size. His hand trembles as he offers it up to her. 'He knew I had it.' His words come in a rush, almost a whisper. 'He said I should give it to you.'

He turns, but AD is already there, moving almost silently over the earth floor. He takes the trinket from the boy's hand as if he hadn't spoken at all. I can see its rounded sides, the dull glow where the faint light hits it, the engraving on its flat bottom. But AD must hold it up to the light and even then seems to have trouble making it out. He squints and his mouth draws tight before he tosses it in the dirt.

'Pretty cheap, your old man,' he says, turning back to the fire. I can see the effort it takes Care not to bend, not to scramble for the discarded object. I make my own move, silent and unnoticed in the larger drama, sniffing at the small thing that has rolled to a stop. No scent beyond the boy. And yet . . .

'Your old man had fallen on hard times, Care.' AD keeps talking, his voice flat. 'Used to be, he paid in coin. Used to be, we could keep what we lifted, no questions asked.'

She's staring at the piece and doesn't respond.

'So where are you going, my girl?'

She stands defeated, a new weight on her back. 'Don't know. South, maybe.'

'South, is it?' AD says the word like it's part of a fairy tale. 'Well, you know you always have a home here.'

He laughs, and the gathered crowd begins to disperse. Care has been dismissed, her potential for amusement – or threat? – played out. I watch as she makes her way toward the doorway before following, silently, along what remains of the wall.

'Wait. Care?' It's Tick. He's hung back until AD moved on and now he chases after her as she leaves the inner room, catching her by the ruined stoop. The light is brighter here and I see how sallow his cheeks are compared to the bruises beneath his eyes. How the skin on his lips peels. 'I'm sorry,

OK? It was right after my mom – well, I had just come back here and all.'

'It doesn't matter.' She shakes her head. 'He's probably right. I probably couldn't have done anything. Only, I would've liked to try.'

Tick nods, and I watch, wondering if the two will embrace. Although he had shrunk from her before, there's something like a family feeling between these two, an attachment that explains AD's jealousy.

'He said something else.' Tick looks up at her. 'Something only for you. He made me repeat it. He said there was too much current. That he was looking for other tributaries.'

'Tributaries?' She's quizzing him.

He nods. 'Like in a river,' he says. 'I asked.' He pushes something into her hands. The trinket.

She smiles and pockets it, then holds out her arms. He hesitates, but he goes to her. 'Take care, Tick,' she says once he pulls away. She searches his face, those dark eyes. 'Stay away from the scat.'

He nods again. 'You're not going south, are you?'

Now it's her turn to shrug. 'We'll see.'

I move in, wanting to get a last impression of this Tick, this boy who seems to mean something to the girl. I smell sweat and dirt and, ever so faint, that chemical tang. I glance up at the girl, wondering if she knows. Wondering if it could be from the building, the close quarters. She hasn't picked up on it, I am sure.

'What's with the cat?' he asks, looking down at me. I freeze.

'He saved me,' says the girl. My girl. Care. 'He's my friend.'

FOUR

As a cat, it makes sense that I prefer to be alone. We are not pack animals, despite sharing the same needs as any other mammal. We hunt and thrive on our own. This partly explains why I am glad to be quit of Care's crew: the derelict building and its rag-tag inhabitants serve no purpose in my life, whatever they may have in hers. And while I would not have minded a brief hunt – the morning's chicken is a dim memory – I am content to have moved on. There will be prey aplenty down by the water.

It is all I can do to ignore the stirrings around us as I follow the girl down the road. She, too, is happy to be gone. She's breathing more easily out here, despite the cold and the damp. Her stride has lengthened, even as the broken asphalt gives way to cobblestone. Whatever succor the group gave her has long since expired, and while I can see that she's concerned about Tick – she's glanced back twice – she is fine without the company of her own kind.

Fast, too. A loud rumble as a vehicle comes by, and she's flattened against a wall almost as quickly as I am. Not ducking, not trying to run – her invisibility comes from her stillness, and the machine passes without a pause. Somebody has taught her this much. When we reach the docks, I'll be ready for a break. I hear scrambling in the rubbish we pass, and I'm too hungry to be fussy. But she keeps on walking and I feel obliged to follow. When she stops at the tracks, I want to warn her. The smell of the metal is bad enough. There are vibrations here. Something is coming. Something huge.

I throw myself against her, anxious to push her away. The air is moving, full of steam and grit. Surely she must hear it now. I look up, searching her face, but she is staring down the track. She cannot hear, that much is clear. But she must see the approaching monster. We must retreat. We must . . .

I cannot help it. I howl as she pulls off her jacket and grabs

me, lifting me into the air, binding me. I twist, wishing once
again for the flexibility of youth. She is moving – heading
toward the noise, the approaching beast so loud I cannot hear
my own cries. She holds me firmly, wrapped in darkness, and
I flash back to the day before. To the dream. Could I have been
that wrong about her?

With a desperate effort I arch back, my teeth finding
purchase in the threadbare cloth of her blouse. It is not enough
– she jumps, holding me against my will. Even as I writhe,
we are rising. We are inside the monster – a word comes to
me: *boxcar* – and as the realization of her purpose hits, she
lets me go and stumbles backward, laughing, as I spit and
edge away.

'Sorry, Blackie.' She looks at the rip in her sleeve and pushes
it up, exposing her wiry arm. 'I'm used to hitching, but I
couldn't risk you bolting and getting hurt.'

I am glaring. I know it, but my fur has begun to settle along
my spine. My ears perk up again, even as the floor beneath
us continues to rumble and growl. To regain my composure, I
groom.

'I meant what I said to Tick, Blackie.' In imitation of my
own efforts, she pulls a comb from the denim bag and slicks
her hair back. Her bare forearm, I am relieved to see, shows
no blood. 'You're my good luck charm, and I'm going to need
as much of that as I can get.'

I am, I confess, abashed. Carefully – the train has gained
speed again and its rocking motion is unsettling – I approach
her. She seems to bear me no ill will for my thwarted attack,
and I once again decide that my instincts were correct. This
girl is safe for me to trust. Leaning against her, I fall asleep.

Maybe we both do. She grabs me with a start, her jacket still
on, and jumps again before I can adjust myself in her arms.
The train has left the water's side and landed us somewhere more
dry. I don't believe this is the south of which she spoke. Her
voice was too high when she was talking to Tick. She cares
for him, but she was lying. No, this is another errand, a journey
I do not yet understand. Then I see her take the trinket from
her jacket pocket, and I suddenly do.

The old man. He wanted her to see this, and it matters for that reason. I do not see how a piece of metal can bring back a living creature and I watch her, curious as to what she will do. She turns it over in her hand and I stretch up to examine it once more. She kneels, opening her palm, and I think how very foolish AD was. This item is small, but solid, with a warm glow that makes me consider its value. Flat on one end, with a bulbous top on the other, it is smooth and round and heavy. Perhaps his thoughts were addled by that scent he had been inhaling. Something about Care's reaction makes me think it was evil. He was more intent on maintaining the illusion of control and he knew Care was set on going.

I sniff the piece. Metal holds little scent – the warmth of Care's pocket, the musk of her muddy hand. And, yes, the tang of the smoke, which had permeated the building. I – and I realize how it pains me to acknowledge this – am unsure how to proceed. Unsure of the importance of this piece. I close my eyes, breathing it in.

Measure. The word comes into my mind as if from a dream. I have overheard it, maybe. It matters. And just as swiftly, I am convinced that Care is on the right track. This piece is a step toward something – something that may not want to be found. My whiskers bristle, tingling with anticipation. We are on a hunt. I am not a pack animal, but this girl has saved me. I have senses that she lacks, and if I can be of service to her, I will.

I do not know how much of this she understands, this strange girl. With one hand she reaches out, and I brace. She sees this. She has known violence, too, and draws back. Wordlessly, she rises and – with a glance at me – crosses the scrub of the train yard and heads down a deserted street.

There's much one can learn, walking in silence with another. This girl, for example: she could be a cat. Like me, she hangs to the side, moving from one area of shelter to the next, all the while surveying the road around her for danger or for prey. Some of this has been learned, I can see. The way she holds one hand out – palm flat – as if to signal me before crossing a thoroughfare. Someone did that for her. The old man, perhaps, and when we make the next turn I see why.

'Oi, you!' A large man stands up, tall as AD but broader. He's been leaning on the corner of a storefront, its brick stained almost black by wear and smoke, and now stands astride, blocking the alley that runs back from the street. He has raised his hand as well as his voice and gestures to us. 'You, come here.'

I don't like him. The volume as well as his size bode ill if he so chooses, but she approaches and so I circle round, watching him and keeping the open road in sight.

'I'm looking for Fat Peter.' She speaks up loudly, her chin raised, but she's not using her own voice. She's softened the consonants to mimic him. 'He around?'

'What's it look like?' The big face is clean but sweaty as it nods toward the storefront with its dusty glass. She turns, and so do I. I suspect she's noticing the jumble of items piled within. Some metal, some less solid. Strands of sparkle laid out on faded cloth. An odd conglomeration of wood and wire that makes me think *guitar.* She probably doesn't notice the movements of rodents in the corner or the thin layer of dust that has dulled even the brightest gleam.

'He's not open?' Maybe she has. I sense her hesitation. This wasn't what she expected.

'Got something to sell, have you?' He senses it too and leans forward, reaching for her. 'Maybe you're the delivery, huh?'

She twists away even as he grabs for her arm. He just laughs as she jumps back, stopping to glare. 'Get over yourself, girl.' He wipes his hand on his coat. 'You're too skinny for my taste, anyway. But if you were looking for a buyer for anything else, I'd move on. Fat Peter hasn't been trading with the likes of you for a while now. He's got better sources, better product coming in than your dockside scat, and you rats are as likely to steal from him as bring him custom. I bet you bite, too.'

His leer is cruel, and I circle closer. If he bends toward her, his broad white face will feel my claws.

'I've got a message for him.' She's standing her ground, chin up, those green eyes defiant. 'Something he wants.'

'I doubt it, but suit yourself.' He nods, and I realize then that he has been standing guard over the alley, the real entrance to the business within. Trying not to touch him, she squeezes by the big man to enter the narrow passage beyond. He's still laughing when I zip past him, following the girl. 'You the rat catcher, now?' he calls after us. She doesn't respond.

'You're here. Good.' Down the alley and she stops, turning to address me. I pause, waiting. 'Don't let him catch you.' She glances back at the ruffian. 'He's nasty.'

I blink up at her, grateful that she has seen what I have too. Perhaps she knows how I ended up in that culvert. I cannot find a way to ask, however, and she has moved on. There's a door in the alley – painted wood set in the brick. She jiggles the handle as I sniff at the corner, where the paint has worn away. The wood is rotten and damp.

'Hello?' Either the door has given way or she has found a way to jimmy it – I think this girl knows some tricks. 'Mr Peter?'

Her voice falls flat in the dark and she steps inside. 'Hello?'

I hesitate. The scent of dust and mouse droppings that billowed out when first she opened the door has been replaced by a stronger aroma. Heavy and sweet and—

'Anyone there?'

I want to bolt. To run fast and low for the river. To find a cranny in the rocks and squeeze in there, glaring at the world until it goes away. I hear the growl rising in my throat and raise it a notch. Surely this girl must notice. Surely she must smell what I do. Discern what I have already deduced.

'Mr Peter? I—' She reaches in and finds a switch. The flat blue-white fluorescents highlight the lazy swirl of dust our entrance has disturbed.

A quick intake of breath. A stumble, as Care steps backward, toward the door. She doesn't scream, this girl. She's come up hard and learned well. She doesn't panic or draw attention to herself – even when she finds a body, lying dead upon the floor.

FIVE

This girl is not a cat. Her actions may be better disciplined than what most humans would display. They are not seamless, however – nor are they silent. Now that we have identified the source of the odor, I step forward to examine it, but she has lost her balance. Although she tries to remain silent, she steps back – into a low table. Like the rest of the room, it is covered with clutter, and her weight, slight as it is, sends the items piled there crashing to the floor.

I wince. The noise is startling, especially considering the size of the objects. Three cylinders – round, with bobble tops – have hit the worn wood floor. They are of various sizes, and the thuds with which they land make them seem bigger than they are. I have only had a moment to examine the odd angle of the man's neck and the blow to the head that undoubtedly bent it so – but I am curious about these objects.

'Oi, what's that?' The door swings open. The alley guard stands silhouetted in its light. 'You – girl!'

He steps into the space, dwarfing it further, and Care cringes. In the moment this has taken to happen, I have surveyed the scene. There is much more here I would like to inspect: the dead man's hands, their fingers curled and white. The scuffmarks on his shoes, which bear traces of dried mud. And those cylinders, which Care's backward scuffle have just sent rolling again.

I am just sniffing the largest of the three – its cold metal surface holds very little scent beyond the dust and oil of the room – when I am interrupted. Care has grabbed me, hoisting me about the middle, and clutches me close. She is retreating, sidling along the wall of shelves and doesn't understand that she is endangering us both by restraining me.

There is no time to be gentle. I twist in her grasp, hissing and spitting. She holds tight until I kick free. I feel my claws rip through her too-thin jacket, but there is nothing for it now.

That kick has given me the leverage I need to launch myself on the attack. Ears back, jaws wide, I fly at the alley guard's face, enjoying for that brief moment the look of horror that I see. This is not my usual process. I would rather explore and understand, keeping myself to the shadows. This is, I assume, a function of my feline nature. Still, this man is a bully. Violence comes off him like a stench, and I take pleasure in my role.

Even as I land, my body mass nothing compared to his, I am in control. With fang and claw, I assault the soft parts of his face until one large hand takes hold of my tail and throws me to the ground.

I hit hard, twisting just in time to land on my feet and jump before his boot comes down.

'Blackie!' I can't risk a glance. This big man is furious, his pink face bleeding, and I brace myself for another leap. I have succeeded in my primary objective. I have diverted him, making him turn. There is a clear path between the girl and the door, but I will have to be quick to avoid taking his wrath on myself. He glares, and I wait, panting. As the faint stiffness in my hindquarters reminds me, I am no longer young, and the last few days have taken their toll.

'Unh!' A loud thud, and with a grunt, the big man stumbles forward. Behind him stands the girl, a black leather-bound volume in her hands.

'Run!' She doesn't try to pick me up again but watches as I veer toward the open door, following me as I clear the alley and turn down a street of broken cobblestones. I am running without thought but not without purpose. The scent of leather, of horses long gone, beckons, and a phrase – *Farrier Lane* – comes to me as I race, her steps behind me. I hold the pace, panting, desperate to recall another scent. A landmark.

There it is – a heady whiff of tar. Another turn and we are back to the scrubby brush of the no man's land. She hesitates only briefly as I dash across the tracks. Of course, her dull hearing cannot reassure her that no train is drawing near. But she lets me set our course as I lead her down the verge and into an area of broken stones and trash. I do not believe she has injured the man from the alley, nor would that blow have hindered him for long. But I neither hear nor smell any pursuer, and so at last I slow, my breath coming hard, and collapse behind the shell of a car, a rusted carcass arcing over a patch of dry ground. She slumps down beside me in this man-made cave, still clutching the leather-bound volume, and places one warm hand on my heaving side.

Immediately she pulls it back, catching herself with alarm. But I am no longer the hissing, spitting demon of the pawn shop. I turn to her, something like a purr starting up deep inside me despite my still-labored breathing. I acted to save this girl, and did so. But she has once more rescued me.

I think back to how she attacked. Choosing a weapon, a moment, and making her one shot count. What's more, she did so without giving warning, without betraying herself, despite what must have been considerable emotion at the time. I look at this girl, her pink hair now falling across that pale and dirty face, and I think again that somebody has trained her well.

'You would have liked him, Blackie.'

I blink. Our thoughts have run on parallel tracks, like those we jumped a few minutes before. That is all.

'And he would've liked you.' She releases the book, that unlikely weapon, and wipes her face with the back of her hand, tears making trails through the grime. The other hand still rests on my back, and under its warmth I feel myself drifting toward sleep.

'The way you went for that creep – I felt like you were protecting me. Silly, huh? But I'm glad you did it.'

She sniffs, and I relax. She is talking to herself as much as to me. To her former mentor, the one who died. Wiping her face one more time, she reaches into a pocket, and I perk up. It has been hours since that chicken, and I have not had the opportunity to hunt. When she draws out a dirty rag and blows her nose, I slump back beside her, hoarding the warmth of our bodies against this hard, cold cave. As soon as I have rested, I can remedy my lack. Here in this urban wilderness, there is prey to be had. Not the songbirds. Their spring calls may taunt me, but even as my eyes close, I can tell they are out of reach in my current condition. I need something I can stalk.

And I need rest. I am tired. I cannot remember ever being so tired. 'I wonder what happened to Fat Peter?' Her sniffling has slowed, curiosity replacing the shock. Her voice grows softer, too, as fear gives way to fatigue, and she shoves the rag back into her jeans.

I begin to drift, dreaming of meat and cream. Of eating my fill and sinking back. Sinking . . .

The balance is off . . .

'Or should I say who?'

With a start, I come awake. Haunted by an image: the three figures, dark against the sky. The world is not my friend, nor this girl's, apparently. I have been lucky. I cannot count on such luck twice.

The girl isn't sleeping. I see her eyes are open and staring into space. Still, my memories have banished drowsiness, and I prepare myself for the hunt. To run again, if need be. We are small creatures in this world, this girl and I. There is much that I would share with her, if I could.

'I mean, if he was giving short count, it could have been anyone. But . . .' Her voice trails off where I cannot follow. Reliving the scene we have just survived, perhaps. Remembering the old man, or thinking, as I am, of food. No matter. One of us must act. I must hunt.

I had to have been a young cat once, but I cannot remember those days, now. My breathing has regulated but I still feel where I was grabbed. My hind legs are sore. I begin to wash, as if the rasp of my tongue could reach the aching joints beneath the fur.

The girl shifts as I do, reaching into her pocket once again for that rag. But as she blows her nose, I see that the movement has dislodged the rest of her pocket's contents. Two coins spin and flatten on the ground. As she reaches for them, close-bitten fingernails scraping them off the dirt with difficulty, a heavier object falls free. The oddly shaped weight that Tick had handed over, the smaller cousin of the cylinders in Fat Peter's shop.

I remember how they hit the floor when Care backed into the table. How their heft had made a solid thud and yet how they had moved, following a circumscribed path from her feet across the boards. I had no time to examine them, to make more than the most cursory observation of that room or its too-still occupant. All I had was that motion. The movement and the sense of weight. This one isn't moving now, though, and so I paw at it, making it roll on the uneven ground.

'Look at you, Blackie. Just like a kitten.' I pause, annoyed. This girl is missing something. Not seeing the importance of the heavy cylinder. Then I smack it, once again, rolling it into her leg.

'You want to play?' She picks it up and I lose hope. If she tosses it for me, I will simply leave. Go find some grubs or a day-blind vole to ease my hunger. But as she does, I see her focusing. Her brows go up and she turns the piece over in her hand, drawing it close to examine the engraving on its flat bottom.

'M,' she reads. 'I think it's an "M," it's in a circle with some kind of design.' She squints and tilts it toward the light. 'Yeah, M. Must be the manufacturer, or maybe it means "metric." One milligram?' she reads, hefting it in her open palm. 'Funny, it feels heavier to me.' She bites her lip while she's thinking, so preoccupied that I can stare right at her. 'Where did Tick . . .' Her voice trails off and I lose hope. If all she can connect this to is that sad boy, I will take off. She has saved me, twice, but I have done all I can. Perhaps our paths will cross again.

'This came from Fat Peter's,' she says at last, a strange energy invigorating her voice. 'It's one of Fat Peter's weights, the ones he uses when he buys. You don't think . . .' She's looking right at me now, but I don't flinch. She's on the right track, I am sure of it, and I blink slowly so she will know that I approve.

'I was supposed to go there, you know. My teacher – the old man I worked for – wanted me to follow Fat Peter. That's what Tick's message meant. We were tracking some street artists – real pros, he thought – who had knocked over a store downtown. They'd taken a fancy necklace – a showpiece, the old man called it. It was probably broken into loose stones. Emeralds, he said. Those are easier to move, and Fat Peter, well . . .'

She pauses. I am beginning to lose interest. The piece in her hand means something. It is real. Solid. But she is talking about people who are gone, and I am hungry. I turn away. There are people out there I do not trust. Men who have hurt me and would hurt her too. Do I dare leave her?

'Blackie, I had a thought.' I think of fish. Of something squirming in the mud of the culvert. 'That message . . . maybe it wasn't shorting someone that got Fat Peter killed, after all. Maybe it was someone who came by looking for work, someone Fat Peter would have seen as easy. A mark.' She bites her lip. Looks at the weight though I do not think she sees it. 'Could Tick have done it?' She isn't asking me. 'Could Tick have killed Fat Peter?'

SIX

S ize does not equal lethality. I am not boastful, but I have no doubt that I am a better hunter and a neater killer than this girl who now sits beside me, her green eyes wide. Likewise, although I doubt that pale child we left at the abandoned building could have taken down the adult male we found at the pawn shop, I cannot completely discount the possibility. Not when I see how Care hefts the piece in her hand – how solid it is. How heavy and cold.

What I do know is that neither of us is thinking clearly right now, and that I have the means to remedy this.

I rise, stretching, and consider my options. Although I had previously noted the signs of prey in the vicinity, I also consider scavenging. This girl must eat as well, and I doubt she has taken anything since the scraps she shared with me. Unlike her, I have the freedom of moving relatively unseen. I could, for example, head back across the tracks. Human habitations offer the best chance of edible scraps, and I can move among them with barely a notice. The brute in the alley would be an exception. He is not someone I would choose to encounter, but he is not seeking me.

I picture Fat Peter's shop, the jumble of objects that I had hoped to examine. Unless you consider the prematurely bloated corpse, I cannot picture anything edible there, nor do I remember any scents other than dust and sweat and a faint metallic tang. And yet, the memory intrigues me and I conjure it in my mind. There was the work surface – a table of some sort – that Care had bumped into. The walls had been lined with shelves. Even the display window had been obscured by shelves, and I had sensed no bolt holes in the old floorboards. Still, the man had clearly liked to eat. And why else would his workplace interest me?

'What is it, Blackie?'

Care is looking at me, and I realize my ears have gone wide

and flat, as they do when I am thinking. Perceptive girl; I can see why someone took her in.

'Is it this?' She holds out the weight, which I lean in to sniff. Nothing, not even the scent of death, has remained on its cold metal surface. She may as well have left it, or returned it to that ragged boy who worries her so. The boy who, most likely, nicked the heavy trinket on some earlier visit.

A boy who was either welcomed in by Fat Peter via that locked front door, or, more likely, had run the same gantlet we did. I look up at Care, wondering how much of this she has realized. We smaller beings do tend to be sharper than the brutes of the world. Still, it may not have occurred to her, as it has, belatedly, to me. The shop we had visited was locked and dark. The alley guard had let us in and nearly trapped us there. If Care – if anyone – had been alone, he very well might have. But he hadn't stopped whoever had come in to kill Fat Peter. He hadn't stopped him – or her – either coming or going.

'I've got to talk to Tick, Blackie.' She's rolling the cylinder around in her hand. 'I don't know if he knows anything, but this came from Fat Peter's. Maybe he saw something – or someone.'

My ears go back. She's not thinking clearly.

'I know Tick.' She's staring into the distance, her eyes unfocused. 'Fat Peter was a creep but Tick's not a killer. If he didn't kill our foster father after what that creep did, well . . .' She turns to me. 'He spoke to the old man, Blackie. He might have been the last person to do so. I need to find out exactly what he said and more – what he looked like, what he *sounded* like. You know?'

I don't. Such loyalty is nonsensical. It serves no purpose. The old man is dead, and were he not, I would scratch him for sending her to the pawn shop. For putting her in danger.

'He always said that everything could be a clue.' She's still talking, which is good in that it means she has not yet left – has not yet resolved to leave – our safe haven by the tracks. 'The way a person speaks as well as the words he says. He'd have been pissed that I didn't look at Fat Peter's clothes or anything while I had the chance.'

No, but I did. Beneath the metallic tang of blood I can still smell the dust and sweat. The pungent smoke and the life-rich river mud on his shoes. All of this I would tell her, if I could. Anything to keep her from returning to that place of death, from confronting the dirty waif who is somehow involved. If only I knew how.

My whiskers bristle with the effort, obscuring even the pangs of hunger. I have lived a long life for one of my kind; the scars on my hide as well as the stiffness in my joints tell me this. A long life alone, but there is something compelling about this girl. Something beyond an imbalance in the scales.

Scales. The word echoes strangely in my head. Of course, the cylinder. Although I do not know how, I can see Fat Peter as he must have been, big belly pressing against the table and his white hands surprisingly delicate as he moved first one then another of the rounded weights. And lastly the smallest – the one Tick found a way to pocket. He is turning toward me. He is talking.

'There she is! Oi!' I wheel around, cursing myself for my distracted state. The guard from the alley is standing on the verge, pointing. Care and I are trapped.

SEVEN

I don't freeze. I react. Only my default response – inflating my size with fur and spit – doesn't have much effect on the man coming over the verge. Red-faced and furious, my scratch marks still showing raw on his slab-like cheeks, he stares down at me. He raises his boot and I know again what it is to face my death.

'No!' Something hits the side of that meaty head hard. The metal cylinder, expertly thrown, falls to the ground beside me, and the ruffian above me stumbles and goes down. I don't need more of a cue and zip up the slope, my claws gaining purchase on the loose soil as he roars behind me. There's a patch of scrub a hundred yards off, past another automotive carcass and a corrugated metal shed, but I hesitate. I can no longer rely on speed. As I pause, Care pulls herself up close behind me, until a hand grabs her ankle and she kicks it off, scrambles to her feet and starts to run again.

'Blackie!' She looks for me and pauses – a bad move, because as she does, another man appears. The brute in the gutter is still howling but the newcomer ignores him, coming up fast and silent.

I can't wait. Neither of us can, and so I take off, heading for that scrub and trusting that Care will have the sense to do the same. Only as I approach do I realize how useless it is. I can dive under the brambles, make myself compact and hidden. She cannot. And by the looks of our pursuer, a few thorns will not be enough to dissuade him.

'Care!' A whisper – almost a hiss – makes her pause. Makes her turn. I slide to a stop, a good few lengths from the brambles. I don't want to see her taken. I do not hope for the impossible. 'This way!'

It's the boy. Tick. He's crouched beside the shed and is gesturing, calling her over. With a glance at me – for confirmation? assent? – she turns and follows, ducking down low

behind the second wreck in the hope that the men will not
notice her change of direction. In a moment, she is gone. But
the big man has rejoined the chase, passing his smaller
colleague. And I am seeing the distance between our pursuers
and myself close. With the girl out of sight, I am less likely
to be in danger. Even the big man is more likely to chase her
down than follow me, although I have no illusions about the
grudge he holds against me – or the cruelty of which he is
capable. I should bolt.

I do. I follow Care and the boy around the shed and see
that he has ducked into a dark opening beneath the train bed.
It's a pipe – a drainage pipe – and my blood runs cold. I
gasp and feel the pressure again – the water that flooded my
mouth and my nose. The cold.

'They went that way!' Care's quick turn – the rusted-out
wreck – they have not been enough. The red-faced thug is
lumbering toward me, his colleague close behind. The choice
has been made. Ears flat, heart racing, I dive into the pipe,
my claws scrabbling on the rusted metal. 'This way!' Their
voices echo in the enclosed space, surrounding me. I am tired,
and I am old. And they are getting louder and closer. I hear
one of them dive into the pipe. The big man – he blocks the
light and I can smell him: blood and rage. But he has to crouch
to enter and that slows him, and even as he reaches for me
he stumbles, his bulk overbalanced as he hurries half bent. He
catches himself with a curse, but it is too late. I have reached
the far end and I am out.

'Blackie!'

I blink, taken aback by the light and pause, panting. I do
not know this place. I do not know its safe spots. Then I see.
Off to the right, Care is running, the boy before her grabbing
her hand. But even as she runs, she has turned to call for me.
She sees me and I am heartened, her voice giving me breath
enough for a last dash.

With long strides, flying low to the ground, I catch them as
they duck into an alley. Close on their heels, I follow as the
boy guides Care around a corner and then to an open door.

I freeze. The doorway is black and low, leading to a basement. I am too winded to scent properly. There is water here

and mold, and something more. I remember the furtive way this boy avoided Care, the odd scent coming off him, and I will her to look at him. To see what I see and to question.

Too late. She follows him down. The pounding of feet grows louder. I dart down behind them and wait, listening to the three of us breathe.

'Tick, what happened? How did you find me?' Several minutes have passed. The footsteps have faded. My eyes have adjusted to the near total dark, and I have grown calmer.

We are in an open space with a dirt floor. Fresh air blows in from the cracks in the far wall. The puddles are rainwater, old and dank but clean enough. I drink my fill, even as Care reaches blindly for the boy.

'Tick, are you there?'

'Hang on.' A hiss and there's light. He's brought a candle – or found one – here in this empty space. 'Care, are you all right?'

'Yeah, thanks.' She smiles at him but she knows better. 'So what's with that, Tick? Tell me.'

The boy turns to stare deeper into the room. He can't see me in the darkness but I can make out the sadness on his thin face. The hunger and something more, something feral.

'I didn't do anything, Care. They knew.'

I hunker down to watch, my ears alert.

'They?' Care makes herself wait. I can hear the strain in her voice, but it pays off.

'Those men – they knew you'd found Fat Peter. They . . . I didn't know, when I told you. When I gave you the weight. Honest.'

She nods. There's more. 'And?'

'AD made me go with them. Told them I could find you. That I would.' He stops and bites his lip.

Care reaches for him, but instead of an embrace she simply takes his hands, turning them over in her own. 'Oh, Tick.' Her voice is sad, out of proportion, I think, to the minor burn marks that stripe his fingers with red welts.

'It's just . . . I get so hungry. But I didn't give you up. Honest, Care.' He's talking more quickly now. He has surrendered some truth to her. 'Not for scat, not for anything. Don't call the services on me, please, Care. The old man really did come to me, only . . .'

Care looks into his face. She is still holding his hands. 'Why did the old man want me to follow Fat Peter, Tick? You have to know more.'

The boy shakes his head. 'He said you would. That it was a lead, like the weight.' A shrug. 'I'm sorry, Care. Really, I am. When I realized what was happening . . . That they wanted to frame you . . .'

He sniffs and Care leans in to embrace him, for real this time. He doesn't pull back as he has before. Instead, he falls against her, crying easily like a child, and she coos like a much older woman as she rocks him back and forth. Outside, the day is fading, and I suspect that these children will both sleep soon. But now that I have drunk, I am aware again of hunger. Dusk was made for hunting, and so I slip by them, invisible in the darkness, to peer out of the doorway.

The city is quiet here and I can hear the rustling of rodents. The few human footfalls have slowed to a walking pace. Still, I slink down the alley, my body low, my dark fur hidden in the shadows. And there I see them, the two who hunted us – the smaller man and the brute with the bloody face. It is dark here in the shadows, and their eyes do not work like mine. Even as they crane around, I do not worry about them seeing me. I can watch them here in peace.

And so I do, piecing together the histories revealed by their voices and their clothes. The stories told by their scents and the way they hold their bodies. They are waiting, and so I wait too, even as my stomach growls in protest.

Their voices rise in greeting as a third figure walks up to join them. A tall man, in finer clothes, nods at their greeting and turns to survey the scene. He cannot see me, any more than they could, and yet I freeze, my breath seizing up inside me.

I know this man. I have seen him, standing on the shore as I was drowning.

EIGHT

I will not flee. I have been a hunter long enough to know how motion draws the eye, and the thought of these three spying me, alone, in this alley makes my fur rise. As it does, I sink low, to listen and to watch.

'Talk to me.' The newcomer – the one I recognize – doesn't waste words. His voice has the tone of command, and his two colleagues exchange a nervous glance.

'It's all good, boss.' The red-faced hoodlum, the one I've scratched, is trying to sound confident.

'Really.' It's a question. Even I hear that, and the two look at each other in panic. The newcomer doesn't see this. Doesn't have to, I assume. He's bending over a match as he lights a cigarette. The brief flare of sulfur reaches me as it catches. More interesting is the quick glimpse I catch of his face, the deep lines around a wide mouth. He'd be handsome were he not marked by his cruelty.

'Fat Peter's not going to squawk to anybody. Not anymore.' The red-faced one again, trying to bluff. 'Randy and I took care of that.'

'And?' The boss releases a cloud of smoke in the brute's face.

'The girl showed up, acting like she knew him. Maybe he tried to turn her out.' My ears flip forward. They are talking about Care. 'Maybe he did.'

'That would be most fitting.' He pauses to pick a fleck of tobacco from his tongue. I find the gesture cat-like and most disturbing. 'If you had her.'

'Not a problem, boss.' The other man, Randy, has a face like a rat I met once. He looks up at his boss, like some dog expecting to be hit. 'We'll get her – Brian and me will. AD's sent the boy to her. The boy will find her – and he'll rat her out. He'll do it for nothing, for a hit of scat. He's got a taste for it, he has. From his mama. Then me and Brian will take care of the rest.'

* * *

My instincts are good, but at times I must fight them. I want to run. To seek Care out and make for safety. To take her away from that child who would betray her. Tick – this Randy must be speaking of the boy who led her into that basement. Led her, I now see, into a trap. Rat, indeed. My tail twitches at the word.

But they are still speaking, and I cannot risk rousing their attention by my movements. Stilling my tail – how unnatural that feels – I begin to back away, ever so slowly. And stop myself as realization dawns. I cannot afford to miss any of their planning. How they decide to spring this trap may be vital to avoiding it.

'The boy will come back,' Randy is explaining. 'AD sent him with us, 'cause he knows her. They ran away together, he said. He took them in at the same time.'

'Yeah? And how can you be so sure he'll rat her out?' The red-faced one has his bluster back now that someone else is on the hot seat.

'She took off without him,' Randy says, pulling a pack of cigarettes from his jacket. 'Besides, he needs the stuff.'

'Good work.' The boss extends a match, its flash highlighting Randy's rodent face. He takes the light, his thin cheeks sucking in to get his gasper started. But even as he inhales, his eyes dart up to the boss man. He's smoking to calm his nerves as well as his fraying lungs. The muscle popping along his jawline . . . the way his forehead is knitted. Signs of tension. He's doing the boss's bidding but he is still afraid.

'Buck up.' The boss has taken a flask out of his coat. He's seen it too. 'Your service won't be forgotten.'

As they pass the flask around I begin to back away again. I don't know how long I'll have until they descend on the girl. Nor do I know how I'll get her to leave the boy. All I can be sure of is that I have to try.

'Tell me again.' Care is talking as I slink back in, her voice soft but direct. 'Use his exact words.'

'I did, Care. Honest.' The boy whines, tired, but I have no sympathy to spare. '"Too much current," he said. He was looking for "other tributaries."'

Care stares as if she could see through him. I think she is seeing someone else. The old man, the one she misses.

'You knew where he meant. Where he wanted me to go.' It's a statement, not a question, but the boy shrugs an answer. 'You gave me the weight.'

Another shrug.

'Why were you at Fat Peter's, Tick?' Her voice has grown softer. 'Did AD send you? He didn't want you to—'

'No!' He interrupts her, speaking too loudly for the quiet space. 'No. AD wouldn't. He knows what happened in the home. Besides, he doesn't deal in skin anymore.'

The way Care's eyebrows lift, I think she is going to argue. I don't blame her. Preying on smaller animals is the nature of things, although there's little meat on this boy.

I'm a bit surprised when she picks up on another of the boy's words. 'Not anymore?' she asks. 'Why not? What's he got going – and what's AD got you doing in it?'

'Deliveries. The usual.' The boy looks up, his face unreadable. 'You haven't been around much, Care. You don't know. Things have gotten bigger. AD's gearing up for more business.'

'Not with Fat Peter. Not anymore.' She sits back and I see my chance. She may be mulling over the connection between these two predatory men. I'm more concerned about the boy. About the men who are waiting less than a block away. I leap to the ground beside her feet, intent on making myself understood.

'Fat Peter must've been working with someone. Someone bigger.' She smiles at me as she says it, pleased with herself for working this out. I close my eyes in satisfaction – and start as I feel hands on my body.

'Ow!' The boy falls back, his wounded hand in his mouth. 'I thought . . .'

'He's a street cat, Tick.' Care is looking from the boy to me. For good measure, I hiss. 'And you grabbed him.'

'I just thought he looked . . . never mind.' The boy examines his hand. It is barely bleeding. 'He doesn't like me.'

'He doesn't know if you are going to hurt him,' Care corrects him and pauses, as if she would say more. I cannot resist another blink of satisfaction. Whether I've put the thought in her mind or not, I'm proud of her. 'So, Tick. You still haven't answered my question. What were you doing out here today?'

'AD sent me.' His head is bent as if he were addressing his injured hand.

'Tick?' Care hears him. I can tell. Like me, she's not content with the answer.

'He told me to go find Brian – he's the bruiser – and do whatever he wanted.'

'And he wanted . . .' She waits. He's staring at the ground, his chin on his chest. 'Tick?'

Nothing, but she's no fool. 'The way I slipped by him – the big guy. What's his name – Brian? That was supposed to happen, wasn't it?' She's talking to herself. I can almost see her thinking. 'He let us go into the shop. He knew Fat Peter was dead all along. He wanted us to find him. He wants us to take the blame.'

She's got it – all but the last step. I'm waiting for the boy to bolt. To signal the men outside. Unless they're already on their way.

I approach him slowly, the low growl rising in pitch as I get closer.

'Blackie.' Care reaches for me, to draw me back, and stops. 'Tick – you were sent to bring me back, weren't you? Or did you—' She jumps to her feet, heading for the door, but I'm a move ahead. I've leaped into the doorway and stopped, frozen. There's nothing. No motion. I look up at her and she turns back into the basement.

'Tick?'

'Don't make me go back, Care. Please.' He's staring up at us, his misery clear in the last of the twilight. 'I don't trust those men, and AD – he's . . .' The tears are flowing freely and I feel Care hesitate. My tail lashes as I take in the street. Soot and ash. That hint of tar from the tracks nearby. Rain, again. But the smell of men and cigarettes has grown faint and far away. And so I sit, wrapping my tail around my feet as Care descends.

'They're not . . .' She pauses. Swallows to keep her voice steady. 'Are they coming here, Tick?'

He shakes his head vigorously, looking up at her. 'This is

my place, my secret. I used to come here when my mom was bad.' We both watch him. Even if he believes this to be true, the basement could still be a trap. 'I've got food here, even.'

He pulls himself to his feet and heads for the wall, where a loose brick reveals a cubbyhole and a plastic bag. The bread he pulls out has mold on it, but he brushes it off and hands it to Care like a prize. She takes it with a nod and, when he pulls out the pizza slices, a full-on smile. To do her justice, she looks for me, but I've seen how hungry these two are. And I know I can do better.

The rain has started up again as I head back out. The men on the corner have dispersed to warmer, drier parts to wait for Tick and Care. I can sense no sign of them, and so I set about getting my own dinner. I don't believe they have given up. They are waiting for the boy, or to stage their own attack. But tonight I am a hunter, too.

NINE

I get back later than I intend, having spent more time than anticipated stalking my prey. Age has definitely begun catching up to me. Age or my recent trauma, leaving me less adept at certain forms of hunting. Almost I feel like I am unused to this mode of survival, as if perhaps I were a house pet or something of that ilk. But when I found my prey's lair – a small, fragrant opening gnawed through a wooden base-board – I felt like myself again. Watching, waiting – this was what I knew how to do. And the results? Delicious.

I had thought about sharing my dinner with the girl. Bread and pizza lack the essential nutrients to be found in fresh meat. However, I am hungry enough that my meal is gone before I can decide, and thoughts of who else might share my interest in these two children drive me back to the basement room before I can obtain more. I need not have worried. Only Care and the boy are there, curled around each other like kittens, their breathing soft and even. I consider joining them, sharing the superior warmth of my body on this chill spring night. The thought of sleeping within reach of that boy, however, keeps me distant and alert, as the rain peters out to be replaced by moonlight thin as watered milk.

'Care, no.' I wake to the sound of an argument. Hushed but determined, the girl and that boy are facing off as they share the ends of the bread. 'Don't make me.'

'You have to.' She gestures with a piece of bread before dunking it in a chipped mug of water. 'Think about it. They expect you. They're waiting. And I've got to find out who they are.'

'But Care.' The boy looks miserable, and the way he's kneading his own lump of bread makes me suspect he's off his food as well. 'They're dangerous. I know it. And if I get caught they'll call in the services.'

'I'm not going to let protective services take you. I promise, Tick.' She chews the bread. Clearly, the soaking hasn't done much to soften it. I can see her jaw working from across the room, the muscle visible under her thin cheek. 'But the way I see it, this is all tied up with the old man. I mean, he wanted me to follow Fat Peter, and now Fat Peter is dead. And someone is trying to set me up for it. But I don't know who, exactly, and I don't know why.'

The boy squirms like a kitten with worms before finally settling on the cold dirt of the floor. 'You don't know that. You don't know any of that.'

'I know enough.' Care is keeping her voice low and her tone steady, but I can hear the tension building. 'The old man takes a job to figure out who robbed that store. To find that necklace. He starts looking into it and he's shot. Shot and thrown in a ditch to die like a dog. But before he died, he left me that message – the one about Fat Peter. And now Fat Peter is dead, too. They're connected, Tick.'

The boy falls silent, his misery clear on his face. I understand his concern. Clearly, Care matters to him. Matters more than whatever threat or promise was made to get him to give her up. But I understand the hunt, as well. My tail lashes as I watch her make her move.

'Look, Tick, we'll be careful. *I'll* be careful.' She's speaking gently now, trying to cajole the boy into complying. 'We'll take off at the first sign of danger and head south. Together.'

'For real?' He looks up, desperate to believe.

'For real.'

I don't believe her for a moment. I'm also not convinced of the boy's renewed loyalty. Yes, he stayed the night without alerting the thugs to her whereabouts, but his allegiance can be bought or beaten, I surmise. When Care isn't looking, he rubs his fingers. Those burn marks remind him of something. Something he wants as much, if not more, than her love.

'Blackie.' She's rinsing her mouth out with rainwater when she sees me. She refills her chipped mug from the barrel that caught it and offers it to me. I stare at her, willing her to take this moment to reconsider, but she misunderstands. She puts the mug down at my feet and backs off, her eyes downcast.

I turn back toward the boy. He's stepped outside, but we can
both see him squatting just past the doorway. It takes little to
raise the fur along my spine, to start the high-pitched whine
that comes before the growl.

'He's OK, Blackie. Really, I know,' she says. For a moment,
I have hope. 'He would never hurt you.'

So be it. As much as I dislike this mission, I will join it. I
do not know if I can keep Care safe if this boy chooses to
betray her. But not only am I more sensible, I have senses far
more acute than either of theirs and I will do what I can.

One thing for the boy – he can move quietly. Although Care
is thin, too thin for a growing child, the boy is featherweight
and knows how to navigate the city. I watch him dart, head
down but eyes alert, from building to shadow. He has the
moves of a prey animal, furtive and quick, but that is nature's
way, and I find myself relaxing. This boy has his own agenda,
I can tell, but he will not blunder into anything. He will not
betray the girl with carelessness.

She's close behind, slower than he is, though I see more
thought in her actions. Again, I wonder at her education – at
this old man whose memory she holds so dear. Not only is
she circumspect, stepping carefully as she makes her way
through the rubble of the city, she is concerned. Not about her
own safety, or not enough, but about the boy's. I see how she
watches him, his thin form darting. How he starts at every
shadow. She sees his vulnerability and it means something to
her. I do not want her to forget what it could mean for them
both.

At least she is aware of her surroundings. I can see that
as we leave the quiet behind and proceed into busier
precincts. As we get farther from the train tracks and pass
the turnoff to Fat Peter's, the broken asphalt and cobblestone
give way to smooth pavement and she begins to walk differ-
ently. She holds herself more erect, her chin higher. When
one young man comments – whether in flirtation or a more
commercial inquiry – she does not deign to answer, instead
tossing off his murmured innuendos with a shake of her
head that sends her pink bangs flying. It's the equivalent of

a tail lash, and he knows it, but I'm grateful to see her pick up her pace and hold her bag closer. Glad to see her hand settling on Tick's shoulder as she guides him down the clean, white concrete. I hang back, using the shadows and the gutter for safe passage here, where all is centered on the patter of hard soles. But she is passing. Taking up space on these busy avenues.

I am less happy here. The loud clatter of commerce offends my sensitive ears, and the vehicles – common here – limit my safe range of motion. Were it not for my color, I would find it difficult to make my way. As it is, between shadow and superstition, I am able to clear a path. More troublesome are the concerned shoppers – women, mainly – who see me speed-ing low and call out as if to give me aid. As we navigate an urban mall – a stretch of concrete blocked to traffic – one even dares to reach for me, her manicured hands brushing my guard hairs before I can escape. One hiss, a green-eyed glare, and she draws back. Still, I have lost precious seconds and must hurry to keep Care and the boy within earshot.

'There.' The boy knows enough not to point, but he has grabbed Care and stopped her. They are standing on a corner, at the edge of a building as sharp as stone and glass can be as I catch up to them, and at the boy's alert they have pressed against the granite wall. There is no place for me to hide here, no shadows, and so I squeeze by them, letting the girl feel my warmth on her ankle. She glances down and smiles at me, her green eyes only slightly darker than my own. The boy does not. He is staring, his eyes riveted on the building across the street, where the storefront is metal instead of stone and the glare from the windows is blinding. 'That one,' he says.

'There?' Care squints at the building. 'Are you sure?'

'Of course.' The boy sounds excited rather than hurt. 'There's not another store like it.' He looks up and I see what he's staring at: a diamond shape of painted glass suspended above the windows,

Care isn't looking at the sign. She's turned toward the boy, and I don't think it's the glare that has knitted her brow.

'Tick, you've been here before?' She's watching his face, and so I open my mouth to take in his – and this city's scent.

'Not this way.' He's sweating, though not with the stench of fear. Some of that may have been the journey; we moved fast and he is still a young child. Some of it is excitement, and I lean against the girl, willing her to be careful. Willing her to remember those burn marks and the strange, acrid odor that even now clings to his skin.

Before I can act, however, he moves. Taking Care's hand, he darts into the street, leaving me exposed. Perhaps he hasn't seen me. Someone has, though. I hear a quick intake of breath and I flatten out, ears back and teeth bared. He's leading Care across the pavement, and so I dash after them, passing them just as a truck rolls by. For a moment, I lose them. I hear the gasps as I pull myself up on the curb. They have taken a less direct crossing, I see. The boy has led her to a corner. Another alley, I assume.

'There they are.' Tick is talking, hanging back as Care appraises the situation. Making myself as small as I can, I peer around the building, expecting that brute or another of his ilk. These back ways are seldom left unguarded.

What I see surprises me. The man looks like several we have passed on our way. His clothing is clean and his jacket shines like that gaudy diamond sign, although it cannot camouflage the belly that age and success have bestowed upon him. Not that the young woman whose cigarette he is lighting cares. She lifts one leg, brushing her foot against her own calf in a signal that transcends species. In response, he raises a hand to her cheek, the glitter of his rings obscuring her dulled eye.

The scene is common. Private, and not what Care expected. I can see on her face that she doubts Tick's information, if not his judgment. This is the kind of man who runs off children like these, I know from some deep memory. If, that is, he sees them at all.

'Wait, is that—' Care pauses. I can almost feel her searching for the right word. 'That's who you're supposed to report to?'

The boy nods enthusiastically. He's done this before. Been paid well, too, or in some manner to his liking. Even as he's brushing back his bangs – they've grown too long, giving him an almost girlish appearance – he's contradicting himself. 'Well, not him, or not directly. But he's the one. They answer to him.'

I sit and prepare myself for the wait, confident that Care will do the same. We may need our strength yet for another dash. Another escape. Clearly, one of the ruffians acts as an intermediary. One or all of them – maybe the brute I recognized – will show soon. But we may have time. Care, Tick – unless they put themselves underfoot, that well-dressed man won't even see them. Which, I realize with the beginning of a purr, is why they are useful. It is why the boy has been recruited.

'What's going on, Tick?' There's a tightness in Care's tone. She is not resting. Not relaxed. 'Tell me the truth now.'

'I have.' The boy's voice rises, although I am happy to see that the burgher has not noticed. He's too focused on his companion. Making his pitch, I gather, before his business associates arrive.

'We've got to get out of here, Tick.' She's grabbed his shoulder. She's pulling him toward her and I look up at her. She's gone pale in a way that the neighborhood, the city, doesn't explain. She starts to back away.

'Care, wait.' He's as confused as I am, and I hear no guile in his complaint. 'It's OK. They can't see us.'

'It's not that.' She turns and walks quickly, head down. 'We've got to— You don't know.'

'What?' He stumbles as he turns and tags after her. She's leaning into the walls now, hurrying as I do, from shadow to shadow. 'What is it?'

He catches her when she pauses at the entrance to another alley, three blocks down. There's a dumpster here and she ducks behind it, only then pausing to lean back on the brick wall and breathe.

'You don't know, do you?' She looks at him, her color returning to normal.

I'm intrigued by the dumpster. It smells of coffee and the rubbish of the wealthy, discarded, half eaten and full of meat. But I smell poison, as well, and the bin is too silent for hunting.

The boy, meanwhile, is shaking his head, his upturned face a mask of confusion.

'That fat guy in the suit?' Care says. 'That's Diamond Jim. He's the one who hired the old man. Hired him and got him killed.'

TEN

'I swear, I didn't know.' Time has passed and Care is still grilling him. 'All I know is that's the place. Diamond Jim's. AD said to go around the back.'

I've folded myself into a neat circle, drowsing while they talk – while he talks, actually. Her voice has become more of a hiss, urgent and angry, and I feel the beginning of a dream coming in. Her questions echo in my own mind as if I had voiced them. Not that she gets answers, in my dreams or waking life. She keeps hammering him for details but he's gotten tired. Tired and hungry, and there's the hint of tears in his voice. 'Honest, Care. I'm telling you the truth.'

She believes him, I can tell. She slumps to the ground beside me, letting her bag slide to the ground, and I lift my head from my tail in order to examine her face. Angry red spots have formed on her thin cheeks but she's staring off into space now, not at the waifish boy who still stands before her.

'Care?' He's shifting from foot to foot, uneasy or uncomfortable. She sees it too, and her voice is gentle when she looks up.

'Yes?'

'Can I – I'll be right back.'

She nods and he dashes off. I marvel at the planes of her face. It should be softer, her cheeks more rounded. And she should be more alert, I remind myself. That boy may not intend harm. That, at least, is the girl's assessment, but he is a small thing and vulnerable.

I stand and stretch, my back arching as I do. She reaches out and her hand is warm. I lean into it, butting my head against her palm and she fondles my ear, running her thumb and forefinger over its ragged end.

'How did you get so chewed up, Blackie?' Her voice is

warm, too, and although she does not expect an answer, I respond as best I can, pushing my head again into her hand. Purring to explain a past I myself no longer remember.

'Care?' We look up. The boy has returned, and it is all I can do not to growl at the interruption. At my own inattention, as well. If this boy could come so close without my realizing it . . .

Care is on her feet as fast as I am. But while she pretends to stretch, peering around the dumpster, I simply sniff the air. No, no other human has come into our alley, and the sounds I hear on the street beyond remain constant in their rhythms, careless of the three of us.

'What?' She yawns, and I realize that last night must have offered her the first good night's sleep in a while, despite the men in pursuit, the boy in her care. My inability to communicate wounds me deeply. There is something about this girl.

'They're there. The men.' The boy looks scared – though whether of Care's response or the men he's referring to, I cannot tell. 'I saw them.'

Care's alert now, as am I. We should run, I know. Find the tracks and keep going, but we won't. I feel my fur bristling, my whiskers alert. With a nod to the boy and a quick glance at me, Care signals, and we set out. The hunt is on.

Some things are easier when you are small. The boy, for example. Simply by dipping his head and hunching over he can appear even younger than his years. His height keeps him below eye level as well. As we navigate our way back up the street, his main concern is not being trodden underfoot as the city goes about its business.

I have the same advantage, of course, and even now, with the sun at its zenith, my color is an advantage. What shadow there is I can blend into, and if I am fast and dart in just such a way, tail low to the ground, the pedestrians avoid me, seeing in my movement something dangerous, uglier even than my feral self.

Care doesn't have this advantage, not with her pink hair and the height that looks like it came on her recently, stretching her slender frame. Not with the curves just beginning to show, despite her too-spare flesh. The confident strut she assumed on the way downtown won't work now either. She's on the prowl, but others are, too, and I find my concern growing as we get farther from the alley. At the first corner, when others march ahead, I feel her hesitate.

'Watch it!' A man in a suit nearly bowls her over. His companion, whose trench coat swings so low to the ground I could grab it, curses under her breath as she detours around us, nearly shoving Care off the sidewalk, bustling by in a cloud of floral scent. I look up at her, concern making me forget my own vulnerability out here on the noisy thoroughfare. The girl must see this. She ducks and scoops me up so quickly I barely complain, so taken am I with my own thoughts. If she could slick back that hair . . .

I raise a paw as if to wash, even as she holds me. I press one ear flat, peering up to see if she is watching. The scent of those passers-by – sharp and clean and foreign – lingers. The city is overrun.

'Care,' the boy whispers, gesturing her over, and she puts me down. But even as she does, she pulls something from her bag. That scent again, of flowers. It is a kerchief of some sort, a square of filmy cloth in the tan of that trench coat, edged in red and black. Care ties it around her head, covering her shock of hair, and my tail resumes its proud loft.

I am less concerned now with the remaining blocks. Instead, I focus on what we will find when we arrive back at the store and what, in truth, we will do. That the girl and I will act as a team is a given. I have come this far. The boy I still cannot count on. While he has not betrayed us yet, I cannot discount a more subtle trap.

Care must be thinking this too – the way she stops short of the alley behind the jeweler's. I am grateful for this caution, for it frees me. Hugging the building, I make my way to the corner. The two thugs who pursued us are there. Brian, the brute, and the shorter, rat-faced one. They are waiting, clearly. The way the big one slumps against the wall, kicking at it with booted feet while his companion paces. I smell cigarettes – several – and nervous sweat. They are muscle, but they are angry and frustrated and do not like to be kept waiting. Though whether they are expecting the man we saw before or the boy who runs their errands, I do not know.

'Care?' My ears pick out the boy's voice and I freeze. If he is going to urge her onward, I will act. If he raises his voice – bringing them to her – I will act. I do not yet know what I will – or can – do, but I have resources, despite my age and size.

'What?' She's peeking around the corner now too. She sees what I see, if not as clearly or with the elaboration of scent.

'Couldn't you be wrong about him? About Diamond Jim?' The boy's voice has tightened. He wants things to be peaceful, to be better. He is tired; I can smell it on him. Hungry, too. 'I mean, you say he hired the old man. Maybe he hired these guys, too. AD's friends. You know, to finish the job. After the old man died and all.'

'He didn't just die.' Care's voice has an edge too, though it's not simply her hunger or her fatigue I hear. 'He was killed. Murdered, Tick. And he wasn't just some muscle you hire, like those losers down there. He was the best there is – a real private investigator. He solved that big heist down by the train station when the cops couldn't get anywhere. And when Jonah Silver was losing inventory and nobody could figure out how? The old man did. That's why Diamond Jim was looking for him, why—'

She stops, catching herself. Her voice has risen with her indignation, and the men in the alley are looking up. I feel my tail rise, my fur start to inflate as the rat-faced one begins to walk toward us. I ready myself for the fight.

'You, boy!' What happens next happens so fast, I am not sure of the sequence. 'It's the boy, boss. AD's kid.'

Tick has stepped into the alley, in full view of the men. And when Care reaches for him, I throw myself at her shins, causing her to stumble. She catches the wall – catches herself – as the man grabs at Tick, who flinches but does not run. If he sees her, if he looks around at all, he sees the fancy scarf. The pattern of tan and black and red, and by the time she rights herself he has dragged the boy halfway down the alley.

'Tick—' She swallows her cry, aware of the futility of the

situation, and, instead, bundles me up into her arms. Together, we watch as the two men take the boy in through the back entrance of the jewelry shop and the door closes behind them.

ELEVEN

'That was the bravest thing I've ever seen.' She looks at me. I do not mean my green eyes to register doubt. My eyes, like those of all cats, are naturally cool. Appraising.

'OK, may have been. But if he was going to betray us . . .' She stops talking. We both saw how quickly the boy was hustled indoors. What neither of us can tell is whether he went by prior agreement or if he sacrificed himself to save Care from discovery. Nor what his relationship to those men – so much larger than he – may have been.

I am grateful to hear Care second-guess herself, although the wrinkle in her brow reveals the pain she feels at doubting the boy. I myself have not drawn a conclusion as to what transpired. As a cat, I see subtleties. Options that the girl has not considered. The men may have simply been inept, unwilling to wait until the boy had sprung their trap and lured Care into their reach. Independent of his loyalties, they may have decided that Care is no longer necessary to their machinations. Willing or not, Tick may be the scapegoat they need, or maybe Fat Peter's murder is no longer even a concern. Or, perhaps, the girl who stands beside me, leaning against the brick of the alley, is correct and the boy willingly gave himself up as a distraction when we were at risk of discovery.

It does not matter. The boy is gone, under circumstances that neither of us can be sure of but which may pose a danger to us. We should regroup. I look up at the girl, willing her to be sensible. To consider the environment as well as her emotions. To act, in other words, like a cat. A hunter, albeit a small one, who knows how to survive in the wild.

'We've got to figure out what's going on, Blackie.' She meets my gaze, although her answer is not all that I would wish. 'I'm sure it's all connected.'

We have retreated, since the boy disappeared, back to the

other alley, but I am not comfortable here. The unfamiliarity of my surroundings plus the sickly sweet aroma are enough to convince me this place is not hospitable to my kind. The odds are high that this space, deserted as it may seem, is monitored, and I do not hunt where I do not know what other predators I may encounter.

'Why would Diamond Jim be meeting with those creeps?' She looks at me as if I might have the answer. I can only stare back, willing her to think. We both heard the boy's theory: that those thugs were performing some kind of service. 'He wouldn't have hired them once he heard about Fat Peter.' She shakes her head slowly. Clearly, she is wrestling with the possibility that her former mentor has been replaced. 'Would he?'

I cannot answer, but I blink to encourage her process. Question everything, I want to tell her. She may be larger than I am, but she is small compared to many in this city. We must be mindful to survive.

Several more minutes pass and I am beginning to despair. If I cannot rouse her, I should take my own leave. This place does not feel safe, and I know there are those who wish us harm. I have not forgotten the man from my dream, and while Care may be questioning the role his colleagues are playing, I do not want to be caught unawares again.

'Come on.' Care pushes herself off the wall and I jump to my feet. Clearly she has reached the same conclusion I have. We small creatures must be alert in order to survive. But as she pauses in the mouth of the alley, I do have a moment of doubt, as painful as that twinge in my hip. She cares about the boy, that much I know. If she seeks to follow him – to go after him within the jewelry shop – will I risk my own safety to follow?

Every whisker is alert as I scrutinize the traffic, both vehicular and foot, going past. Every current of air brings me information. I will weigh them all. Only then will I decide—

And the choice is taken from me, once again, as the girl grabs me around my midsection, lifts me up and holds me close.

'*Naaoh!*' It is not only humiliating to be lifted so, it is disabling. No matter how stiff my hindquarters might be, I can still jump and run and slash. Even this girl would be better off unencumbered by me, were I to leave her and not lend my teeth and claws to her defense. And yet I try to keep in mind her intentions as I squirm in her grip.

'Hang on.' She presses me close as she dashes into the street. I do not mean to claw, but as I see the onrush of traffic, I struggle for purchase and connect only with the denim of her bag. Still, I will kick. I will jump free. I will not let this child betray me and—

We are across. I have seen the startled faces turning toward us as I cry. Felt her hands clench in my fur. But now she is running, maybe not faster than I could go, but farther at this pace. Within minutes we are beyond the bustle, back in shadowed, narrow streets that seem both safer and more familiar. As we approach one building, its façade striped with damp, she slows, and I prepare once more to leap.

She releases me and I land on all fours, hissing. My bared fangs, wet with spit, must seem a poor rejoinder after recent events, but I do not like being surprised. I have been a victim of malice and not of mishap, of this I am certain. And while I want to trust this panting waif, I cannot condone such treatment – such blatant disregard of my feline dignity.

'I'm sorry, Blackie.' She nods, acknowledging the righteousness of my complaint, and just like that, I feel myself settling. It helps that she has turned away, the arrogance of a direct stare mitigated by modesty. Or, no, she is fumbling with a door. She presses a brass lever and, with a sidelong glance, slips inside.

I follow, as surely she knows I will, and climb behind her up the worn stairs, the filthy linoleum worn concave by untold, tired feet.

'Hang on.' She searches through her bag and pulls out a ring of silver slivers. I watch, curious, as she slips first one and then another into the nicked keyhole. The hallway is too dark for her eyes. She works by feel, one hand tracing the opening, the other working the pick. I find her face to be of more interest than her hands. The way her brow has furrowed, the working of her teeth on her lower lip. These are not signs of sadness nor the worry that has eaten at her before. She is thinking, this girl. Detailing the process in her mind. Remembering, perhaps, other hands – older and more deft – manipulating the metal just so.

And with a click, the memory is complete, a broad grin wiping out the worried frown. As carefully as I would wish her, she inches the door open. Leans to listen . . .

And I am in.

'No, Blackie!' She reaches for me, but it is kitten's work to evade her now. Her poor senses may still be in doubt but I can hear and smell the emptiness within. The dust of days has only just been sent floating; the rodents in the baseboard scurry, shocked. I do not know this place but I sense we will be safe here.

With a leap, I gain the back of an ancient couch and mark its horsehair fabric as my own. It tears with a satisfying rasp and I am nearly done by the time the girl has finished her own examination of the room, collapsing on the seat beside me with a heavy sigh.

'You would've liked him, Blackie,' she says. I do not think she can see me. The light in here is dim, the windows shaded, and she is facing away. 'He liked animals. More than most people, maybe. Then again, most people didn't like him. Too big for his britches, some said. Even the cops – they thought he showed them up, made them look bad at their own jobs. The old man made enemies. AD warned me. He said the old man was past it. That he really was too old.'

I bristle at that. How could I not? This talk of age and infirmity hits close to home. The girl feels me shifting and misinterprets. 'I'm sorry. I know I startled you, grabbing you like that, but I had a bad feeling. I wanted to get away – to get away and think. He always told me to trust my instincts. Told me that I was responding to stimuli – to senses I didn't even know I had. That's another thing you would have liked about him, Blackie. And he – well, it's too late now. But I don't think he told anybody else about this place. I think we'll be safe here, at least for a while.'

The day has passed its zenith and the office is both quiet and shadowed. I expect her to sleep and prepare for that myself.

But she is restless, rocking the old sofa as she pushes to her
feet and begins to pace.

'I should never have let Tick go.' She runs her hand through
her hair; the pink stands up like a cockscomb. 'I'm all the
family he has. The only family he can rely on, anyway. And
AD isn't . . .' She stops, her thoughts getting the better of her,
and shakes her head. 'I mean, if the old man hadn't found me
. . . hadn't singled me out . . .'

I watch her, curious about her process. She is working out
a problem, I can tell. But whereas I would choose to sit and
watch – to wait, still and silent, for a movement, for the prey
to reveal itself – she must stay active. I see that, and consider.
For all her size, she has been a prey animal. Such activity
must have been vital at some point. If she now seeks to hunt,
however . . .

'Hang on,' she says. I cock my ears. She has rushed over
to a cabinet and I turn, my eyes following her as she crouches
low. This is hunter behavior. This is how stealth turns to profit.
But no. She has opened a door and pulled out – can it be?
Yes, the aromas announce themselves even before she turns,
a grin making apples of her wan cheeks.

'Supplies.'

There is something complicated here, with metal and a small
machine, but she masters it. The scent that reaches me first
– an aged cheese – is only part of the feast, and before long,
Care has revealed both fish and fowl.

'Anchovies,' she says. Her nose wrinkles despite itself, and
I realize this will be my portion. The chicken – a pallid version,
cold and cooked – seems a poor substitute, but I will not
complain when she takes that as her share. The cheese she
slices between us, leaving the bulk of it intact in its waxy red
casing. I cannot stop gorging, my purr almost obscenely loud.
The girl makes her own noises, though, and for a time we are
of a like purpose. We eat until we cannot consume more, and
then we rest.

'The old man.' She leans back in the one wooden chair,
shaking her head. The memories are fond now that her belly
is distended. I have licked my whiskers clean and settle down
to hear her reminiscences, the full meal making me sleepy. 'I

forgot that he kept this place so well stocked. He was always prepared.' She's sleepy too. I can hear it in her voice. 'Which is why . . .'

Her voice drops off. I glance up. Her eyes are still open, and rather than push back, she pulls the chair up to the desk where I lie, my forepaws tucked neatly away. 'He was careful, Blackie. Always. Kept great records, too. They're all here.'

She opens a drawer to bend over it. As I hear her leafing through paper, my eyes begin to close, opening only briefly as she hauls a thick folder out onto the desktop beside me.

Some of the pages she flips through right away, moving them to the side. I sniff them, curious, but smell only dust, the faint scent of tobacco and something other. The last man to handle these was ancient – older even than Care imagines – and he was cautious. I get no tang of fear or nervous sweat. In fact, the odor is pleasant, like a familiar blanket or a remembered kindness, and as Care begins to read I shift over to the discarded pages, nestling down on the pile.

'What's this?'

I look up, eyes half open, at the girl's question. She is holding a sheet up, her brows drawn together in a bunch which then releases as she exhales, flattening the paper down on the desk before her.

'It's code, Blackie,' she says as I once more drift toward sleep. 'I forgot. He didn't trust – well, he trusted me. I think. I mean, he taught me his code. He only took cases that he could verify; that he knew about first-hand or that came from a previous client. He thought that way he could manage things. Manage the risk.'

She keeps reading while I settle down. The papers make a good, warm bed, holding my body heat and cushioning the wood of the desk. Except for the occasional rustle or a soft sigh, the room is quiet and I begin to doze. We have food, of a sort. We are protected from the elements, from the chill that comes as the sun drops. We are inside. Care has closed the door behind us. The lock she picked and opened. The walls . . .

It's a trap.

I jump with a start that sends the pages flying. Before I

know it, I'm on the floor – spine arched. Ears back. Ready to attack.

Only there is no enemy before me. None that I can see. Only Care, who has slid back, her eyes wide with surprise.

'What?' She blinks. The sudden nature of my response has left her nearly wordless. And I . . .

How can I explain? I'm not sure I myself understand the sudden terrible conviction that shot through me. I spin around but my eyes merely confirm that which my other senses have already told me. No, there is nobody – no enemy – behind me. Certainly not the shadowy figures I was certain were there – was certain I had recognized a scant moment too late.

I sit, my mouth still open as I pant. As I take in the air with its scent of dust and paper. Of Care and of another – the man who spent his time here. He left his scent in sweat and exhalations. Not scared, no, but careful. One who in his own cautious way marked this place as his own, as surely as my claws rent that sofa back. Before . . .

'I don't know what got into you.' Care has risen from her chair and is now retrieving the pages that I scattered. 'You scared the crap out of me, you know that?'

I begin to wash. My default behavior, I know, and yet I cannot explain the sense I had – the certain feeling of impending doom. A dream? Perhaps. At any rate, my startled leap has raised more dust and I do not want it settling into my fur.

'I keep thinking of what Tick said, what the old man told him. "Too many tributaries," if Tick even got it right.' She's picking up pages, bouncing them together to make them line up straight. I finish my bath, both dust and tension dispelled. 'I guess I was hoping – hang on . . .'

She stops, crouching, and looks at the page in her hand. 'A tributary – that's a kind of river, right?' She looks back up at me as I settle once more in my nest. 'There's something here called Rivers Imports. It was one of Diamond Jim's references – one of businesses that told him about the old man. Only I don't think the old man knew any Rivers Imports – it just says "Mister" and then a question mark where there should be a name.'

I do not know what she expects from me, beyond a sounding board or companion. And so, as she pulls the desk chair back and begins once more to read, I let my eyes close again. I am clean, my belly full, and as I slip into what I hope will be a dreamless sleep, I feel a purr of contentment envelope me. All is well.

TWELVE

When I wake, I am alone. I know this because I wake as do all my kind – instantly – with a beast's perfect awareness of his surroundings. The availability of prey, the presence of larger predators, environmental change of all kind – they flood my senses at the moment of mindfulness like a light coming on in a dark room, not that I have much experience with lights. Or with complete darkness, for that matter. And yet, that is the image that comes to mind. Perhaps because I am in such a room, recently occupied, and the girl has gone.

I am not, at first, concerned. I have made my toilette, and she must hers. She had previously found water in an adjoining chamber, and I assume she has gone there. The building is not unoccupied. Alongside the distinct murmur of the city's voices, I hear the rumble of plumbing deep within the walls. And so I stretch and groom, my sleep having left the fur on my right side slightly matted, and then dismount from the desk. The girl has left me the remainder of the cheese, alongside a shallow bowl of water. I pause momentarily, weighing the value of these dry scraps as a lure for something fresher, and then I eat. While there are rodents in the vicinity, the human presence is keeping them in check. The day is ending. Even beyond the darkening of the shadow that falls upon this building, I can feel the growing chill. Soon enough the city will be quiet, and then the hunting may commence.

Still, I am not quite easy. Not as the gloom deepens and the girl does not reappear. The plumbing has grown quiet; the rush of water through the recesses of the walls ceased and the occasional footfall down that worn linoleum replaced by the nervous scurry of lighter, unshod steps. I should begin my hunt: there is a crevice behind the desk that smells ripe with possibility. And yet, I am concerned. My earlier dream haunts me – the shadows of men. The surprise. The attack. And my sense of the growing darkness does not help. The girl is not a cat. She is vulnerable and she is alone.

I ascend the windowsill with a leap and stick my head under the raised pane. The sightlines are bad here. Off to the right, the glow of dusk reflects red off brick; to the left, the dark of the alley. The breeze brings me what I need, however. I smell the ebbing of humanity, the quieting of the traffic. And then – yes! – the girl.

Only she is in distress. I catch sweat and the bitter scent of fear. I can hear, over the distant hubbub, her labored breathing as she runs.

I must rely on my eyes, my least favorite sense. I peer down – there is a ledge of concrete, decorative at some point, perhaps half the distance to the ground. It appears to be solid, although I see how the edge has worn and crumbles. And so I gather myself up, twitching in anticipation, and I jump. The ledge holds; my paw pads grip its grainy surface even as my claws fail to penetrate. The scent is stronger from here and I catch a glimpse of her. The scarf she had donned has fallen back and she is hurrying, like some frightened mouse. Only I cannot ascertain who pursues her – or what.

One more leap and I am on the street, hitting the pavement a bit too hard for comfort.

'Blackie!' Passing by the alley, she has caught the movement and races down to scoop me up. Hissing, I retreat. This is no time to compromise my movement, and she freezes in response. Ignoring the look of pain on her face, I make my own approach, brushing against her shin to reassure her as I take in the scents and sounds of the street. No, there is no pursuit, and so I lead the way back out of the alley, pausing at its mouth. I am pleased to see her hesitate as well, to see her taking in the diminished traffic before she ventures forth. She has resumed her furtive mode, leaning into the building, the better to pass unseen. At the entrance, she barely opens the door, and when we both slip in we begin to hurry again, me bounding silently up the stairs as she keeps pace, her breathing hot and hard.

'I don't understand it.' Once inside our sanctuary, she closes the door and locks it, leaning against it as if to add her slight form to its force. She has taken a bottle from her jacket and drinks deeply before pouring some in my dish. Water, I am glad to see. It has a different tang than that from the nearby tap, but it is clean and so we both drink. 'I knew him, Blackie.'

She slumps on the sofa and I look up at her. She does not need my green eyes for prompts, however. Something has happened, and without the boy here she seeks to unburden herself to me.

'I couldn't figure out this Rivers thing, so I went to see Jonah – Jonah Silver.' She takes another drink and licks her lips. I am right about her fear. She has been running, but her pace is not entirely responsible for her quickened breath. 'He was the last client the old man finished a job for. I worked with him on that case, Blackie. It was my first real case. And I thought . . .'

She pauses. Unlike me, she has a face that changes as thoughts pass through it, like clouds in the sky. Or reflections in a puddle, perhaps, obscuring the depth beneath. I see hurt as well as fear, and beyond it all, confusion, which makes its way into words.

'He knows me. He congratulated me, Blackie. I was the one who noticed the lack of damage to the storeroom lock – the fact that nobody had forced it or picked their way in.' She flexes her hands in a gesture I recognize. I, too, flex my claws, remembering a successful hunt.

'I mean, I kind of think the old man saw that too, but, anyway . . .' She shrugs. 'I thought he'd be doing great now. Now that we solved his loss problem, figured out that it was an inside job. But he's not, Blackie. He's barely keeping his head above water. The place is a shambles. And personally, he's a wreck. I mean, when he saw me, he looked like he'd seen a ghost. I thought, you know, maybe he'd heard about the old man and he was worried about me. Maybe he'd heard I'd gotten hurt too. But I think he was scared for himself. He said something about Fat Peter . . .'

She pauses, as if considering the possibilities. Remembering the lies that the dead man's hulking guard seemed ready to spread.

'Jonah can't think that I had anything to do with that,' she says, shaking her head. 'He doesn't. He can't. But he knows about Fat Peter, and that those creeps are looking for me. I think he knows more, too. I told him about Tick and he said he'd heard nothing, but he was lying. I can tell – I mean, the old man taught me what to watch for. It's funny, some of it. Like, you'd think that people would look away, only they don't. If they want to convince you, they stare at you. Hard. And they raise their chins a little. And when I asked him about Rivers Imports, he started to sweat. I could see it, Blackie. Beads of sweat broke out all over his forehead, and he got all twitchy.

'I was trying to find out more. I mean, he owed the old man big time. And I thought he liked me. I thought he'd help me when I explained about Tick. But when I asked him who was in charge of Rivers – the name of the man who referred Diamond Jim – he lost it. He nearly kicked me out, Blackie. I mean, he grabbed some bills from the register and shoved them at me, but then he pushed me out the back. He really spooked me, the way he was acting. I ran all the way back here.'

This is a lot to absorb, and I find myself regretting the nap that kept me from accompanying her. This girl is brave, and she has learned some skills. But she has no sense of smell, and her hearing, well . . . I should be glad that she has survived this encounter. 'Twitchy' does not sound promising. I need more information, and put my face up to her hand to see what I can gather. She misinterprets, pulling me onto her lap. It's awkward. I am too large for this, and she is too skinny. My hind legs hang over the sofa and I must restrain myself from using my claws to secure purchase in her threadbare jeans.

'Hang on.' She shifts, pulling me more fully onto her thin thighs and begins rubbing my neck. It's a pleasant feeling, her warm hands smoothing my fur, but I have work to do. I run my nose over her other hand, mouth slightly open to take in all the flavors of the day. Sweat, fear and a mix of varnish and rust. That former client's shop might be rundown, but he is working hard to save it. 'Are you looking for treats, Blackie? I'm sorry, I was in such a rush, I didn't get anything else to eat. Stupid, probably.'

I look up at her, willing her to understand that I do not think that. That, in fact, I wish she would be more circumspect while those thugs are on the loose. She, after the fashion of her species, misinterprets.

'You know "treats," huh?' She smiles, which only makes it worse. 'I wonder if you were a house pet once?'

I jump to the floor in disgust and she rises. 'Look, I've got some coin. Let's see what we can get. Unless you'd rather wait here?'

In response, I rush the door as she opens it. She chuckles as we descend the stairs, her earlier fright forgotten. I must be careful, I realize. She seems to derive comfort from me and that may put her off her guard. Better to keep my distance, I decide as I bound down the last flight ahead of her. If she has been followed, I will do what I can to alert her and to stop the attack.

The man is rank, scent coming off him in waves. I smell him before we reach the lobby – before he has even reached the door. I freeze as his odor hits me, blinking as I work to decipher its mix of filth and perfumes, chemicals and the very animal scent of death.

Too long. When the building door opens before us, it is all I can do to dart to the side. From the shadow of a doorway, I wait, willing Care to be as alert as I am. Willing her to be aware. Her sense of smell is sadly lacking, this I know. But surely she will have heard and will wait out this intruder. Surely she has the sense of a three-day-old kitten.

'Mr Bushwick, good to see you.' No, she's taking another tack. Walking slowly down the center of the stairs as if she owns the place. I wait to see her play.

'Oh, hey, kid. You're . . . that kid, right?' The man who has stepped into the lobby nearly dwarfs it, his obesity exaggerated by the coat hanging open over a shiny three-piece suit. The coat has a fur collar, which he fondles as if he were stroking a pet. A dead, poorly cured pet. 'You worked with the old man?'

'How do you think I recognized you?' Care has a half-smile on her face as she stops, still three steps above the ground floor. She's waiting for the newcomer to respond, positioning herself where she's slightly taller than him. It's a good play, a dominance play, and I settle back to watch.

'Yeah, of course.' He pulls a handkerchief out his pocket and mops his head. He's sweating despite the chill in the air, and I wonder at the coat with its dead, cheap collar. He takes more time than he needs to with the handkerchief, and makes no effort to shed the coat. Rabbit, I believe, though the scent is primarily of acid and rot. Something else as well – something that makes me think of mice and fledglings too weak to fly. He's stalling, I see that now, and hope the girl notices as well. 'Hey, sorry for your loss.'

'Thanks.' I see her making a mental note, acknowledging that he is aware of the old man's death. 'So what brings you here?'

I wince. Better for her to have waited. The sweat and the procrastination were already building up the pressure.

Still, he answers. Her youth, her gender and her slight build give her an advantage in that he discounts her. 'When the old man – ah – passed, he was looking into a thing for me.' He strokes the collar, one hand lingering. It seems to give him confidence. 'A job. I gave him some papers to get him started. You know, a lead. Anyway, I need them back.'

'He was doing a job for you?' Her eyes narrow. She doubts him. Doubts herself, too, I believe. There's something wrong here, but she's not sure of herself. 'You came back to him?'

'Yeah, kid.' He sees her hesitation. 'A load of coats went missing. I think he was going to handle it himself. Maybe he thought you hadn't earned one yet.' He gives her the once-over. His eyes would linger on her thin body, I believe, but her dead-eyed stare soon turns him away. 'Anyway, he never got around to it, so I'm going to put in for the insurance.'

'Insurance?' Care is eyeing him in a way I know. Taking his measure. It's not just the coat, too heavy for the weather.

The cheap, badly cured fur. There is something wrong with what he's saying.

'Yeah, insurance.' He's talking too loudly now. Stressing the word too hard. 'These were the real deal, kid. Not that Chinese dog or rabbit or whatever it is. But you wouldn't know the difference. Maybe in a few years.' The leer again, forced this time. He can't keep himself from looking beyond her. Looking up the stairs.

'Anyway, it's legit. And I really need these papers I gave him. For, you know, customs. I figure he kept them in his office. The office he keeps here.'

'Wait, who told you that?' Care asks. 'He never saw clients here.'

It's too much. He smiles, his information confirmed. 'A little bird,' he says. 'A little sparrow down by Diamond Jim's.'

'You saw Tick?' She can't help herself. She comes forward – the desperation in her voice doing more to lower her stature than her descent in the eyes of the fat, overdressed man. 'Where? How is he?'

'He a friend of yours?' A greasy grin spreads across the round face. I flex my claws. 'Yeah, you're both on AD's crew. Funny, I never put that together.'

'Where is he?' Care's voice has gone flat. If this man has any sense, he'll hear the warning in it.

'Cool your jets. He's fine. AD's got him working. Making a living. Which is more than I guess you're doing.' He eyes her, and I can imagine what he sees: the tattered, dirty clothes and the pallor of her thin cheeks. 'Still, you could earn.'

He licks his lips. My ears go back.

'I've got a job.' Care's chin goes up but it's pride that I hear, not deception. 'A career. I'm taking over the old man's cases,' she says. 'So, no, you can't look through his papers. But if you're looking for someone to help you retrieve what has gone missing or locate the lost, I'm your gal.'

She's quoting someone – the old man, presumably. The words have a grand sound in her mouth, though. They serve to put this sordid suit in his place. He pulls his feet together.

Stands up straighter and looks at her with newly opened eyes.
'You? You're taking on the business?'

'Yes,' she says. 'Yes, I am. And to start with, I need you
to tell me where you last saw the boy, Tick. And also what
you know about a company called Rivers Imports.'

THIRTEEN

We celebrate with tuna. A can each, as well as an orange soda for the girl. That man Bushwick hadn't been much help, but Care did her best with him, and she seems to have enjoyed the process as much as it discomfited him.

'Did you see how he was sweating, Blackie?' She wipes her mouth, her smile popping right back up. 'He didn't want to tell me where Tick was, but when I described Diamond Jim's and his muscle, he thought I already knew. That I was testing him. I'm glad Tick's OK.' She turns somber in a moment. 'At least, so far. I don't like him being there, though. I know he can't go back to his mom. Not now. But working for AD? Even if he's got him over at Diamond Jim's, that's not a good environment for him.'

She glances at me, but I understand. I smelled that bitter scent on the boy, and I have lived long enough to understand something of human weakness.

'Bushwick's scared. When I asked him about Rivers Imports, he pretended he didn't know what I was talking about, but he did. He looked like he was going to have a heart attack.' She stops and looks at me, and for a moment I believe she sees me – sees that I understand and would like to contribute. 'It could be a business thing. But if that's the case, why's he so scared? I don't care if he's changed his name or set up a shell corporation or whatever. I know about "doing business as." The old man taught me all that, and it shouldn't be a big deal. But it is, Blackie. It definitely is.'

I want to tell her about the fur, about the corrupt stink of the man. I do not know how. I think of prey animals and how I would teach a kitten, but I come up blank. She has seen his fear, and I try to be content with that. Still, my tail lashes the air as she mulls over his visit, as she considers the meaning of names and the truths that may lie behind them.

'It's got something to do with the paper. He wants that file, or whatever it was he left with the old man, but not for an insurance claim. The businesses down by the docks don't file for insurance. And when I told him I'd be taking over, he didn't look happy. Maybe he doesn't think I can do what the old man did. More likely, he doesn't trust me.' She rolls the words around slowly, thinking them through. 'No, there's something else going on – something else he wants from the old man's office. And I wouldn't put it past him to break in to get it. We should find it and clear out. I mean, *I* should find it.' She wipes her hands and looks around. Sighs.

'I don't want to give this place up, Blackie. I mean, maybe I really can take over. The rent's paid up till the end of the month, I know that. And if we leave . . .'

She doesn't finish. Doesn't have to. Bushwick had the gloss of a pampered house cat, accustomed to having his way, but there is something off about him. Something driving him. 'Nothing I can do about it tonight, though, and I need some kip. I'll barricade the door. And at first light, Blackie, we'll see what we can find.'

I watch her as she sleeps, careful that she's fully out before I do what I must. It's pleasant, I find, to perch on the sofa's back as she curls on the cushions below. In sleep, she becomes younger. A child almost, her face losing its taut watchfulness as it relaxes. Even her body appears softer, more childlike, her knees pulled up and one hand lying open on the pillow. As her mouth opens slightly and her breathing deepens, I dismount the sofa's arched back and land softly by her side. It is warm here and her breath is sweet. I lean in, my whiskers coming close to those chapped and worried lips, and must pull myself back. It is her youth, I suspect, that draws me. The change I have witnessed once more from the guarded young animal of the evening to this open and tender child that urges me to give over my plans. To fit myself beside her and let her wake to the softness of my fur. I am not a house cat and have no memories of domesticity. Of kindness at the hands of others. And yet I understand its allure.

Which, I recall, is why I must not linger. Turning from her face, with care I sniff her palm. She has told me what matters to her, but I want to know for myself what happened during her outing. Besides, before that greasy suit took off, she took his hand and shook it, although – or perhaps because – it disconcerted him. I do not think she did so for my benefit, but I will make use of her gesture, examining what traces he has left.

I am glad I have eaten. As his attire suggested, Bushwick is self-indulgent. The big man has a fondness for bacon and eggs, as well as other meat products that I cannot name. His corpulence could have told me that, but there's another scent beneath the grease and salt that is more disturbing – one that had been masked by the cheap fur and the overbearing cologne. The bitterness could be explained by illness: this man indulges himself to an unhealthy extreme. But when I factor in the sweat, beyond what the stairs up to the office merit, I sense the acid has come from more than indigestion or, perhaps, both the indigestion and the self-comforting with food spring from an external stimulus.

This man may appear prosperous. I do not understand exactly how I am able to judge the value of his clothes. To know, as well, the impression he seeks to convey. But I sense that this is true, just as I understand the smell of his hand reveals something other than moneyed comfort and a need deeper than the hunger to consume the city's riches. Scent does not lie: this man Bushwick lives in fear.

He also, and this I find most strange, has not had contact with the boy Care misses so. As lightly as I can, I walk the sofa's length, taking in every scent he has left from their brief interaction. In my mind, I run through that strange meeting: the man on an errand, stopped apparently by the appearance of a girl. No, he was lying about Tick; perhaps about many things. What I would like to know is why.

With a lightness that belies my age, I arc over the sleeping girl and attain the floor. If only she had been sleeping when he came by, I would have answers as well as questions. Though as I leap up to that desktop, I am mulling the most challenging of all. Why, that is, I did not examine the man more thoroughly when I had my chance.

I pause to consider this, wrapping my tail around my feet in a move both reflexive and comforting as I list the possibilities. In part, I know, it was fear that stopped me from accosting him. Fear for her, that is. Unlike that brute at the pawn shop, this man was not a killer of dumb beasts. I would not have turned my back on him, not without expecting a sly kick, but he posed no real danger to me. To the girl, though, he could have been a source of evil. His lasciviousness boded ill, and his love of money and of comfort worse. He would trade in human flesh with no more compunction than he would devour an animal's, and Care's youth and frailty would only add to her marketability in his all-consuming world.

In part, my own fastidious nature may have been to blame. Even now, the stench of the man makes my ears flicker back. The fact of that fur, as well, offends me. Not the source – some are made to die, just as some to hunt – but the care, or lack of it. When I kill, I do so cleanly – a quick shake to snap the neck. A bite to pierce the skull. Although it is reasonable to assume I have offspring, I have no recollection of teaching a kitten to do the same. Never had to prolong the last agony into the panic and squeals that marked that pelt. It is not what I do. I hunt alone.

Or I have, until now. Which may, ultimately, be what was at play today as I stood back to watch. The girl is intelligent and has had some rudimentary training. But she is not a cat, and now I regret my wasted deference. The opportunity lost as I, the hunter, stood aside. My vision is not my strongest sense, and yet I was acting in a most un-feline fashion. Did I consider an attack? Or was there something else about this man, about this shopkeeper, that kept me in the shadows? It is a question for another night, I decide finally. The girl has started to stir and I do not know when I will get this chance again.

First, the papers. Care has been through them, and her scent lingers. She has found soap to wash with, and the impression of her warm, clean fingers makes me pause over certain pages. It is not sentiment that holds me so. While I consider my senses superior to those of any human, and certainly this child, she has the advantage of me in one way: I cannot read. And although I sense the import of these papers, I receive only the barest hint – as if in memory, forgotten, from a dream. No, I seek out those pages with which the girl has lingered. It is her interest in them that marks them for me, and when I find the one over which she exclaimed, I pull it free, gently piercing its corner with one extended claw.

It is one of the newer pages. The scrawl looks hurried and the writing brief. Still, it had some significance. She held this one so tightly she left an indent, and I run my nose over the marks. She sweat holding this, and there is a faint mark of water – a trace of salt – in the corner. I sniff that too, though it leaves me both confused and saddened. I would turn away if its mystery did not compel me so. But as I close my eyes, I get another, fainter trace. Tobacco from a pipe, its ashes tossed carelessly as the writer puffed. The nicotine was soothing and it helped him concentrate when sleep was not an option. I imagine him sitting in that chair: the old man as he must have been, resting his pipe here – the darkness of a burn marks the desk's edge – and scratching away at this paper mere hours, perhaps, before his death.

This is what drives her, more than defiance of AD or fear for the trades he might apprentice her to. She seeks some connection with the old man, an understanding of his end. I settle on the page to absorb what I can. This quest has led her to another dead man – Fat Peter – and perhaps cost her the boy. Yet she will continue; I can read that in her as easily as I can spot a mouse.

I have been a fool. Abandoning the desk, I return to the windowsill. All I can get, I have gotten from those pages, from this room. I am not a house pet, nor will I ever be. What I am is a hunter, more experienced than this poor child, and yet I am hanging back? No, the night is mine. The girl is safe for now. Warm and fed, the door blockaded against any intrusion.

The window is low. She has closed it some, against the cold, but with my feline flexibility I can work my way beneath the lowered pane. I judge the leap more accurately this time, landing with the grace of my species despite my age and despite the stiffness that will not shake off. One last look up at the window, still and dark. If all goes well I will return by morning. But now the quarry waits.

FOURTEEN

t's no great feat to track the suited man. If anything, I would prefer more of a challenge. The time I spend with the girl already threatens to soften me, to take away something of my feral edge. But although our unwelcome visitor reeked as well of the usual vices – alcohol, the must of badly stored cigars and a particularly pervasive cologne – what I stick to is the potent combination that sets my ears back. The odor of that pelt – dead fur and, now, wet wool – overlying the very personal scent of his fear. As I pass the night haunts of his kind, the other scents are common. Where they don't confound each other, they explain themselves. One would want to dull one's senses around such loud and uncongenial company, the numbing effect of the drink covering the poor quality of the leaf and vice versa.

I am not surprised that my pass takes me back across the tracks and down toward the river. But this man did not travel by back alleys or by boxcar. No, despite the anxious sweat – or perhaps because of it, afraid of the enclosed car, the metal machine, the box – he seems to have sauntered, making his way down the wider avenues, even as they grow rough and loud.

He would not have been alone. As the night progresses, I pass revelers – some in couples, others in crowds. One group catches my particular attention, their voices growing louder even in the time it takes me to make my way up the block. I do not need their volume to know their placement, the slight movements as they laugh and swing at each other in jocular role play. Three men, deep in drink. Despite their inebriation, I am wary. Males in their first flush of strength, they are ready for the hunt, and I, though a predator too, am smaller than they are. Where once I may have ignored such men, I do not now. Not since my vision of the other night, that dream of three.

But this trio is another such. There is no one leader, taller than his companions, and seemingly no one guiding intellect either. As their voices fade behind me, they talk of women and I cannot help but think of Care. In a year or two she will be seen as sport by such as these. I cannot help but hope that she sees them as I do, all bluff and noise and cheap cigars. I recall the trace of scent on those papers, a leaf both mellow and fragrant, and wonder again at the character of the old man, the one who died. What he would have done for the girl, if he could.

I have no time for idle musings, however, and must seek this Bushwick's scent. I open my mouth, taking in the damp of the air and all the fragrance of spring. An opossum has her burrow somewhere near. Has taken prey and given birth. Life and rot and – yes! – the sharp tang of sweat and fear as well. Bushwick has passed here, where the track is confined between cobblestones and concrete, his scent mixing with the cinder and ash of the mechanical beast.

The scent is muddled – the train, the river damp. It matters not – I am on familiar ground. A name comes into mind: Dock Street. And I have found his lair: a warehouse at the edge of the nightlife district, bordering the docks. A closed block of brick, it poses a challenge, but not an insurmountable one. Although Bushwick's trail leads to the street, I make my way toward the back, toward the river. Halfway there, I find my ingress. The scrabbling of claws leads me from the gutter to a vent of some sort, where the mortar has been worn away by a slow and constant drip. Had I not recently fed, I would find good hunting here – this is not only an opening into the building, it is a source of water for creatures of many kinds. As it stands, I pass through, pointedly ignoring the timid stares from the crevices. For tonight, my ears signal my disinterest. Let there be a truce.

I hear the frightened chatter as I pass by. The denizens of this space know well how to read my signals. This is how they live, but I cannot blame them for their nervous skittering. As I believe Care has learned, trust is a gift given only once.

I do my best to tune them out. I am hunting bigger prey, and once I am above the basement I know I have him.

Bushwick, the man in the suit, has been here recently. His scent is fresh: new tobacco – newly lit, that is, but stale – the fetid fur and even more, that bitter undertone that makes his human sweat so sour.

It is almost too strong. I close my eyes as it washes over me and find myself clinging to thoughts of Care. She has sensed something of this man, has tested his bluff with her own will and found him wanting. Still, he has experience on her and the power of a suit and a big cigar. She does right to be wary of him, although if I can find his weakness I will do what I can to bring proof of it to her.

Tick. That is whom she fears for most, the reason she let her guard down with the suited man. Ears up, I listen. These walls jump with life, but I tune out the rodents and the grubs. His breathing would be softer than the large man's, his foot-steps quicker and more light. Starting with the corners, I search for any trace of the boy. For his powder-soft child scent or the acrid tang that had also marked him during our brief acquaintance. *Scat*. The word comes to me. Of course. But there is nothing of the boy or his drug here, not even the second-hand scent of one who had come in contact with him or his few possessions within memory.

With the silence my kind are known for, I scale the stairs. Here a hall is lined with offices and wooden doors left half ajar, their daytime occupants heedless of the outside world. Bushwick is king here. I catch his scent on every door; every surface holds his ashes. I imagine the scene by daylight: workers scurrying as those rats did before me. Bushwick prowling at his ease. And yet not – that fear scent again. The tang of sweat. He is a big man, overdressed in his shoddy fur, but there is more to his stench than overheating, than vanity. I am on Bushwick's territory, his base of operations, but he is not comfortable here either.

This is a mystery I would unlock, and so, with paws and stealth, I make my way through the remainder of the floor to see what scares him so. The first room sends me reeling. Scent so thick as to be maddening. Tobacco: the leaves in back already rotting sweet. Bushwick and his minions have not cottoned onto the leaks that weakened their foundation. They do not know their store is going bad. This, I realize, as I retreat back to the hall, must be the source of the man's power – there is too much here for his personal use. Too much, even, for the revelers I passed on the street. The man must bring this foul leaf in to distribute throughout these streets.

The next chamber has been better secured. Against men, however, and not a cat who can contort himself through even the tightest space, around a loosened grill and in. Bushwick was more careful with the venting here, and as I drop to the floor I understand why. Once again, I am enveloped immediately by an aroma so strong it sets my ears back. Prey animals once. Or . . . I blink in the darkness, dim even for my eyes, and make out three figures. Men. No, mannequins; faceless and cold, despite the coats draped over their – I see now – decidedly female bodies, set before a sofa steeped in the funk of flesh and ash. I think of Bushwick's collar, the way he stroked its cold, dead fur, of the reek that nearly sent me reeling. Of the woman outside Diamond Jim's. For a moment, I wonder if I have grown used to the miasma. The smell of fear and death and commerce. The trade in flesh of many kinds. Or . . . wait, did Bushwick not say that such as these were missing? Could this room or others like it have held more? Is that why the stench has faded? I examine the mannequins, their forms so cool and still. All are covered; all are clothed. This stage has been set for its tawdry drama, and it has not been disturbed.

And then it hits me. What I have *not* scented here matters as much as the odor that now enrobes me. I have not found Tick or any trace of him, despite the suited man's insistence that the boy sent him to Care. Nor, I realize, have I gotten a trace of the old man, the subtle spice of his good pipe tobacco or the indescribable warmth Care sought on those pages. Not in these rooms, at any rate. Nor, I suspect, were these coats ever missing, despite what Bushwick has told the girl.

Why this lie should threaten him so, I do not know, but logic suggests a connection. As surely as rats will find water and weak spots and rot, so too will men link money and power. And while this chamber – this entire building – appears full of the goods of commerce that the city craves, there is something wrong here. Bushwick is not enjoying the fruits of his success. He is seeking something, something he has lied about, and there is some element of that search that has left him in fear.

FIFTEEN

Getting back into the office is more challenging than leaving it, and not simply because of the distance or my sore hind leg. Although I do not like to admit that I failed to consider the specifics of how I left – or how I might re-enter, I am forced to as I sit in the alley, eyeing the wall before me. The brick is pitted; the years and the grit that cycles down this alley have left their mark. But even that crumbling surface will offer little purchase for my claws, and the ledge is simply too high for me to jump. I do not need to test this hypothesis, as I am quite capable of judging both height and distance and have no illusions about my capacity at this point in my life. Which is not to say I have not already tried it, to the amusement of a muskrat who has since, wisely, made himself scarce.

It is not yet dawn, although the shadows of the street have begun to sharpen with the coming of day. The girl, from what I can hear, is still within. Still asleep, most likely, the scent of her former mentor and the lock on the door both granting her a peace I do not think she enjoys often. I would let her remain at rest, gathering what strength and solace she may. And once she wakes, then I would warn her, by what means I have not yet devised. I would turn her away from this Bushwick and his false quest. She is curious, I know, and more than that, desires to prove herself. To set herself up in the field her mentor was training her for. It's a sensible development, promising longer health and greater autonomy than any of the other options that have been suggested. Watching her eat last night reminded me of how limited her resources are, how restricted her skills for survival.

Still, I would have her seek another task – another field if not another mentor. This Bushwick is not a thug like those by Fat Peter's, but he – his warehouse – stink of something

worse. No, this is simply another form of trap, although she
does not see it. Another source of filth that would use and
discard her, like so many soft and living creatures used
thus before, though this brings me to a deeper fear: that she
sees the trap and knows it for what it is. Her mentor was a
hunter, of sorts. That much I have gathered. This girl – Care
– is on her way to emulate him, to mimic his skills. Not
simply for a livelihood but for her own satisfaction. She
seeks redress for her mentor. To avenge him and solve the
mystery of his death, and that is the most dangerous motivation of all.

The foot traffic in the street is picking up with the light,
and I retreat to the far side of the alley. In shadow, I am
less likely to be spotted, and from here I can make out
movement within the room. An arm as she stretches. Her
face, pale in the sun, as she turns around. I feel a pang of
what might be regret as I realize she is looking for me. That
she might experience concern at my absence. Already, she
mourns one companion and fears for another. I cannot add
to that burden.

I mew.

It is an undignified sound, both high and without distinction in terms of meaning or intent, and I hear it fade to no
effect. Still, I realize as I see her head turning, as I see her
seeking my sleek form, it may be my best chance. And so
I call again – not a simple mew but a caterwaul. Putting
my body in it, I let out a resonant yowl that would have
passers-by turning were the day a little later, the street more
trafficked.

'Blackie?' My ears, more acute than hers, hear her
perfectly as she wheels around, searching for the source. I
cry again and she comes to the window, opening it to reveal
her matted hair and sleep-swollen eyes. 'How did you . . .
Hold on.'

I retreat to the shadows, aware of how I have exposed
myself. That man Bushwick is a coward but he has too close
an affinity with death for my comfort.

'There you are.' Care is at the mouth of the alley, wearing
a man's broadcloth shirt over her jeans. She has run a hand

through her hair. The pink stands up like a flag while the rest of her slouches, relaxed and – dare I say? – happy. The rest has done her good, the safety of a known environment an antidote to the horrors of the day.

I emerge to greet her, my tail high, when the sudden rush of footsteps causes me to freeze. She spins – either the sound or the sight of my sudden change alerting her – and I hear a quick intake of breath.

'Tick!' She sobs with relief as she wraps her arms around the boy who this time has run to embrace her.

Tail down now, I circle. I would not be caught in this alley, and I do not trust this boy who has buried his face in that borrowed shirt. He reeks of dirt and sweat and the musty smell of Fat Peter's storefront, where perhaps that body yet lies. He is scented, too, by that pungent smoke.

'Tick, look at me.' Her nose buried in his hair, the girl has smelled it too. But the face that looks up at hers is stained with tears and dirt. A mark the size of a man's ring is purpling beneath his eye, and she loses her resolve. 'Come with me,' she says. Keeping one arm around the boy to guide him, she looks back at me.

I meet her eye and take a step forward. She will know I am with her, that I will not leave her alone with this boy or whoever he has brought with him. If she has the sense to realize I do not trust him, then she will know, as well, that she should not either.

Against my better judgment, she leads him around to the front of the building, holding the door for him to enter. I follow as they go upstairs, but when she opens the office door I dart past with a hiss. The boy recoils, as I intend, and this gives me the moment I need to reconnoiter. Nothing has changed that I can smell or see, and I experience a moment of gratitude. The boy was not a decoy, at least not for this kind of trap.

As they rumble in, I take a seat on the windowsill. From here, I can observe. I also, if need be, have an exit at my back. The boy settles on the sofa where Care has slept. She has gone to the cabinet where she keeps her small store of food. It is hers to share, and so I do not protest. While she busies herself with openers and bread, he eyes me as suspiciously as I do him.

'That cat doesn't like me,' he says.

She doesn't comment. My hiss spoke for itself.

'He's mean. Why do you keep him?'

'I don't "keep" him.' She answers without turning. 'He just showed up.'

The boy squints and I wonder about his eyesight. Then I realize I am sitting with the sun to my back. He is trying to read me as he would the girl – or any of the other humans around whom he circulates. As if my cool glare would reveal my thoughts.

'But you let him in.' The boy seems hurt by this, as if we were competing for a limited resource.

'He's company.' Care returns, the canned meats we have feasted on now spread between layers of bread. She has kept some aside for me, I see, and brings it – in a shallow bowl – over to the windowsill.

'The old man said you could learn a lot about people from the way they treat animals.' She puts it down but does not attempt to touch me. She is learning. 'Especially if they thought no one was watching. Besides, he liked cats.'

The boy makes room for her on the couch and reaches for his plate. Even as he eats, however, he keeps glancing over at me. 'There's something spooky about this one, Care. I swear, he's watching me.'

The girl looks over at me but she denies it. 'He's just skittish. You must smell funny to him.'

He shrugs, and as they eat I settle in, tucking my paws beneath my body. The boy is at ease. The time is right.

'So, what happened, Tick?' Care keeps her voice level, although I can hear the tightness of stress in its upper register. The tears, that bruise. 'I thought we'd lost you there.'

She says it as if it were a joke, a counter to that note of tension, but the boy shudders. 'You know what AD says.' He looks at his sandwich, as if the meat has suddenly gone bad. 'We've all got to earn our keep.'

Now it's her turn to put the food down. 'Tick?'

'It's not what you think,' he says, his voice petulant. 'It's my job to run errands. To do the small things. You know.' He picks up his sandwich again, but I cannot avoid the suspicion that he is dissembling, avoiding the meat of her unspoken question by offering a lesser or partial answer. 'Brian and those guys, they needed me.'

I wait for her to pounce. He has left himself open, both in terms of the nature of his tasks and their seeming cessation. The girl is no fool. She can see as well as I what he has implied. His presence here is not of his own volition, or not entirely.

She does not question him, though. Instead, she goes to the larder. When she returns, she is holding a box of biscuits. In the moments it has taken her to do this, he has wolfed down the rest of his sandwich. He eats like an animal, afraid to make himself vulnerable, unsure of when he will have such bounty again. As she offers him the cookies, he looks up at her. For a moment, his face is open, and I understand her reasoning.

'They don't want you messing around with this, Care.' There is fear in his voice. Fear for her, I believe. For the moment, he has forgotten the sandwich. The cookies. Everything but her. 'Fat Peter? The stuff the old man was looking into? They got someone else to take care of it. Someone, you know, big.'

He pauses. Swallows. He puts down the cookie before he speaks again. 'They knew I'd told you what the old man said. That I'd sent you to Fat Peter. I mean, I didn't mean to, but—'

'It's OK, Tick,' she interrupts, and I feel my fur start to bristle. 'I'm not working for Diamond Jim. Not AD either.'

He shakes his head and I can see he is near tears. 'That doesn't matter, Care. It's not the job that they care about. They don't want you asking questions. "Keep that girl of yours from poking her nose everywhere." That's what Brian – the big guy – said to AD. They're . . . I don't like them, Care. I think they're dangerous. I think they'd hurt you. I think maybe they hurt the old man.'

Care nods, acknowledging a truth. 'I think they did, Tick, but it doesn't matter.' She looks up and, for a moment, our eyes meet. I get a flash of light – the sun, reflected in her unshed tears. 'I'm going to keep looking into it. I'm going to find out what happened to the old man, and I'm going to make them pay.'

SIXTEEN

Tick doesn't like that, and neither do I. He protests loudly, however, while I wait and watch, considering my options. Care is a smart girl, and this is not a smart move. We who are smaller must be careful how we hunt. *Whom* we hunt. At the very least, she must realize that her declarative outburst – stating her purpose to one who has admitted being a pawn – is foolish. There is nothing to be gained by revealing your next move. There are many things I will never understand about humanity, and this kind of self-destructive gesture is certainly among them.

'Care, you can't.' Tick is on his feet. He has taken her hand and is shaking it, as if he could wake her sense of self-preservation. 'These guys, they mean business. They don't want you nosing around.'

'Like they didn't want the old man nosing around?' Care's voice has gone cold. She holds her hand still. Holds his. 'I think you've just told me what happened, Tick. That creep, Brian, he wanted the old man out of the way. The old man must have realized he was the one behind the jewelry theft. I knew he was onto something.'

'No. It's not like that.' Tick shakes his head now, unable to keep still. 'Brian and his guys – they didn't rip off anything. They don't need to. In fact, Diamond Jim is working with them now. Like he was working with the old man. And he's doing good. Business is better than ever, he says, and I believe it. His shop is full up with everything you can imagine and—'

He stops and stares at his feet.

'What?' She leans over him, concern replacing the anger of moments before.

'He even paid me, Care.' He looks up sheepishly. 'In coin and everything.'

'To come find me?' She's catching on. I even see her sniffing the air around him. Searching for that strange and acrid scent.

He shrugs. 'He didn't want you bothering Brian and those guys. He says everything is all right. Just . . . quit poking around. Please, Care.' His voice is pleading. 'He'll have jobs for both of us. Paying jobs. For coin. But you got to stop asking questions about everything.'

'And Fat Peter?' She's looking at him as if from a distance, her eyes hooded and cool.

Another shrug. 'They're handling that. You know he was mixed up with a lot of things. He just—' Tick looks up. 'Nobody thinks you did it, Care. Not really.'

'But everybody thinks they need to tell me to back off.' She's talking to herself rather than him. This makes me purr. 'Everybody says that everything is fine.'

She sends the boy down the hall to wash and as soon as he's out the door she starts shoving papers and other items into her bag. 'I don't know, Blackie.' She talks as she works. 'First, Fat Peter is killed. Then Bushwick comes by, and now Tick.' She hesitates over the food but shoves that in, too. 'Seems to me that whatever the old man was onto is still going on – and I'd be a fool not to see it.'

'Care, what are you doing?' Tick walks into the room as she rolls another of the old man's shirts into a ball.

'I don't know if I'll be able to come back here,' she says, shoving it into her bag. 'No matter what I told Bushwick.'

'Who's Bushwick?' His confusion appears genuine.

'Another visitor. Only he came by to get something, not deliver a message. And I bet he'll be back.' She folds the top over her carryall and pauses. Our eyes meet, and I can see that hers are clear and hold no tears. 'So it's time to move out.'

Tick accepts this without comment, only looking at the uneaten wrapper of cookies. 'Take them,' says the girl.

They're in his pocket in a moment. 'Thanks,' he says, his voice soft. 'Where are we going?'

'We?' She smiles. 'Tick, I don't want to get you more involved in this.'

'You're not going to send me back, are you?' He looks sick at the prospect. 'Not to AD or . . . or . . .'

'I'm not calling protective services. You know that.' She

reaches for him and turns him toward me. 'Why don't you go back to that basement of yours? Maybe you can take Blackie. That way you can keep him safe for me.'

'No!' The boy pulls away. I can't say I'm unhappy, though I would have gone. I would have used the opportunity to understand the forces acting upon this child. 'I'm not leaving you again. Whatever you do, Care, I can help.'

A moment's appraisal, and then she speaks. 'OK, but if things go bad, will you promise to run – run and don't look back?'

He nods.

'We can meet in that basement if we have to. I don't know if this place will be safe.' She turns toward the windowsill but I've already jumped off. I wait by the door until she opens it. She pauses then looks back in the room, as if remembering its former occupant, and for a moment I see it through her eyes. This was his lair once, the man she misses so.

'So where are we going?' Whether it's the cookies or the company, the boy has regained his pep.

'I want to check out Fat Peter's place again.' She has put her melancholy behind her as she leads us away from the business district. Although the day's traffic has picked up, the roads we are on are quiet and pitted, with only the occasional truck rumbling past. 'There's got to be something there and I didn't get to examine it.'

'Care . . .' There is fear in the boy's face. Something else as well. 'There won't be – you know Brian's guys cleaned it out.'

'I'm not looking for money, Tick. Or any of AD's crap, either.' She bites the word off, an edge in her voice. 'I'm just hoping that whatever the old man wanted me to see is still there.'

The boy doesn't look convinced but he keeps up with her, half running to match her pace as she strides back toward the tracks, toward the shadier side of town. She walks quickly, determined, and I dash to keep up, moving from shadow to shadow, watching the street before and behind for unwanted companions or the curious.

By the time we reach the pawn shop the morning sun shines full and bright, reflecting like a beacon off the dead blank window, its frayed curtain faded to dust. The light can't make this street look clean, but it does illuminate the alley that runs behind the stained brick building. The guard of the other day has gone, and Care's picks make quick work of the door.

Although she stands right inside it, her arm out to keep the boy from moving in, I slip easily by. She is right to show caution, but I sense no life in this empty room – nothing larger than a rat, at any rate, and those make themselves scarce at the sound of human feet, accustomed as they are to those both larger and more bloodthirsty than my two companions.

'Blackie, careful!' Startled out of her own watchful appraisal, she steps forward as I jump. The table that held the weights has been righted and set against the wall, although its surface is now empty of all but dust. It is the shelving behind that I wish to examine. The scent there is both more complex than the mix of filth and blood on the floor, and older.

'What is it?' The girl has the sense to follow my lead and leans over the table. I have pressed myself flat to reach under a shelf. There is little in my way. The boy was right: the thugs have cleared the shop of most of its contents. The ancient guitar, missing its strings, and the tarnished hookah are gone, as are the balance and its brass cylinders, the companions of the one the boy had pocketed. What does remain is trash: a china figurine; a dancer, her extended leg broken at the foot; an inkwell, chipped and dry. And a trace of the fragrance of a hand, pressed under here quickly and in duress. It held none of the bitterness I smelled on the boy, but rather something more. Not the blood and terror of the warehouse. No, this is something different but related. Another element of sweat. Of human turmoil. Could it be . . . fear?

'Is something hidden under there?' I am shoved aside as Care's hand reaches beside me, feeling blindly in this cramped space. Her aroma – warm with feeding and with soap – obscures the trail and I back out, annoyed to have been displaced. 'Is that what you're trying to tell me?'

'Probably a mouse.' The boy is watching me intently, his gaze straying from my twitching ears to my restless tail. He is learning to gauge my displeasure. 'I think you bothered him, Care.'

'Nonsense.' She leans in, groping heedlessly. 'Wait, what's that?'

I am on my feet in a flash, ready to take on the scent. She pulls out a scrap of paper, orange, with printing on one side. The boy crowds close, pushing me aside and preventing me from putting my nose up to its surface.

'It's a ticket,' says the boy, reaching for it. I growl, ever so slightly, but he is too distracted to heed my warning and does not put it down. 'One of Fat Peter's tickets. It must have fallen back there.'

'Unless he hid it.' The boy looks up as Care says this, his eyes wide with doubt – or fear. 'The old man always said to question what I find,' the girl goes on to say. 'To not take anything for granted, or assume that something was an accident.' She reaches for the scrap and turns it over in her hand. 'It's blank – just the number and M on the line for Mister or Miss. Maybe it is just a scrap.'

She tucks it into her pocket before I can get to it, but her purpose too is thwarted. 'They took the books.' Her voice is flat with disappointment. 'Of course.'

Beside her, the boy fidgets, shifting from one foot to another. I eye him with distaste. He is old enough to have mastered the basics of toiletry and self-care. But no, instead of excusing himself he appears intent on getting the girl's attention. I close my eyes, the better to concentrate on the faint whiffs of scent still in the air. Beyond the grime of the dilapidated shop, beyond the blood and fetor of Fat Peter's last struggle, there is something heavier – a deep funk. I close my eyes to concentrate and see before me three silhouettes, the tallest one in black.

'Care.' Tick draws two syllables out of the word, the whine in his voice as bothersome as a fly. I do not wish to remember this dream, but if I must, I would prefer to do so quickly. 'Care, I don't like this . . .'

I flick my ears. He should take heed but even the girl is

preoccupied. As I seek to withdraw, to consider the possibilities of this fetid male scent, I hear her moving about. Poking beneath the table, as if to uncover some other cubbyhole or hiding place, some remnant my infinitely more acute senses did not already detect. It is too much, and I would focus. I turn my back.

'Someone's coming.' The boy's whispered warning sends a cold chill through me. He is right, of course. The vibrations of multiple feet announce the intruders even before we hear the slide and click of the lock. I catch myself – the lure of that memory had been intoxicating – and leap to the floor, leading the two children into a back passage where a closet, its contents rifled, sits open.

'Tick, here.' Following me in, Care crouches down, but not before first enfolding the boy in her arms. The closet is empty, save for an old sack, which the girl drapes over her shoulders and the boy. Ungrateful, he pokes his head out and reaches for the door, which she has left ajar.

'Leave it.' Her voice is soft but she knows enough not to whisper; those breathy sounds would carry too well in this enclosed space.

He freezes, not at her command but at a creak and thud. The newcomers have entered the little shop. Their steps are heavy – they are men – and from the way they tread, unafraid to make their presence known.

We squeeze back in the closet as they put down their bags. I hear wood splinter and the crack of porcelain as the figurine tumbles to the floor.

'There's nothing here, boss.' A voice made tight with tension. 'That was his hidey-hole, where he kept the good stuff, and look, you can see.'

More footsteps and then more cracking as the henchmen open more of the wall.

'It's like I said.' The voice a little breathless now. 'We turned this whole place upside down.'

The leader – his stride betokens confidence and good boots – does not respond. Between the clatter of tools going down, going back into their bags, I hear him humming softly to himself as he paces. He walks slowly, his steps measured, and it is with growing trepidation that I hear him move toward the front, toward the window. I do not know what he seeks, but I sense his calm. He is gathering information. Breathing in the room. I can almost see his breath add its fog to the grime as he peers at the junk still waiting there. At the street outside.

'Maybe there never was anything.' Another voice, trying for calm. 'Fat Peter was pretty careful.'

'Hmm.' A low rumble of dismissal and more steps. The sound of a sigh or – no, the sweep of a hand over a surface. The worktable. Does he sense the marks we have left in the dust? The signs of our shared search and discovery? Or will he attribute the passage of fur and paw to some starving feral, another denizen of the city whose agenda does not interfere with his own? It is possible. I cannot hope.

'It's not like the old man needed anything to go on.' I feel Care stiffen beside me. I would will her into stillness if I could. 'I mean, no proof or anything.'

More footsteps. He has walked away from the table but the fur along my spine is rising. A shadow falls across us but the chill I feel has little to do with the blocking of the sun. He has entered the hallway and stands too near our hidden space. I lower my eyes and trust the girl has the sense to do the same. It is dark in here, particularly now that he has blocked the sun, and we are low. And yet we dare not risk a flicker of movement. Of reflection. My whiskers feel the air, judging the space, hoping for a back door, an opening. I smell the boy's fear, and the girl. A hint of masculine sweat.

'Besides, it's Bushwick's neck on the line if anything does turn up. He's the one who's got the most to lose.'

More steps, lighter and hesitant as the first speaker, the higher-voiced one, comes close in agreement. 'And he's doing his own search. If there's anything, he'll find it, boss.'

Another grunt, this time of agreement, and the light returns as the tall man walks away.

'There's nothing here, boss. Nothing but junk.' The girl exhales as the men gather up their tools. I hear footsteps on the broken china and the wood. The creak of a door opened

casually and held that way. Fresh air rushes in and I too begin
to breathe again.

'You want me to lock up?' The subservient one again, his
voice querulous. His companion waits in silence.

'No.' One syllable, deep and sure. 'Torch it.'

SEVENTEEN

The stench is staggering and makes the threat all too clear. Gas or paraffin – sharp and flammable – and the sounds of splashing as the two goons go to work. The scrape of a metal cap being screwed on.

'Hey, give that here. No sense in saving that. That's evidence.' The can is tossed. It bounces against the work table as the men make to leave, the last of its contents spilling out onto the floor. 'Hold on,' the louder ruffian calls ahead. The bite of sulfur. The hiss of a match, and our hope is dashed. The sound of the door closing is almost lost in the woof of heat and light.

'Come on!' Care stands, tossing the sacking aside, and then falls back, coughing. Already the air is thick with dark, oily smoke.

'Care!' the boy whimpers, curling himself into a ball and giving me an image of how he must have been when he was younger. How she must have protected him.

'Here, take this.' She rips the burlap and shoves a piece at him before tying a scrap over her own face. 'Tick, look at me.'

He looks up, still whimpering, and she takes his hand. With a glance back at me, she pushes the door open. The fire is climbing the front window, devouring the moth-eaten curtains. With a pop and a crash, the glass breaks, but the air rushing in only makes the flames roar louder. I do the sensible thing, retreating as far as possible. The air down here is still breathable, the wall solid against my back.

'Blackie!' Care's voice carries over the roar of the flames. There's an urgency in it, but when she reaches for me, I hiss. I have faced death by drowning. I do not want to burn.

'Care?' The boy is crying. Either that or the fumes have made his eyes stream, those big eyes looking up at the girl who has one arm wrapped around him. 'Please, Care?'

Another crash, louder. The shelving above the worktable or perhaps the wall itself. My ears lie so flat on my skull I no longer hear the difference.

'Hang on.' The girl takes up the remainder of the sacking and flings it at me. My claws catch as I smack it away, and no matter how I twist and writhe, I cannot break free. She has grabbed me and, I think, stood up. The heat is crushing, the smoke intense as she lifts me off the ground – as she moves, as she leaps. I am tossed sideways. Upside down. The sweet-hot fug of melting plastic and of blood blinds what senses I have left as the world spins and I howl and rage, waiting for the piercing blow, for the heat. This girl has betrayed me. She has turned on me and I am blind. The light makes shadows on the sacking. Three men watching and the pain . . .

We tumble. I fall hard, my limbs immobilized by my tangled claws. I hear the grunts of others near me.

'He's gone.' A man's voice, flat and cold. No, it's Care. 'They're gone,' she says, and suddenly the cloth pulls back, freeing me and revealing a face black with soot and striped with tear tracks. The shadows of my dream. Behind her, a dumpster smells like rotted fish. Like heaven. We are in an alley, sheltered from the street where a crowd is gathering. Where sirens, too late, pierce the hubbub. The boy, crouched beside her, coughs and spits.

'You OK?' She's asking him but watching me. I hiss again. Reflex from the scare as I step from the fusty sacking with a sneeze. I have no reason to love humans, nor they me. But this girl deserves the best from me, and so I sit and wash my face as I consider our next step.

'No, Tick, I don't think we can go back to the old man's place.' With a glance back at the shop, its stained brick black-ened further by the billowing smoke, the girl urges the boy forward, away from the fire. Away from the crowd. We are heading toward the river. I can smell it. Despite a gentle rain, we are not returning to the upstairs room. 'Not till Bushwick has found what he wanted or given up.'

The boy is sniffling, shaken by the fire. Care has her arm around him, but that's poor shelter. We walk a few more blocks, until the boy begins to stumble, and then turn into another alley. This is a good one: a tunnel of brick, with openings at both ends and the ruins of a doorway that keep us above the puddles. But the door behind us is bricked over as well, its ancient outline impervious to Care's picks. And the overhang that should have shielded us has begun to drip. The wet is slowly soaking, permeating my fur, and I feel the toll of the day. For Care, though, it's the quiet whimpering that makes her turn; makes her draw the boy close and share her warmth.

'I don't think they knew we were there,' she says. It's not comfort. She knows, as do we all, that our presence would not have deterred them. Knows as well that Tick has failed in his errand and worse awaits him if he returns. 'Though I do wonder what they were looking for.'

She fishes around in a pocket, coming up with the scrap. She's slouched against the wall and so it is easy for me, now, to put my nose leather up to the paper. Too late. I get smoke and ash, the tang of the accelerant. Anything else is gone.

'It's probably nothing. A scrap that got lost.' She turns the slip of paper over in her hands. 'Unless it isn't.'

The light is fading and she squints. 'Hey, Tick. You spent time at Fat Peter's. Did you learn anything about his system?'

'What?' The distraction does him good, but as he reaches for the ticket, I feel her hesitate. He is a child and may be careless, I see her tell herself. She does not want to think more.

'Here, look at this.' Keeping hold of the paper, she stretches it open for him to see. Tick blinks at the symbols printed there. They make no more sense to him than they do to me, I suspect, but he tries, biting his lip as he strives to find a meaning in the marks.

'Tick.' Her voice has gone soft. 'Have you forgotten everything I taught you?'

'No.' The boy is annoyed. 'It's just – shouldn't there be something next to those . . . you know . . .' He points.

'Where it just says "M"?' Her voice is soft. She isn't looking at the ticket any longer. Instead, she reaches over and lifts the boy's chin. 'Tick, what exactly did AD have you doing?'

He shrugs. Pulls away and tucks his hands under his thighs.
I do not think it is a response to the cold.

'Tick.' I trust she has noticed, as she had spied the burn
marks days before.

'Messages,' he says at last, when the wait grows too long.
'Errands. You know. I'm small and nobody notices me, AD
says.'

'Is that all, Tick?' She hears what I do: the boy is not telling
her the entire truth. 'I know Fat Peter didn't like girls much,
but—'

'No.' The boy pulls away, embarrassed rather than angry.
'You think that's the only reason anyone would want me. You
think that 'cause you're a girl, and if the old man hadn't picked
you, AD would've had you on the block. But I've got skills,
too, you know. I'm fast and I know my way around. That's
why Brian wanted me.'

The girl flinches at the casual reference to the thug. She
hides it from the boy, though. He's wiping his eyes, wiping
his face of the rain and mucus that make tracks through the
soot and grime.

'So Brian knew you from Fat Peter's?' She's careful in her
use of the name, but she manages. 'You've worked for him
before.' She's slowly piecing this together. I could have told
her about their commingled scents back at the pawn shop.

The boy's eyes dart up to her face and down again. She
sees it, too, but her interpretation differs from mine. 'I'm not
sending you back there, Tick. Don't worry. But doesn't it seem
odd to you that someone like Diamond Jim should be connected
to Fat Peter?'

The boy shrugs his thin shoulders. 'The old man worked
for them both.'

'The old man didn't work for Fat Peter. Fat Peter was a
source.' I hear pride in her voice. 'Like AD.'

The boy looks up again. This time, he doesn't look away.

'That's how I hooked up with the old man,' Care explains.
'He came looking for AD one day when you were – when
you were still searching for your mom. Said he wanted
someone to do some work for him, you know, like he used
to. AD laughed him off, though. He told the old man that he

had better prospects these days. Better coin and more fun, too. The old man wasn't happy about that.' She's talking to herself now, but I can see it. Her mentor recoiling on his dignity. 'I tagged after him.' The ghost of a smile plays around her lips. 'I mean, I had you to look after.'

It's the wrong phrase. 'I can look after myself.'

'Sure you can.' Care keeps turning the ticket over in her fingers, further obscuring any useful information. I huddle back in the doorway. I'd like to keep my eye on this girl, but the rain is not letting up. 'Hey, Tick,' she says after a few minutes have gone by. 'What say we go over to Diamond Jim's and you show me what's what?'

'Care, I don't want to.' His voice is winding up as if tears are on the way.

'I said, I'm not sending you back. I just want to look around on the sly, like. See what we can see, you know?' She grins and the boy grins back. He looks younger with a smile on his face – they both do – though I imagine she is fully aware of the risk she is running. I remember too well the bite of the accelerant. I remember, as well, the silhouettes of my dream. Still, I cannot let this girl face this danger alone.

Brushing her wet hair off her face, she stands and holds her hand out to the boy. I stand too, shaking off the water that has beaded on my guard hairs.

The two humans turn at the movement. 'I don't know what to do with him.' Doubt pinches her face.

'He probably thinks we're going to get food.' The boy knows better than to reach for me, but when he bends for a rock, she takes his hand.

'Tick, no.' She pulls him back.

'He's just some ratty alley cat.' There's a sharpness to his voice – a nastiness assumed to hide his fear. 'Besides, he hates me.'

'He's with me, Tick.' She reaches for his shoulder. Pulls him around to face her. 'You don't hurt animals. You don't hurt anything weaker than you are.' He tries to pull away but she holds him fast, determined to make him listen. 'You just don't.'

I dart ahead of the pair as she releases him. The street

beyond the alley has grown quiet, the sirens long since gone. I do not need to turn to be aware of them passing by me, of them veering to the right, back toward the smoking ruin. We are going downtown, back to Diamond Jim's, with a sullen boy as our guide.

EIGHTEEN

'Y ou don't go in the front.' The boy is reciting, his words clipped and formal. Another lesson learned from a heavy hand. 'You never go in the front. That's for show and for the nobs.' He nods toward the fancy storefront as he talks. We're across the street and several doors down. The traffic here is still considerable, but the grime on these children – along with the stench of smoke – makes other pedestrians give them a wide berth.

'But Brian and his boys keep watch on the alley, right?' She puts a hand on the boy's shoulder, as if to restrain him. She doesn't have to.

'Uh huh.' His voice sinks to nothing and he licks dry lips. She notices. I see her glance down at his face, her own growing more drawn. I would have her focus on the shop opposite. We have approached Diamond Jim's from the high street this time and stand there now, surrounded by commerce and noise. This is not a comfortable setting for me, and I have pressed myself back against a building to escape the mindless bustle. This area has one saving feature. Down here, the entrances to the buildings are separated from the street by planters and columns. The base of one provides sufficient shadow for me to disappear into, the benefit of my dark fur and the dim light, already fading with the day.

'What . . .' she starts to ask. The question remains unfinished. The tumult on the street announces a new presence. A threat. Care glances around and sees me backing further away. I am already secreted, my presence concealed from passers-by. She follows my lead, however, and steps back, pulling the boy with her. They cannot take refuge behind the planter but there is shadow beside the pillar. From here, we can observe.

'It's him.' Tick's whisper sounds loud in the tight space. Louder certainly than his previous admission. I leap to the top of the planter to see, only to feel myself pushed back by the girl.

'Blackie, no!' I turn and spit, my hiss less loud than that foolish boy, and she draws back abashed. But it is too late. The newcomers have passed into the shop, using the front door despite Tick's memorized admonition.

'I told you.' Tick leans forward, peering into the street. 'That cat is bad news – and we shouldn't be here, Care. We should go.'

He steps out, ready to run, and Care follows. 'Tick, I need to find out what those men were looking for – what Bushwick was looking for – if I'm ever going to figure out what happened to the old man.'

'What happened to the old man?' The voice behind her makes Care turn so fast she nearly tumbles. 'What happened to the old man is he got old. He got careless and he forgot that when someone tells you to leave well enough alone, you should do it. Speaking of, I thought you were going to head south, my girl.'

AD is standing there, grinning, his long arms crossed before him. I sink back one step, then two, into the shadows as he unfolds himself to pull a small square of foil from his pocket. 'Good work, Tick,' he says as he tosses it to the boy. 'Though you certainly took your time.'

NINETEEN

The girl gasps – that is all. But in that quick intake of breath I hear everything: dismay, disappointment, fear. As near a sob as a hiss, and of much less use, as it broadcasts her vulnerability when she should be warning this man off.

These men. Although Care is focused on AD, focused on the boy, whose thin wrist he now holds, I see the two emerge from the shadows. The ruffians from before step up behind Care, blocking her exit. Blocking too any aid I might provide, though in truth in such a setting, I do not see what I can do. We are in the heart of the city, on a thoroughfare busy with traffic. And although the pedestrians flow like water around the five still figures, I cannot assume they would pause for me.

One woman, however, looks over. Care's face is a mask of pain, and the woman sees it. She would speak, I think, were it not for the two enforcers. Brian – his face still showing the traces of my claws – glowers, and the woman ducks her head. Carries on, the drama on the street not of her making.

'Tick?' The girl has found her voice, and in that one word puts all her grief and longing. 'What did you do?'

'He grew up,' AD answers for him, the boy himself keeping his head down. 'Got himself more street smarts than you ever had, darling.'

I watch in frustration as the shorter of the two lackeys – Randy? – clasps a beefy hand around Care's upper arm. He needn't worry. She is not trying to run except, perhaps, to the boy, who has pulled free only to kick at the sidewalk before him, aiming one scuffed toe at a spot even I cannot see.

'Tick.' She is pleading, a note in her voice like the mewl of a nursing molly.

'I told you, Care.' He looks up now, no happier than she but at least, for now, unrestrained. 'I told you to stay out of

AD's business. You didn't have to get involved.'

'What business?' She twists in the villain's grasp. It doesn't break, and AD only laughs. 'What does this have to do with you?'

'Didn't you hear what the old man said, Care?' AD's tone is softly mocking. 'All that tricky talk about the balance being off? It's all quite simple, really. Fat Peter had his fat thumb on the scales. He ripped us off once too often. Ripped off other people too, and not everyone is as forgiving as I am. Right, Tick?'

He clasps the boy's shoulder, hard enough to make him wince. Care starts forward again at that, and this time the rat-faced one must pull her back.

'Leave him alone.' She's getting angry now, fury focusing her earlier confusion and despair. From my place of safety behind the planter, I cannot see the color in her cheeks but I hear the steel coming into her voice. She is outnumbered here, however, and any of the three men could master her. I stare at her back, now as stiff as my own, and will her to control herself. To remember her training, which has stood her in good stead thus far.

AD pulls the boy close to him, his hand wrapping around that bony shoulder. I see the child look up at AD and then at Care. He appears to be near tears, although I do not understand the conflict that pulls at him.

'It's not that simple, Care.' AD is smiling. He has gotten her where he wants her and is driving at some end I cannot see. 'It's no longer just up to me.'

'I'll drop it,' she says. I can hear in her voice what this costs her. What she is willing to give. 'Just let him go. I'll drop the old man's case and quit poking around Diamond Jim's. I promise.'

AD laughs again but there's something hollow in it. He's doing it for show, although I do not know why.

'The old man? That's rich.' He looks beyond Care to her captors and I brace for a further violation.

'You always did have a wild imagination, girl. No, this is a simple case of a cheat being caught out. A thief who has to pay.'

Care shakes her head, confused. 'What are you talking about?'

'We can't make things right until we check all the markers off, now can we, Care?' His fingers tighten, digging into the boy, but the child holds still, more frightened of his captor than of any pain. 'Maybe I let things slip once, but I've got another chance now, haven't I? 'Cause it seems that Fat Peter wasn't the only light-fingered member of our crew working the room.'

The boy whimpers, though whether because of AD's grip or the threat in his voice I do not know.

'Is it something Tick lifted?' Care digs her hands into her pockets. Doubt clouds her face as she tries to remember. 'He never— He just goes for the small things, AD. He wouldn't take anything serious.'

AD laughs again, shaking his head as the hand on her arm tightens. Despite his paternal approach he has no love for this girl and is enjoying her discomfort.

She knows this, from long experience, I believe, and fights the urge to pull away from her captors. The rat-faced one rifles through her bag, looks up and shakes his head. A flash of understanding lights her face.

'Wait,' she says. 'I have it. Somewhere.' She roots through her clothes until she finds the ticket, offering up the battered scrap of paper on her outstretched palm. AD barely glances at it.

'I don't want your ticket, my girl.' His voice is cold with scorn. 'Though I am curious what you had to pawn. I've got coin enough these days, and more on the way. No, Care, I'm looking for something else – something that belonged to Fat Peter that you've got.'

Care freezes and then breathes a phrase: 'The ledger.' Her exhalation is too soft for human ears but I catch it, envisioning a book, large and leather-bound. Care's weapon, with which she felled the brute behind her, the one who would have made short work of me. I can still see her standing there, brandishing it in both hands. And, yes, she did run with it, despite its weight.

'That was an accident, AD.' She's speaking fast. 'I didn't mean – I took off with it.'

'Yes, my girl. We know that.' AD nods and the other thug comes forward, taking her other arm and wrenching it out of her pocket.

'Wait, no—' Care protests, too little, too late, as they start to turn her toward the street.

'Officer, there!' It's the woman, the one who walked by. She is leading a uniformed man, a bully in his own right, up through the crowd. 'Those men!'

Head down, the cop passes her by, his face set on violence. He's too late. The two goons have stepped back, into the street, their caps low over their faces. AD, meanwhile, has melted away, leaving Tick and the girl on their own.

TWENTY

'All right, girly.' The bullish cop stands, legs akimbo, before Care. 'Now what's your game?'

She takes a step backward, into the planter, and I dash around to the concrete pot's far side.

'Officer, no.' The Good Samaritan grabs his arm. Not hard enough to dissuade him, but he pauses. 'She's the victim here,' the well-dressed woman explains.

'Really?' He turns back to Care. She has begun to sidle away but he extends his billy club, blocking her retreat. 'Phew, you stink. You want to tell this nice lady here what you're really about, girly? You and your pimp, bringing your dirty business down to the clean part of town?' His brows go up as he spies something on her, something I cannot see.

'Officer—'

'Hold on.' He dips his club into Care's jacket, the pocket she'd been digging in only moments before. When he pulls it out, there's a cloth on its tip – tan and black and silky. The scarf she had used to disguise her hair. 'Using that fire as cover for a bit of work, eh?'

'Is that a—' The Good Samaritan reaches up to her own neck, as if any of us could have spirited part of her wardrobe away.

'That's how they work it, miss.' The cop turns ever so slightly, eager to explain to a grateful public. 'One of 'em creates a distraction. Maybe even set that blaze, then – hey, what's this?'

I am not above the obvious. Although I have no doubt that the officer speaks the truth in a general sense, I do not believe my companion has played that particular game. As he was speaking, however, I saw my opportunity and grabbed it, jumping down from the planter to rub against his leg. It's a risk, for sure. A man like this one may wear a uniform but underneath he is similar to the minion doing AD's bidding.

The sole of his patrolman's shoe is thick, his leg heavy with muscle and fat, and I must remember that I am no longer quite as quick as once I was. Indeed, I feel him shift in preparation for a kick and play my final card.

'Mew.' I keep my voice soft, plaintive, as I peer up at the matron, blinking my green eyes in feigned affection. 'Mew,' I say again.

The cry she emits is not what I expected. A squeal of hatred or disgust, she recoils as if I were verminous or as rank as a poorly cured pelt. I am taken off guard, it is true, but so too is the officer. Having already checked his initial aggressive reaction to my unwanted advance, he has not yet resumed his wide-legged stance, and in that I see safety. I cannot purr. That is beyond me at this time, but I can lean in, and do, throwing myself against his shin.

'What the hell?' The man looks down. If only the girl would seize her moment, not hesitate from concern for me. I stare up at her, willing her to go. 'Hey, girl!'

Too late, my gaze has drawn his attention back to Care, even as she had begun to sidle by his still-outstretched baton. 'I'm not done with you!'

With a glance to me that seems half apology and half despair, she pulls back farther even as he reaches and steps toward her. And as he does, he forgets that I am there.

The woman shrieks as he stumbles, tripping over me. His steel-toed boots lift me up but a lifetime of training, as well as a lower center of gravity, serve me well as I scramble from beneath his flailing figure and head for the gutter, running fast and low and keeping the girl in sight.

She takes off like a rabbit, darting around corners and people to elude pursuit. But where a rabbit does this by instinct, I see sense in her flight – a quick appraisal of the landscape guiding her choices as she skips one alley to duck down another, a delivery van providing cover as she squeezes through its torn rear fence. I follow, of course, although the beep-beep-beep of the van signals its backing even as I clear the tires, making the chain link's gap almost too dear a risk.

She slows after that but keeps moving and I see her head

turning, that mop of hair a beacon to her foes. I will her to go to ground, not least because of my own fatigue: the prolonged sprint has winded me; the ache in my side becomes a piercing with every panting breath. She has become used to hunting, to being in pursuit, but now she is the prey. I would that she seek safety. That she hide.

Then I see it. She is not merely running, fleeing heedless of the danger. She is adjusting her course, a destination in mind. These streets carry some memories in their perfume – the smell of leather, of horses long gone and, more faint and farther off, tar – and soon I realize that I, too, know our path. We are nearing the train yard, the wasteland where we found safety briefly once before. And where, I realize, the fur stiffening on my neck, we were also nearly trapped.

She pauses at last, bending, hands on knees, to gasp in air, and with a last effort I reach her, moving from the gutter to the open street to catch her eye.

'Blackie.' Despite everything, she looks pleased, a smile brightening her pale and sweating face. 'I thought you—' She stops and shakes her head. 'No, you couldn't have, but thank you.'

I approach, tempted for a moment to rub her legs, to feel her warmth against my heaving side. Instead, I sit and wait as my own breath grows steady again. This is not the time for sentiment, nor would I have her recall the ploy that I have so recently used.

'OK.' She nods and pulls herself upright. Walking now, she heads down the street. It is quiet here, far enough from the center of commerce that the pedestrians and police are less of a threat. But no part of this city is without some life. I notice with approval how she looks ahead, leaning to peer around each building before we pass, checking that the fire escapes and windows are as blank and quiet as they appear.

I check as well, though with other senses more acute than sight. A quick scan, using ears and nose, and we would appear to be alone, the day too early still for the dealers and their shills, the whores and petty thieves who make such borderlands their home. Some are still uptown, hiding under the mantle of respectability, on the hunt. Others wait in restless repose, sheltering inside these husks of buildings. I hear their muttered sighs and snoring, as much the soundtrack of the city as the scrambling of rodents in the drains. I do not sense any undue interest, however. No suppressed breathing, no footsteps shadowing ours. Unmolested, we reach the train tracks, and as the girl slows, inspecting the terrain, it dawns on me what she is after. What she, in her frail human way, is stalking.

'It's got to be here, Blackie.' She leads me this time across the tracks and to the pitted junkyard where we had sheltered. 'The ledger AD wanted. I ran with it, I remember, despite its size. I thought – never mind what I thought. I was thinking more of a weapon than of what the thing actually was. But maybe that was smart of me.' She pauses. 'Or maybe I got Tick in deeper because of this. Maybe.' She stops and wipes her face with her hand as if to block out the memory of betrayal. 'Maybe this is all my fault.'

I do not understand her logic. I can, however, see the pain in her, the wincing need that brings tears into her eyes again, and I react, leaning into her now with the affection I withheld before. I relax her, I can feel that, the way my superior warmth and the softness of my fur cause her to unclench just a little. I wait, even, for her to lift me, and will myself not to fight the loss of agency in service of a greater good.

She kneels, her palm flat against my back, fingers curling to where my side still aches and it is my turn to tense, to anticipate what pain she may unknowingly cause.

I need not worry. One touch and she has stood again, craning her face around as if to memorize this patch of dirt and refuse. Or, no, to recall it.

'Here,' she says as much to herself as to me. The rusting shell where we had stopped looks much the same, its detached door still propped against its trunk. She walks up to it but I leap ahead. Our foes have been vicious rather than wily, but I will take no chances.

As she pokes around the wreck, I examine the stony ground where we once sat – the cold metal the girl had leaned back on – letting the damp air bring me all its mingled traces. She soon begins emitting the sounds of frustration: a grunt, a sigh, even as she lies belly-down on the earth to peer beneath the rotted chassis.

Although her search appears to be fruitless, mine is less so. There is much to record here: grubs and rot and a decay of a more alchemical sort as this giant machine breaks down. The rain and cold of the previous night have washed away the scent of our earlier sojourn – all I get of the girl is from her close presence, still sweating from our run. There has been another human here, though, and someone close – familiar. A clean, sweet scent, like that of a child but with a hint of something bitter. The breakdown of rust mixed with motor oil, perhaps, or . . .

'Tick!' Care's voice startles me more than I care to acknowledge. I have not heard the boy, nor been aware of another presence. However, there he is – hanging back by the train track, as if he still might consider a run. 'It's OK, Tick.' The girl calls out to him, using the soft cadences one does with a spooked animal. 'Come here.'

The boy looks up, hopeful, at the entreaty, but an animal wariness remains and he approaches slowly. Head down, he kicks the ground as he walks, like the child he is. A dangerous child.

Care waits, sitting back on a rock. I circle, not trusting this unfaithful friend, but for the life of me I get no sense of any others. No sense of the villains who would make quick work of us here, with no civilians to witness.

'How'd you find me, Tick?'

The question surprises me. I had thought her focused on the book – Fat Peter's ledger – and I am gratified to hear that she shares my curiosity about the boy.

'I followed you.' The boy looks up, a glimmer of pride lighting his face. 'I've been doing it for a while. Same way I found the old man's place.'

The girl blinks, the surprise knocking her head back. She hadn't thought to question his appearance the other morning. The boy doesn't seem to notice, so desperate is he to make his case. 'I started doing it just to prove I could,' he says, a pleading note creeping into his voice. 'That I'd be good at detecting, too, you know? I wanted you to see that I could do this, and—' He pauses, his face dropping to the dirt. 'I didn't like that you left me behind.'

He is lying, of course. Prevaricating as all good dissemblers do, confusing the scent with a dollop of truth. That he did not wish to be excluded, I believe. That wish, in fact, may have ensnared him into AD's plans. However, he did not follow Care – not this time – and I wrack my brain for the means to tell her so. A low growl begins to rumble deep inside me, involuntary but to the point. If I were to approach this boy I would frighten him, and so I hold back, waiting. I have other goals than revenge, and terror will not win me them. Observation, on the other hand . . .

'You got here awfully fast.' Care tilts her head, as if to signal that her statement requires an answer, and my growl subsides. This girl knows something of interrogation, though her senses lack the acuity of mine. I start forward, creeping slowly. I would get the scent of this young traitor. Read for myself his recent travels and abode.

'I had a head start.' The boy flushes, his pale face turning red as his contradiction catches up to him. 'I mean, I followed you the other day – when you left Fat Peter's. I knew you were going there, Care. You'd just left AD's—'

He stops short, the name of the gang leader a ghost standing between them.

'And AD sent you after me?' Her voice is so soft now, as gentle as the touch of my whiskers as I come up behind the boy. This close, I see that he is shaking, his tiny frame trembling in his oversize rags. Whatever the men have threatened, it has stayed with him. He reeks of fear and sweat, and of that acrid sharpness. The chemical tang almost obscures another scent, dark and earthy. The boy has soiled himself recently. The funk clings to him like the shame that makes him hang his head. I do not believe he dissembles now. This boy is wretched. A tool of those savage men – nothing more.

'I'm sorry.' The whisper barely reaches me. The girl, still ten feet away, cannot have heard, but still she starts at this, rushes forward, garnering through some undetermined sense the meaning of his words. But I step in between them, glaring up at her with fierce concentration. Pity is a luxury, I want to tell her. And a boy may be a victim and a tool both, more dangerous for his apparent weakness.

She steps by me to take him in her arms, even as I growl. And as she does, I see her reach into his pocket to retrieve the foil-wrapped packet AD had given him, the source of that acrid scent.

'It's just to sell, Care.' He struggles in faint protest. 'I wasn't going to smoke it.'

'Tick.' She holds him still, ignoring his protest. 'You don't need this. You're not your mom. What you need to do is tell me what you did with the book.'

TWENTY-ONE

'You do have it, don't you?' Her voice is low; her question direct. The boy continues to stare at the ground. 'Tick?'

He nods. 'I saw you drop it the other day,' he says. 'Before Brian and Randy— Before they came for you.'

Care looks thoughtful as she works back over the memory of our escape from Fat Peter's – and our brief respite here. I recall the smell of the volume, the black leather worn soft by the pawnbroker's hands, but do not know how the girl disposed of it once I fell asleep. I watch her face for my answer. Yes, what the boy says apparently fits with what she remembers.

He sees this as well and begins to spill words like water.

'I thought you'd want it,' he says, doling out his explanation like an offering to win her back. 'I mean, I know how you feel about books.'

From my vantage point several feet away I see a pained expression pass over the girl's face. The boy has evoked a shared memory, that much is clear. I can only hope that this touchstone does not cause her to lay down all of her defenses.

When she fails to comment he goes on, eager to fill the void. 'I came back here while I was . . . while I was on my errands,' he says. He looks down as he says this. In humans, this could indicate shame. It may also be a ploy of distraction, an adult usage I do not think beyond this hard-used child. His next words support this. 'I didn't think that AD would care.'

AD. I have come to hate this man, and not simply as the source of that foul-smelling substance. He has a power over this child – over the girl as well – that I fail to understand, and that I believe he will use without compunction. From my vantage point I watch the girl, waiting to see her reaction to his words. The mention of their former colleague – no, leader – should be warning enough that this child is compromised, and yet I have reason to be concerned. Emotion makes this young woman vulnerable, no matter how well schooled she may have been. Its influence, as much as the persistent sadness, is a sign of how that training was cut short.

'AD.' She sighs, and in her voice I hear the echo of something I cannot explain. Not the nightmare vision that I wrestle still to understand, but something other. There is longing and sadness, and I see her face go slack for a moment. 'Tick, you can't go back to him. You know that.'

The boy's shrug is eloquent in its way, dismissive of her concern and powerless all at once.

'When we first came to him, he wasn't so mixed up with all that crap.'

'He always used and cooked, too.' The boy speaks and my ears prick up. Would that Care's did, too. His tone reveals an allegiance she would do well to mark. 'And he's doing great.'

'He's doing—' She shakes her head. The fight, it seems, is one to which she is accustomed, one she will not win today. 'Tick, where's the book?'

He smiles as if he's won and nods his head back across the tracks. I stand and lash my tail, willing her not to act on his lead. Those thugs have tried to snatch her here, in open land, and failed. How easy would it be to lure her into a confined space? To subdue her in some hideaway, away from passers-by or their uniformed henchmen? She turns toward me and sees my back begin to arch. She pauses. 'Tick?'

'You remember the basement where we spent the night?' He points to the drainpipe. To the brick beyond, more ruin than building, and thick with the shadows of the fading day.

She nods, assessing his words – her options. She wants the ledger, and I confess to curiosity about that worn black leather as well. Still . . . she stares at Tick, but he has already turned.

'Come on,' he says. She follows.

I keep close as we cross the wasteland, flanking the boy but out of reach. I stay before her, in her sight, ready to react. I will not flee at the unexpected but rather sound the alarm – what alarm I can, with howl and hiss and claw. It is not much of a guarantee, but I owe it to the girl. In truth, my aching side reminds me, I am hunting now on borrowed time, and while I do not understand just how our lives have become intertwined, I respect it – the debt owed from one lone creature to another as the roles of hunter and of prey shift and mutate like the shadows in my dream.

'This way.' The boy ducks into the pipe and I steel myself. This is too like a trap, its narrow, unlit passage perfect cover for all manner of evil. A trickle of water, opalescent and polluted, flows out into the rocky dirt and I sniff at it for signs of movement. Signs of life.

'Don't, Blackie.' She has come up behind me and mis-interprets. 'That's not healthy.' She bends to touch me – no, to pick me up, and I must leap ahead. I will do her no good couched in her arms. If I am ensnared, so be it: at least I will give warning. But as soon as I descend, I see the graying light ahead. The day is fleeting but this tunnel, at least, is not obstructed and so I dash through it and beyond, whirling as I do to catch sight of any ruse or ambush. There is nothing. An unseen crow mocks us from the lowering clouds, and that is all.

Care emerges behind me, blinking, her trepidation clear as she cranes her head.

'I told you.' The boy sounds petulant now, his value doubted. 'It's my safe place – mine alone.'

He turns and wordlessly we follow, my guard hairs up and senses keyed for trouble. Down pitted streets where cobble-stones show through broken asphalt, we make our way. Only the puddles here give evidence of the passage of machines, their oily stench almost as overpowering as that of the foil-wrapped packet that Care has taken from the boy. It hangs between them, I can see, as he glances back and as she shoves her hand once more into her pocket. But he moves freely, without the cramped and desperate look I remember from their former colleagues – from AD's crew, almost a child again as he jumps across a pothole and skids on greasy stone.

And then he stops, one hand out as if to still us, too. A trick he has learned from Care. We pause, waiting for his signal. Waiting, too, for the ambush that will finally arrive. Three men. I now have names for two – Brian and Randy – and while I do not share the human's reverence for naming – my own now lost to time and water – I find some comfort in the

knowing. These are the brutes who would see me dead. There
is peace in clarity. Satisfaction in my knowledge.

'Tick?' The girl's voice is soft, barely a murmur. After a
moment, he responds.

'All clear,' he says, stepping into the street. I pass in front
of Care, mindful as I do of the superstition about my kind,
half remembered, and pause for a second, waiting. No, there
is no other movement here, no watchers waiting, and so I turn
and follow, freeing her to walk as well. We cross the street
to a familiar entrance and descend to Tick's basement hideaway
at last.

'Here.' On his familiar turf the boy becomes an eager child
again, heading straight for the pile of bricks where once he
had his stock of food. 'I came here when they let me go. When
I got away.'

He moves two bricks, one in each of his dirty hands, and
then two more, before pulling out a large flat shape wrapped
in rags. Peeling the cloth back, he reveals the ledger and hands
it, proud as a prince, to Care, who immediately takes it over
to where a gap lets in the last of the afternoon light.

'Let's see what's gotten AD all riled up,' she says and
pauses. 'Thanks, Tick. You did well.'

The boy glows, despite it all. And Care opens the book.

TWENTY-TWO

I am, as previously noted, a cat. And while this means I possess senses more keen than those of many creatures, as well as the ability to reason and to evaluate that which I observe, I do not read. And while I doubt the boy's ability to do so either, despite Care's obvious concern and tutoring, I see no point in huddling with her as she examines the ledger, murmuring as she runs one finger down each scribble-filled page. Instead, I examine the cover, rubbing my jaw against the tattered binding to capture its scent – its essence – and begin my own analysis.

Leather, but better quality than expected. Fat Peter may not always have been the small-time hustler that his shop suggested, not if he kept his accounts in a volume such as this. Though considering his trade, that dusty window full of junk, it is more likely that the book came in as collateral – some poor accountant too tangled in his own numbers to have anything else to offer as his bond.

I sniff the cover again, open-mouthed, and close my eyes to better take it in. The quality of the hide and its deep perfume reminds me again of the man I had trailed and his own badly cured pelts. He had been afraid, this man who had accosted Care, the stench of fear overpowering those sad, dear furs even in his own place of business.

What had he been seeking? My companion has surmised, with reason, that his stated goal was not his real one; that this man – this Bushwick – has most likely by now searched the office where her mentor once offered sanctuary. Did he find that which he sought? Did he seek it for himself, as he had said, or for another? The deep warmth of the leather calms me, but I am mulling over that stranger – the third man at Fat Peter's. Did he seek this ledger, too? Was he affiliated with the treacherous AD, or was there something other here at work, something that I have as yet failed to grasp?

'Look at the cat,' the boy whispers, but I ignore him. 'He's totally asleep.'

'Shh.' Care would silence him, though for the benefit of my supposed rest or to aid her own concentration I cannot tell. 'Come here.'

She does not speak to me, and so I continue with my cogitations. The boy, however, climbs over to where she sits and folds himself under her arm. My eyes remain closed, of course, as I persist in my analysis. My ears, however, twitch, registering every motion, even as the boy's lips begin to move, sounding out the words and symbols held before him.

'Do you know what this means?' The girl's voice is soft, though her concern is more for the child cuddled close than for my supposed slumbers. 'These numbers here?'

'The items?' The boy is guessing, and she prods him further.

'What do you see?'

'Three four eight one oh.' He makes the numbers out slowly and then stops. 'Three four eight one one.' Clearly, she is moving him down the list. 'Three four eight one two.'

'Very good.' The sound of paper as she turns a page.

'Three four eight one four,' says the boy, and I sense rather than hear Care start.

'Wait.' The page again. She is turning back. 'Well, Fat Peter skipped a number, Tick. That seems unlike him.'

More pages turn but she ceases to speak. I have shifted again. The last of the afternoon sun now rakes the basement floor; the shadow of the two children stretches along the uneven dirt and I align myself with that, my sore side absorbing what is left. The light gives precious little warmth, but what there is my fur absorbs. I think of those pelts again. Of that strange fat man and all his clothes. These children could use half as much. They could use my fur, were things to come to that. I do not see what they have that he would want. Nor Fat Peter's role in such transactions as would interest him.

'No, he never skipped a number.' Care is speaking to herself as much as Tick, but I hear him turn to look at her. 'There's no item listed. No name, either. Just—'

'Do you think this is what the old man found out?' His question seems so guileless, but I am instantly alert. This boy turns like a centipede, slipping into corners. He has even bragged of this, if only Care will remember.

'Maybe, Tick.' She's thinking – of his absences, I hope. Of his time with AD and Diamond Jim's men. 'You're sure about what he said?'

'Something about weighing down the scale,' the boy repeats. 'And that Fat Peter's not on the same level. I think that's it.'

'Fat Peter must have been involved in the theft from Diamond Jim's. Why else would the old man have passed that along?' she asks, as if not expecting the boy to reply. 'Maybe it's as simple as that – and that he was killed when those thugs found out. They wouldn't have had the old man's technique but they'd have their ways. And if they even suspected him . . .' She doesn't say more. There is no need. We all saw what became of Fat Peter.

In her arms, the boy begins to squirm. Discomfited by the memory, perhaps. Or by some knowledge that he dare not share.

'What is it, Tick?' Care sits up and I do as well, taking in the scene before me. The boy does not stand; does not pull away as if to answer a call of nature. Instead, he stares first at me and then, my green gaze too cool for his liking, at the pile of bricks that had concealed his prize. 'Tell me.'

He bites his lip, as if to keep the words inside.

'I don't know, Care.' He doesn't look happy. 'I mean, maybe I got it wrong?'

The girl nods. 'You mean the old man's message? Do you think AD heard it? Or . . .'

He shrugs, not willing to say more.

'Fat Peter's death isn't your fault,' she says, her voice soft. 'Everybody knew Fat Peter was no thief. If he were involved with that necklace, it was as a fence – a resale man. Everyone knew he could move stuff. But, maybe, if he paid someone, gave out credit . . .' She nods, the possibilities becoming clear. 'That might explain a ticket not entered in the book, a marker for those emeralds, especially if he expected Diamond Jim to send someone looking. Someone tougher than the old man.'

She thinks on that for a while. 'The old man wouldn't have taken the job if he thought he was setting up an execution.

Diamond Jim must have kept that from him, and that's pretty hard to do. So maybe Fat Peter knew something else, something about who commissioned the job or why they hit Diamond Jim. But if so, why . . .'

Another pause and then she turns, slowly, to appraise the boy.

'Unless the jewels came to him first, before he found out where they were from. Fat Peter never could resist a bargain, and if a thief brought him something nice, he'd be hard-pressed to turn it down. Especially if he could get it cheap – if he could bully the seller down to a rock bottom price.' Her voice fades as she sorts it out. 'And then, if he found out; if he wanted to return them . . . Tick?' An edge has crept into her voice. She tries to hide it, softening her questions with a singsong quality. 'Did you steal from Diamond Jim? Did you maybe do a smash-and-grab, a quick pocket and hare, perhaps? Please, tell me.'

'No.' He's shaking his head so hard, his overlong hair swings back and forth. 'No, I don't do that anymore, Care. You told me what could happen and I don't want to go back. No way. Not even if I'm hungry. I don't steal.'

Her voice grows softer and my fur begins to prickle. 'What about that little weight you gave me, Tick? The brass thing? Didn't you pick that up, maybe, at Fat Peter's?'

'I didn't.' His lower lip sticks out and I fear tears. 'He gave that to me. Honest.'

The girl bites back the obvious response. 'Maybe there's a silver lining,' she says instead. 'I never did like you hanging out there with everything that went on in that shop of his. And it was probably one of those flash boys who brought the wares to Fat Peter. Nobody will cry when one of that crew washes up on the riverbank. I wonder who the old man was looking at? Was there some big money on the other end of the transaction? Diamond Jim's wares are major league and that necklace sounded grand. Even once he broke it up, Fat Peter must have had somebody in mind for the stones.

'Unless . . .' She reaches for the ledger again. 'Unless they were on consignment.'

'What do you mean?' The boy sits up as she starts to leaf

through the pages. The sun has moved, and so I join them. The basement is damp after the recent rains, and the shared warmth is welcome. 'Like on order?'

'Exactly.' She runs her finger down a page. The light has grown dim and she must lean forward to make it out. After a moment, she pauses to dig into her pocket. The rumpled ticket is the worse for wear, and she holds it flat, squinting at its surface. I cannot resist a look myself, but as I jump up on the windowsill, the better to view the tiny scrap, my shadow falls upon it.

'Hang on,' she says, standing. Reaching up to the open well, she leans on the sill beside me. The markings are clear to me, although she struggles to make them out. Would that we could combine my eyesight and her comprehension. 'Eight one three,' she says. 'And no name on the line.'

Back to the page then, and she nods with something like satisfaction. 'The missing entry – the one Fat Peter skipped – it's got to be tied in with the stolen necklace. The old man always told me: "Never trust a coincidence."'

She sinks back to the floor, the ticket in her hand. 'So maybe Diamond Jim hasn't gotten the emeralds back yet. And maybe this is what those creeps were looking for.'

'Wouldn't Fat Peter have given that up?' Tick isn't looking at the ledger. He reads Care instead. 'I mean, if Brian or Randy showed up to hurt him?'

'You'd think.' Care goes back to the ledger. 'Maybe things got out of hand. Maybe he died before they could get the info. That could be why they still want the ledger.'

She sits there quiet, deep in thought, the boy by her side. This is their circle, the rules they know. But something is eating at the boy, something besides hunger and his own filth. He's fidgeting again, and while she reads I examine his face – the way he chews his lip. I mutter softly, a murmuring rumble to break her reverie, but it's the boy – agitated, alert – who looks up.

'What do you mean, send a message?' He's blinking, afraid.

'You know, to keep everyone in line.' I see her concern on her face. She was speaking without thought, though the idea that she would be able to shield this child from the harsh reality of their environment seems risible. I grumble a little louder, just enough to make the boy turn.

'But that's – that's what I did,' he says. This bothers him, although I cannot see why.

She pulls herself upright, the book forgotten on her lap. 'What do you mean, Tick? Tell me.'

'I told you.' In the fading light his eyes are dark and shadowed. 'I carry messages. That's what AD had me doing.'

'I don't mean that kind of message.' Care leans in as if to comfort the boy and stops herself. 'Wait – Tick, do you know something about this?'

'I just . . . It's a job, Care. You said so yourself – I needed to find a job. And AD said I could go anywhere. Get by anyone. And I'm fast, too.'

'What kind of messages did you bring, Tick?' She's making an effort to keep her voice steady. 'You need to tell me.'

'Most of the time, it was something small,' says the boy. 'A thing – you know, a token. Like a book of matches to old Jonah.'

'Jonah Silver?' She's been taken by surprise.

The boy nods.

'No wonder he's so down in the mouth.'

'But he didn't have a fire, did he?' The boy seems proud of his role, though the threat makes my ears flip back and down. 'He got the message. He knew what it meant.'

'He knew all right.' The girl is thoughtful. 'Was that what it was for Fat Peter, Tick? Was it a book of matches?' Her own voice is nearly silent, all breath and tremor. 'Was it the red brick – or the bloody knife?'

He shakes his head and sniffs. Shoves his hands into his pockets as if to find the answer there, or perhaps something of comfort – some small, fine thing to call his own.

'It wasn't like that, Care. It wasn't a – you know – a threat. It meant, "It's time," he said – Fat Peter said. He was all worked up about it. Excited, like. He tried to . . . you know.'

'Oh, Tick.' She folds him in her arms at last as he begins to cry, and holds him until he calms. Only then, when his breathing has grown regular once more, do I hear her murmur.

'Time? Time for what?' She pauses, hearing her own question.

'And why no token?' In the growing gloom she doesn't see how the boy looks away. How he opens his mouth but doesn't speak.

Instead, she is lost in her own thoughts. When she speaks again her voice is breathy with memory. A voice so distinct I feel I can hear it as well, a growly kind of baritone, soft but sure of its impact. '"The measure is off," he said.' A ghost stands behind her, his breath in her words. '"Fat Peter isn't on the level." The old man told you to tell me that. He knew Fat Peter owed somebody, but by then it was too late. Someone else knew that he was getting that message. Someone got rid of Fat Peter. The question is, who? And why kill the old man as well?'

The boy only shrugs, the darkening room quiet but for those ghosts.

TWENTY-THREE

Morning finds the girl roused and ready, shaking her younger companion at first light. I've been awake for hours, of course. Hunted, bathed. But although I find myself wondering about the boy's duties and the role he may yet play in this girl's life, I keep my thoughts to myself, content to sit on that ledge and sniff the air, all the while keeping these young humans within earshot.

'Come on, Tick,' she calls to him while rummaging in her sack. The boy is slow to wake. He's been dreaming, I could tell her. Though whether the night phantoms that haunted his sleep, prompting the twitches and moans of a prey animal under attack, bear any relation to the scene I have relived, the water's edge and the silhouettes, I do not know. 'We've got to go.'

'Where are we going?' He takes the piece of cheese Care hands him along with the wrinkled apple. I perk up at the sight of the cheese, remembering its salt and grease, and Care slices off the rind, placing it on the sill before me. It is more wax than cheese, however, and I leave it. Perhaps it will draw something more toothsome still, especially once these two have moved on. My side still aches from yesterday. My hindquarters are stiff and sore, and I have no desire to trot around after this girl as if I were some kind of dog. This seems to be our base for now, dry enough and reasonably safe. I will wait here and hunt again, gathering my thoughts until these two return.

'I have an idea.' Care looks around before locating the loose bricks of the boy's hiding place. That she then unpacks her bag and places her extra clothes, the few treasures she has taken from AD's, in the space confirms my deduction: this is to be home for the foreseeable future. I fold my paws beneath me and prepare to nap.

'I think . . .' she says, turning back to the boy, to us, '. . . I want to call on George Bushwick.'

'Who?' The boy stands yawning, his question a delaying tactic. But I am no longer at rest. The memory of Bushwick's warehouse, the stench of those pelts, has banished thoughts of sleep. There was something – *is* something – wrong with that man, reeking of fear and death. I cast my thoughts about for some way to communicate and find myself twining around the girl's ankles, willing her to listen as I mewl out my complaint.

'Hey, Blackie, it's OK.' She picks me up, burying her face in my fur. It's an uncomfortable sensation, being lifted off one's feet, and although the warmth of her embrace is pleasant – I am not immune to the affectionate gesture and the rubbing of her face against my side translates – I struggle to be let down, twisting in her grasp. 'You didn't eat your cheese.' She has noticed the rind and reaches for it before I can bat it away. Strict economy delays her further as she retrieves her bag to stow the waxy morsel. I close my eyes in frustration. Not being able to communicate directly seems wrong, somehow.

'I don't think he wants you to go out.' The boy surprises me, although I suspect he is speaking from selfish reasons. The grey dawn has grown no brighter and I smell rain as well as fog. 'He likes that we're warm and dry here.'

'He didn't know the old man.' Her voice has acquired an edge; some combination of anger or fear makes her want to push this boy. 'But it's more than that, Tick. Bushwick came looking for something the other night, something he thought the old man had. I don't know if it was that pawn ticket or something else. But until we get to the bottom of it, those jerks are going to keep coming after us. They're going to start looking for you.'

The boy shuts up at that, although he stares at me as if I am to blame. Because the mistrust runs both ways, I leap, once again, to the sill. Despite my earlier plans, when the girl takes off, I will tail her. If I can, I will stay out of sight. It is my deepest hope that she does not know about this Bushwick's warehouse, that she never goes to that place of fear and blood. But there is an air about her – determination, fate – that I recognize. This girl is on the hunt, and I will not let her hunt alone.

'Come on, Tick.' She ushers the boy out the door as I watch from my perch. 'First, I want to go back to the old man's place. Bushwick's probably been and gone by now, but maybe I can figure out something by what he's taken. If there's anything left.'

So far, so good. I trot behind them. The boy is still sleepy and they proceed at an easy pace. She is speaking, as much to encourage him as to explain, I believe. Her voice is musical and soft.

'I don't know why he lied, but I'm pretty sure that he didn't have any outstanding business with the old man,' she is saying. 'Still, that tells us something. The old man always said to look at the absences – what are people not telling you? What are they lying about? That's where you find the truth, he said.' They walk in silence for a block. The fog is lifting but the clouds are growing thicker, as if all the dampness of the day is gathering overhead. 'Why would he even come to the—'

She stops, her back stiffening in the cold morning. 'Tick, why did you talk to Bushwick? Come on, I know you know him.'

The boy has stopped walking, too, but he kicks his worn shoes at the cobblestone before him, the thin canvas sliding over the grey stone.

'Tick?' Something about the action alerts her. I, meanwhile, have found a ledge, also stone but elevated from the roadway. It offers a dry perch from which to watch this little drama. 'I know you told him about the office. He told me. But why were you speaking to him at all?'

'I carry messages.' His voice is nearly buried, his words addressed to that unfeeling stone. 'I told you that.'

'Messages, Tick?' The effort she expends at keeping her voice level makes it tremble. I hear this. The boy must as well. 'Both ways?'

He nods. 'Intel, AD calls it. Things he wants to know.'

'Like where the old man had his hiding places?' Another nod. 'But how does Bushwick figure into this? He's not one of AD's usual clients.'

A shrug – more eloquent than any of the boy's words. 'Intel

is like gold, AD says. It doesn't lose its value and it goes to the highest bidder.'

'I don't get it. The old man didn't mess with AD. Didn't mess with his business.' She pauses, a memory flitting across her thin, pale face. 'He always said he was there to help people who wanted it, not the ones too foolish to know better. And George Bushwick, well, he wasn't the kind of client we were likely to see again.'

'Who is he? I mean, what's he do?' Tick's questions break into her reverie. She's been thinking aloud, and his question smacks of a diversion. Still, she answers.

'You don't know?'

He shakes his head.

'Business. Import, export – a little of everything. He wanted us to do a job for him a little more than a year ago – last July, maybe August. It was pretty much open and shut. He was bringing in whiskey – some high-test stuff that was below the radar of the inspectors. Only he wasn't getting what he'd paid for. I gather he'd figured out that the seller wasn't ripping him off – and, no, I don't want to know how he did that – and he wanted the old man to find out who was messing with his product at this end.'

The boy looks up, waiting. Care has started to chuckle and the boy gasps. In their world, I gather, justice delivered is usually not a laughing matter.

'It was his own fault, Tick. His own fault all along.' She shakes her head before explaining. 'He was bringing in whiskey and then rebottling it. Selling it to pubs that didn't want to pay the tariff to be legit, you know? But he was doing it in a storage facility made for dry goods. In summer. The hooch he was bottling ended up being lower proof than he wanted and tasted funny to boot because it was evaporating. He'd gotten too big for his business and he'd gotten careless. Boy, was he angry when the old man explained it. He didn't even have to go down to the warehouse to check it out.'

We've reached an intersection and she hangs back, motioning for the boy to do the same. 'The old man said there was a lesson in that.'

'People are stupid?' He's playing up to her. Smiling.

She smiles back, even as she shakes her head. '"Look beyond the obvious," he told me. Look for what isn't there – like a proper procedure – as well as what is.'

She leans out into the street. A truck is unloading wooden crates, each as wide as a man's arms can reach. At least, as wide as those of the scrawny workers who wrestle with them, taking turns climbing onto the truck bed. A beefy grunt calls out orders, his voice obscured by the train rumbling just beyond.

'Come on, Tick.' She puts a hand on his shoulder and leads him out onto the sidewalk. She's straightened up now, assuming what I think of as her downtown walk. Tick scurries to keep up, but even as he does he turns toward her.

'Care?' he asks.

She looks over.

'What's evaporating?'

'Well, see that puddle?' She points across the street where the workers are finishing up. Or would be – one of the two, a hunched, scrawny man, has dropped a crate, splashing the dirty water over the cobblestones.

'You!' The crew chief points, yelling. His voice is clear now. 'That's it. That's the last straw.'

'But I—' A raised fist cuts the protest short. The scrawny worker backs away, into the street.

Blat! The honk of an air horn as the next truck pulls up makes the man jump. He stumbles on the broken stones, falling, just out of the tires' path. 'Watch it!' The driver yells out the window, adding an obscenity for good measure.

'Are you OK?' Care runs into the street, reaching for the fallen man's arm. He pulls back as if from a blow and turns. His face is a mass of bruises; his eyes large and sunken. 'Mr Silver?'

He blinks at her then takes her hand as she helps him to his feet. 'You again,' he says. 'I'm sorry. What's your name? Care?'

She nods. Tick has hung back and so have I, watching from the early morning shadows.

'I'm sorry,' he says, then stops. 'You shouldn't be here.'

'Why?' Care sees something in his thin and battered face. 'What happened? Why are you working here?'

He brushes himself off front and then back, working almost as carefully as I would. Only from the state of his clothes and the thinning hair that hangs over his collar, I do not think he is by nature as fastidious as I. He is wiping his hands off. Looking everywhere but in her face. There's a story here.

Risking traffic, I leap to the cobblestones. Scent may tell more of his tale than this man is willing to share.

'I lost the business,' he says at last. He is looking down at me, and I approach gingerly. This man does not appear cruel, but those who have been kicked are prone to pass that violence along. 'It's gone.'

'But—' Care shakes her head. 'I just saw you. At the shop.'

'Then you know.' Chin up, he seems determined to sustain his pride. I pass behind him, sniffing at his cuffs. 'You saw that we were in trouble.'

'Well, yeah.' Care's brows bunch together, as if tangled by the questions waiting to form. 'But – to be here? Loading the trucks?'

'I have debts to pay.' His voice has settled, pride steeling the resignation. I smell the mud he has splashed through this morning. Sweat and, yes, blood. He has his shoulders back, his spine straight, but I notice the slight wince – the intake of breath. It is his own blood, dried on his body, that still marks him. 'Obligations. And you shouldn't be near me.'

Care waits. Stands still as Tick stares off down the street. Such occurrences are not uncommon in this world, where the small and the weak are easy prey.

'What will you do now?' she asks.

The first truck starts with a grind of gears. The second pulls up, but this skinny man doesn't turn – not even when the bully calls to him.

'Hey, you there!'

Care pivots. Hands on hips, she takes a step past the muddied man and raises her voice. 'What do you want? You fired him.'

A laugh. 'I ain't gonna pay him for loafing, that's for sure. There's work to be done.'

She turns back to the gaunt man. He wipes his hands again

and nods to her. 'No rest for the weary,' he says, a ghost of a smile creasing his swollen lip. 'Good to see you, Care, despite . . . Well, thank you – thank you for everything.'

We watch as he goes back to the truck. The foreman laughs as if at some private joke as his new man clambers onto the truck bed and reaches for a crate.

TWENTY-FOUR

The girl remains silent as we circle the block, her face as opaque as those cobblestones. The boy, by contrast, becomes noisier as we walk on, leaving the back streets for the bustle of the waterfront. He dances around Care, peppering her with questions which she ignores, and turns instead to commenting on the changing scene as the traffic grows busier. He seems particularly dismissive of the people whom we pass, in their monochrome suits and leather shoes. The coats, especially, he remarks on, disparaging their daytime drab. But he is eyeing their good wool, I see, and I detect a note of envy, despite his insults.

It has been a cold winter, I gather – recent events have erased my memory of anything but rain and a freezing flood. As he speculates about the passers-by – their proclivities and paychecks, their expenditures for fur or suede – it occurs to me that he is seeing a different side of this street. He is looking for the nightlife that must dominate here once these office drones have had their day. The idea that these workers may be the same preening peacocks who strut about after dark seems foreign to him, and I understand the concern Care has for his education, for his future.

I am uneasy about our journey. In part, because as we left the back ways for the more commercial avenue, my path became more difficult. A cat on a quiet street appears natural, a necessary part of the fauna, with a job – no, a responsibility in this industrial area. A cat among the busy urbanites? A freak. A nuisance at best. A rogue attracting attention and, at worst, violence. I do not want a repeat of the scene down-town, especially here where the desire for order – in the guise of civility – is much less in evidence than on the cleaner streets we have left behind. I am timid here, darting from shadow to shadow. Although the pain in my side has subsided to a dull ache, I find myself falling behind. On such a busy thoroughfare, as the day grows bright, there are too few safe places.

My dread grows as Care proceeds across a slate-paved plaza. A scent of alcohol and sick seems out of place and yet familiar. When I detect the perfume of an opossum, the leather of my nose twitches in response. I know this place, these broad walkways. This is where I followed Bushwick – Dock Street. The way to his warehouse. The night market looks different under the sun's glare, although it sports the same tidal pull of commerce and greed. The boy catches up with Care. He knows this place, too; his comments on the toughs and their dolls express a certain yearning. This is the arena he aspires to, though not in its mundane dress.

Suddenly, my reluctance makes sense. There was evil here – the stench of death and fear – and I would keep this girl from it, if I could. Despite the constant footfall, the open stretch of stone, I dart ahead to stand before her.

'Blackie.' She shakes her head as if I were the boy. 'I thought maybe I saw you. Damn . . .' She looks around, as if for an escape, and my tail perks up. My ears. 'Where will you be safe?' She's talking to herself, without expectation of an answer, but I must react. She seeks to store me, to stow me away for my safety, when I am the experienced one in this venue. I lean in, straddling her foot with my body. This has the advantage of stopping her while I deliberate, as well as expressing my allegiance. But no, too late, I recall our relative sizes – I feel the hands on my side and twist. The sore place makes me, perhaps, a tad more vocal in my protest than I would like, but it does no good.

'Shh.' She holds me up, close to her face. Her breath is warm in my fur, her heartbeat steady. I settle, and as I do, I feel her shift and turn. She is putting me in her satchel, asking me to be quiet. Rather to my surprise, I am.

'What are you waiting for?' The boy's voice comes from her other side. He has not, I realize, seen our meeting. Has no idea that I am secreted in her bag. I shift and feel her arm through the worn denim, emptied now of her clothes and few possessions. This could be a useful vantage point, I realize. I am hidden here and yet close to her. Even the boy, whom I do not trust, is oblivious of who travels by her side. And – yes! – I test the cloth with my claw. If need be, I can rend this carryall. I have had too much of traps in this life and while I trust the girl – trust the heart I still hear, steady, through her side – I have no such expectations of this world. Not for myself alone do I fear. This girl may need me, yet. For now, however, all is well.

'This is the one.' She's talking to the boy, having already explained about taking stock, about checking the surroundings. He's too smitten with the verve and zest around him to pay heed. Here, on the downtown side of the river, many paths cross, their combined scents and sounds an intoxicant to the unwary.

I confess I hunker down as she ascends the stairs. Through the loose weave I can barely see the brick beneath us but I remember its dampness and the way it crumbled where the water had gotten in. The girl leans back and the bag sways as she pulls on a door. Better for us both if I could have led her through the mouse hole from the alley, through the dark and secret entrance to this evil place.

'Oi!' The voice rings out, a man approaching across an open space – the lobby with the stairs. 'Girl!' Closer now, and she stops so short I slap against her side and her arm descends to hold me. Does she fear that I will struggle or call out, and thus expose myself? I prefer the thought that she finds some comfort in my solid warmth. 'You can't come in here.'

'I'm looking for Mr Bushwick,' she says. I can tell by the tone – the breath in her body – that she's standing chin out, trying to look brave. 'I've something for him.'

'Do you now?' The inquisitor turns salacious; in his voice I hear his greasy smile.

'Intel,' she says, the syllables hard. Direct. 'Something he's been looking for.'

Nearby, I hear the boy mutter. He must recognize his own words but she reaches and pulls him close. She fears his going off – his being hurt – when she should be cautious of the damage he may do.

'Wait here.' Footsteps, work boots on worn linoleum, the

give of rot beneath the floor softening the heavy tread. Through the weave I spy the stairwell leading up. The scent of death is faint here – too many men and too much commerce. Ash and mud and sweat converge. I do not see the man, but as a door squeals shut I feel Care move. She is following – no, she is turning to watch – and she heads toward the steps.

It is not only the movement that makes me grip the cloth, my claws ready for a fight I fear will come. But no – it's the squeal, and Care jumps back again. The breeze of an open door and another voice, familiar in its threat.

'This one, huh? Well, what have you got to say for yourself, girl?' Not the big bully – not Brian. I sniff the air for smoke or that chemical tang.

'Bushwick came to see me.' She's dropped the title. Gauged her audience and pitched. 'He was looking for something. Something he lost.'

Smart, this girl. She doesn't trust the story about the job and so she has kept the old man out of it. She's setting bait as sure as that cheese I had hoped to leave.

'And what has the big man lost that you can help him with?'

I feel her arm move. Her hand rises to her throat and my ears go back with trepidation. She is not speaking. She has lost her nerve.

But no. The speaker laughs. Randy – the smaller of the thugs. 'You looking for some sparkles, girl?'

'No,' she says, her smile clear in her voice. 'But Bushwick is. Tell him I found what he came by to look for. Tell him I know where it is.'

Footsteps and some murmured consultation just beyond my ability to hear. I am hesitant to shift much in this sack, and the girl's arm, while steadying, blocks some of the impressions I would ordinarily receive.

'What are you talking about?' Tick's whispered query lets me know both men have retreated to a safe distance. 'What are you going to do?'

'It's got to be about the heist. The necklace,' she answers, her voice low but clear. 'Bushwick must have been looking for the ledger, too. The old man always said: "There are no coincidences."'

'Girl.' She starts, turns. No, she hasn't been overheard. 'Come here. You can go up, see the boss, but not this little brat. He's filthy, and the boss doesn't like his things getting dirty.'

I brace myself as the bag sags. 'Wait for me outside, Tick,' she says, bending low. Through the loose weave, I see him nod, his eyes large with worry. 'Around the corner.' He nods again and opens his mouth, but she cuts him off. 'Give me an hour, no more. If I don't come out, bring the ledger to AD. Tell him I wouldn't let you have it. Use it to save yourself.'

She rises before he can reply, holding me close to her side as much for reassurance, I believe, as to keep me still. Up the stairs then, but then a turn. She's not heading toward the room of coats, the badly cured furs, but down a hallway opposite. She's walking quickly but she doesn't speak. Doesn't engage the ruffian whose heavy tread leads the way.

'In here.' An intake of breath – a reflex as she considers the door, a room, a trap. I think of the room with the coats. The couch. The stench . . . But then she steps inside and I relax. The light is different here, even through the bag – brighter and more diffuse. An office, then, with large windows. The scent confirms this: tobacco and men. Stale but not rancid.

'If it isn't little miss detective.' Bushwick, his voice full of swagger. Fear, too, though it is faint now, buried beneath the tobacco and the beer. 'She's got her own sidekick now.' From the sound, he's seated, leaning back. Of course, he wouldn't rise for a girl like this. It's not simple courtesy, it's dominance. 'And she's got a delivery for me.'

'I have information.' She calculates her speech, doling out words. I do not know what she understands of politics or of power, but she has incorporated the basics. She is asserting herself. My ears prick up, curious more than alarmed. 'You were seeking some paperwork?' She pauses before the last word, letting him see that she is aware of his lie.

He laughs too loudly. Too obvious. 'Paperwork? Come on, girl. You've got it or you don't.' He licks his lips. 'Don't be stupid, girl.'

'I don't have it with me.' She articulates the last two words carefully, emphasizing the distinction. 'I know where it is.'

A bark. No – a laugh, forced and lacking humor. 'You amuse me, girl. You've got spunk. Maybe you do have a future on your feet. You could run errands, maybe. I could use a trustworthy messenger.'

Silence. He's thrown her off, as he doubtless intended. I feel her intake of breath, readying her next sally. 'I've been made aware that others want it, too, you know.'

It's a risk. AD and this slick monster may be in league. But the man before her only laughs some more. 'You hearing this, Randy? The girl is trying to strike a deal.'

A squeak and a shuffle – and a shift in voice. 'You don't know who you're messing with, do you, girl?' He has leaned forward. I can almost feel his breath, heavy with meat and his own importance. 'You really don't have a clue. Look around.' I feel her move slightly. She doesn't dare disobey. 'Does it look like I have to bargain with gutter scum like you?'

This close to her body, I can feel her tremble as she takes a breath. By the time she speaks again, however, her voice is steady. 'I have the ledger, Mr Bushwick. The ledger you've been looking for. It's in a safe place, and not—' A pause. For effect, I believe. The girl is growing more confident with each passing moment. 'Not in my mentor's former office.'

He doesn't respond, not right away. And when he does, his voice is different. Distant. He is leaning back in his chair, but more than that is at work.

'You thought I was seeking a ledger?' The laugh cascades out of him like a marble bouncing down stairs: cold and hard. 'I came by your late boss's office because I had mislaid something. A trifle, a detail. And while I appreciate your desire to please me, I fear you've picked up the wrong idea about what I was seeking – or what your role could be. No, girl, I don't need anything you may have or think you've found. I've got everything I need. It's you who should be asking me for help. I could use an eager young thing like you.'

The last words come out slow, the proposition in his voice as obvious as the implications.

'I guess I was mistaken then.' The girl speaks up, and I confess I am proud of her. 'I had reason to believe you were looking for an accounting, shall we say? But if not—' She turns so fast I lose my balance. And she stops. I hear breathing in front of her. Blocking her way. 'I came here in good faith.' She is making an effort to hold her voice steady, only I hear the slight tremor.

'So you did, so you did.' Bushwick must have made a gesture because the breather moves. 'And as I've said, you've got spunk, girl. But don't let it go to your head like it did with your old man. You keep coming to me with whatever goodies you find and we'll get on fine, you and me. When you're ready, I'll have a place for you in the organization. When you get tired of playing at detective.'

He's laughing again, calling to his man even as the door shuts behind us, and this time Care rushes down the steps, her worn shoes slapping on the linoleum as she runs.

'Hey, girl!' It's the doorman, but she keeps on going, out into the sunshine and down the stairs. Only when she's around the corner does she stop, taking a great breath in what sounds for all the world like a sob.

'Care, there you are!' The boy is here, for good or ill. I shift and mew, ready to get down. 'What happened?'

She's panting, fright rather than exertion. I call again and scratch at the fabric. She sinks to the ground, her back against the building, and I jump free. It has been a disturbing visit and I feel the need to groom. One asserts order however one can.

'He threatened me, Tick. And he pretty much confessed to having the old man killed.' She pauses but I can imagine her train of thought. Bushwick views himself as a fancy man, despite his cheap furs and low-life companions. He's quite capable of ordering violence, although he's unlikely to have committed it himself. There is something wrong, however. Something about how he presented . . .

'And he didn't care about the ledger. Maybe there was something in the old man's office.' She's talking to herself now more than to the boy. 'Something I missed.'

I neaten my ruff and begin to work on my leg. It feels good to stretch after all that time being carried. My fur is falling back into place.

'I think he's behind the heist, Tick,' she says at last. 'I think he got the necklace – paid those jerks to steal it, most likely. And now, with the old man and Fat Peter dead, he's neatening up the loose ends.'

I pause, my leg extended, struck by her phrasing. Struck, as well, by the logic of what she says. Yes, it makes sense. The man has a business large enough to incorporate many kinds of contraband, and gemstones would be more compact, easier to transport than those stinking ratty furs. What I don't understand, I realize, as I return to my grooming, is why the man should still smell of fear – and why he views this one pale girl as a threat.

'So what now?' The boy is on his feet, anxious to move. 'You want me to bring that book to AD? I mean, if he wants it so bad.'

'No.' She shakes her head, scowling. 'I don't understand what's going on with it yet, Tick, but it's worth something. I need to put it together before I present it, case closed, to Diamond Jim. The old man always taught me to watch out for the loose ends, to make sure I had everything in place. I think I need to go back to the old man's office. See if I can figure out what Bushwick was really looking for.'

The boy, accustomed to obeying orders, stands at the ready, but when Care looks down at me I remove myself, just far enough to make my intentions clear. Concern flashes briefly across her face as she realizes I will not be compliant, and I experience a twinge of regret. I do not want to cause this child any sadness. However, I do not wish to be confined again, no matter how benign her intent. As she begins to walk, retracing

our steps to the back street, I trot along in full view, the better
to reassure her, aware of her gaze as she watches my upright
tail.

It is my fault, therefore, that she is caught in an inattentive
moment and I spin, hissing, as an arm reaches out from a
recessed doorway, pulling her into its shadow.

'Care!' The boy raises the alarm, jumping away from the
hands while I crouch, readying myself to attack.

'It's me, Jonah!' The man in the shadow pulls back, hands
open and up, releasing her. She sways and rights herself,
staying still within the shadow as she considers him. He looks
too much like a splayed frog to be threatening, but his smell
is foul. Sharp and gritty all at once. It irritates my nose and
eyes as I pass behind her, settling into a low growl. 'I just – I
wanted to warn you.'

'Warn me?' Care's been spooked but she's curious. I feel
her lean forward on her toes; her head tilts up with the question. My pose does not change, though I lower my growl to
listen. He has not harmed her – not yet – but that does not
preclude a trap.

'I shouldn't.' Even from below, I see the whites around his
eyes. He's the one who's afraid, his face drawn and darting,
peering out into the sunlight and back again. I step forward
to sniff his cuff. It's worn and dirty, frayed as if by claws, and
rank – soaked in more than filth and sweat. 'The boss sent
me to get a crowbar but I saw you and, well, you were good
to me. You and the old man. You couldn't know . . . Bushwick
– he's the big boss now. He's the one who . . .' He swallows
and points to himself. Whatever happened, it's still too raw to
articulate.

'The matchbook?' She keeps her voice low but he still
winces as he nods. That smell – it's kerosene – under the fug
of smoke. Kerosene and something else – cloth or paper.
Maybe wood. The stench of a life's work taken and destroyed.

'You have something of theirs. I heard them. You've got to
give it to them.' His words come in gasps, his breathing rough
as he looks around. 'Please, Care.'

'I can't.' Care's words are gentle but the man starts back as
if she's hit him. 'You knew him, the old man,' she explains.

'There's something in it if they want it that badly. Something that could explain why he was killed. If I can just decipher it—'

'Decipher?' He looks at her as if she is speaking an unknown tongue. As if he were the beast, not I.

'The sequence,' she says. 'Fat Peter had everything in order, so I think they're straightforward. Only one is missing.'

'That's it – that's the one!' He's excited. He reaches to grab her hands.

'Can you read it?' Care picks up on this, color rising to her cheeks. 'Can you read the ledger?'

'Ledger? What ledger? You mean Fat Peter's? What does Fat Peter's ledger have to do with anything?' Care is staring, confused. The man leans in, all sweat and desperation. 'It's the marker they're after. You've got to give them the marker. Then you'll be able to get away. They'll let you go, I think. Now that the old man's gone, they'll let you go.'

'No, wait.' Care shakes her head, her hand going into her pocket. 'I tried – they don't want the ticket—'

'It's not a ticket.' He spits the word. 'It's the marker! The marker they're after. They need it for the deal.'

'The deal?' Care examines his face, leaning in despite the stench, despite the way he has begun to shake. From my vantage point I see the cords on his neck. See as well how he swallows once and then again. 'Jonah, is that what happened to you? Did you try to do a deal with Bushwick? Because the old man and I, we thought we'd set you up. This city, it's hard on people, but we thought . . .'

'No, no.' His head hangs down as he shakes it – weighted, it seems, by sadness or by memory. 'No, I kept it straight. I refused. I thought I could protect him but now there's only you.'

Down the street, an engine growls and male voices shout. The man jerks back, a puppet on a string, and turns. The light coming in from the alley's mouth illuminates his eyes, the cracked lips that he keeps licking. He cranes his neck and then turns back.

'Give them the marker, Care.' He takes her hands once more in his. Squeezes them tight, a father or a teacher imparting words of wisdom. 'Give it up, and then run.' A quick glimpse back toward the noise. The engine. Shouting. 'Run as fast and as far as you can.'

He steps back into the street, a look of grim determination on his face, and is gone.

TWENTY-FIVE

'Where's Tick?' She spins around, eyes wild. The man's disappearance has spooked her.

I watch, unable to explain. The man, more scarecrow than live threat, had frightened the boy when he reached for her. She heard the boy's yell, his warning shout. That she did not notice him backing away was a lapse. Now he has run, though to safety or to her enemies I cannot tell, as she turns again, locking her eyes on mine. 'Blackie, did they get him?'

That is the wrong question, as foolish and one-sided as asking that frail man whether he had given in to temptation. Though he, at least, explained that it was his reluctance to act that ruined him rather than some desperate gesture. I would that the boy were as unwilling, but I cannot in good conscience vouch for him – for either his intentions or his moral strength. I lash my tail, once back, once forth and hold her gaze, willing cool by example. Willing her to consider.

She slumps back against the wall. I have failed. 'Damn it, Blackie. I don't know what Tick heard – or what he'll do.'

Unable to offer counsel, I rub against her ankles. This seems to calm her, and for a moment we are at peace. The shouting has died down, the truck has left. The thin man either back at his labors, or silenced for his trespass, I do not know. It is interesting, this absence of sound. Like the absence of an action, it may have a meaning, as the lack of something – of a marker – means a life.

I am pondering this as the girl pushes herself off the wall to stand upright. 'Blackie.' She brushes off the red brick dust. 'It's time for me to take control.'

I don't like it, the way she strides off down the street. She's talking to herself, head down, heedless of the bustle around her. It's broad daylight, and with the sun the city's denizens have come out, taking to the street for their business and their leisure. Groups of men on the corner rake their eyes over her, as slim as she is, her confidence pulling their eyes as they smoke and laugh. She's on the border of adulthood, I can see, her attitude swaying the balance. A hackney driver calls to her as she crosses in front of him, while a suit – his gaze as greasy as his modish hair – ignores his companion to watch her pass.

I do what I can to keep up, dashing from shadow to doorway, availing myself of the preoccupied rush to skirt both vehicles and feet. I would abandon her, in this setting, were it not for her mood. Midday in the open, she ought to be safe – safer than I – but I do not like the tension around her. She fears for the boy, I understand, even if I do not share her concern. More than that, she is settling on some plan, some course of action. I see once again why her mentor must have chosen her. She is strong, this girl, her determination the biggest thing about her. But it is foolish to simply walk through the city this way. Like me, she is a small creature, a hunter only on a limited field. Like me, she must practice stealth, must take care if she is going to survive.

'What the—' The boot appears from nowhere, and I dodge it only by leaping into the gutter. 'Filthy beast!' I scramble to distance the agitated voices and must swerve and dash to avoid catastrophe in the street. By the time I have reached safety – the underside of a vendor's cart, a shadowed place both cool and dark – I have lost the girl. I am also, I am embarrassed to note, panting. There is nothing to be gained by dying out here, I decide, and instead tuck myself into a niche by the wheel well, to wait out the crushing mob and, perhaps, to think.

I understand the girl's vexation. Her courage was discounted, her offering – that ledger – rejected as of as little value as any trinket that a street waif might pick up. She is frustrated, I can tell, by her inability to negotiate with that self-satisfied miscreant Bushwick. She does not comprehend him as I do – the rancid sweat, the fear he barely holds at bay – but she does not like him and sees him as a hindrance, blocking her way.

This I know, and it makes me concerned for her, for the

bluff she may attempt. She may have started on this path out of grief, fear and loss prompting her to avenge the old man she so dearly misses, but she has added another impetus along the way. As she told the smug man, she seeks to take over the old man's business. She wants to finish his assignment, to solve the crime he had been hired to investigate. It would be a tall order for a full-grown male. For a young girl, it is madness.

But – as my eyes close in the cool shade – she may yet have a chance. Another type of female, supported by societal strictures and accustomed to its cosseting, would have given up by now. This Care is tough. She is smart, and as I have noted before, she has been given the rudiments of training. No, it is not impossible that she should achieve both her aims. The obstacles she faces are formidable, however. Not only Bushwick but her former colleague, AD, the leader of that rough assemblage by the docks. Which is why I do not trust the boy either. He loves Care. I am not so removed from social intercourse as to miss that. But his allegiance is, at best, divided. She must keep in mind that he has disappeared once more, and that fear may not be his only motivation. How easy would it be for him to lead those two thugs up to her, whether wittingly or not? If AD sent him scurrying, if he were careless – or chose to be for a moment blind – those two brutes could follow and then flank him. And Care, preoccupied by her hunt, might perhaps be heedless, be searching for connections between a jeweled necklace and those who may have seen it last. Not until all chance for escape was lost would she look up and see them waiting; hear the cold laugh as they made their final approach – the two henchmen stepping forward to complete their vile task.

I can picture them with ease, tall and looming against the light. The two bullies approach first, stepping each to the side to better set their trap – to seal off any hope of escape. The one in the middle does not speak, and too late I recall that cruel sneer as he comes toward me . . .

I wake in darkness, the shade beneath the cart matched now by shadow on the street. Shaking the dream like dust from my fur, I peer from my sanctuary. The day has passed, the traffic calmed. Above me, the vendor is pulling in his wares, folding down the awning that protected his display. The vibration must have woken me, though I cannot discount the possibility that its creaking collapse may also have sparked the dream. No matter – it is time for me to set out. The girl needs a companion she can trust. Already, I may be too late.

Twilight, with the long cool shadows of early spring, and the streets are quiet. I consider the scent of people passing, of their animals in leash and harness in the business of the day. I spy, as well, others of my type. A nursing mother – her hunger and desperation have driven her out wide and early. I mark a corner; she would know of my passing regardless, but vow not to hunt, not here. Three kittens I can sense, too large for milk alone. The humans who come here, their buildings full of grain and cloth stuffs, should be grateful for her attentive nature.

I steer clear. While I am subject to the usual urges of my nature, there is nothing for me here. The female is of single mind at this point, her energy focused on her young. In truth, I realize as I continue on – her scent fading on the cold stones – I do not care. As I trot, my ears picking up the sounds of the nocturnal world waking, I ask myself if, perhaps, this is the result of age. A dulling of appetite. I try to recall an earlier time of heat and urgency and find I cannot.

I pause, in part to take in the air, mouth open, for all its richness. In part because this thought has troubled me. I have no memory of my life before I came to myself in that drainage ditch. Before the . . . incident, for lack of a better word, that nearly killed me. Perhaps the girl was right, and I was at some point a pet. My fur bristles at the concept: to be servile. To beg. But as I ponder, I see myself, suddenly, contemplating a fire contained behind a screen. I feel myself warm and well fed and – dare I say? – complacent.

No, I shake it off. If that was my life, it is over now and has left me with my senses, at least, intact. I raise my head, the damp air intoxicating with its riches. Perhaps I am not too battered, too tired, too old.

And then, at last, I find her – the girl. Not in person but in scent, the trace of fear near gone from her trail of sweat and thought and dust. I begin to follow and then stop, pausing as the evening fog begins to settle.

It is not her trail. To my fine senses, her scent is such that I could track her through the city. It is my deductive powers that stop me, here on the frayed edge of this massive city. I could follow, ducking around corners in the dark. To do so is not the best use of my time or my instincts, however, tagging along, always a beat behind. And so I leap onto a window ledge, its glass long since gone, and wrap my tail around my feet to think.

The girl is on the hunt. My senses tell me she is traveling quickly and on her own. That does not make her invulnerable, and I have seen both the size and the tenacity of her enemies. What I need to do is anticipate her moves. One young girl, nearly a woman. For a street cat who has, apparently, survived for years, this should not be too difficult a challenge.

She seeks the boy. Therefore, first I consider the basement where they have sheltered. It is also there she left the book and its continued security, as well as her questions about its utility, might draw her back there. What she does not consider is the boy who found it for her, and who may have drawn his own conclusions about its worth.

I leap down to the pavement and set off. The city reveals itself to me through sounds as well as scents, and I can hear the nighttime revelers begin to gather blocks away. I have not forgotten my last visit to this area, this middle ground between the city and the river, and I plot my path accordingly. The girl is older than her years in many ways, and I tell myself she will devise her own route.

But as I round a battered dumpster and slink through the torn chain link at an alley's end, I wonder. Her mentor's office was her last stated goal, and it is a sanctuary, too. Perhaps it is my concern about the boy, about his familiarity with the basement and the book, but I find the thought of that other, more ordered space appealing. Perhaps it is the creak and ache of my old bones, seeking peace and warmth. I think of a fire again, the roaring contained behind a hearth. I think of my standing – a cat of the streets, a feral, a beast – and pause again. No matter, it is a place to start, and I alter my path, leaving behind the boisterous waterfront for quieter streets. If I cannot trust my instincts, I am dead already, one more casualty of the growing dark.

TWENTY-SIX

The building's door is propped open, the brick inside smelling more of mud than of a human hand. When I see the rags left on the floor, a drying pile left in the shadow of the stairs, I understand. I am not the only creature seeking shelter in this damp and rainy spring. The occupant has gone out, seeking food or solace, but he wishes to return, and no one here has bothered to forbid him entrance.

Up the stairs, I pause before the office. The door – what there was – has been shattered; splinters of the old wood have landed a body's length away. From inside, I hear movement. Something heavy – a chair, that desk – is being moved. Papers catch and crackle, caught beneath. Not lifted, then, slid. One person, light.

I approach and note her scent, even as she curses, softly, beneath her breath. Care, alone. Tail erect, I step into the doorway, waiting for her to turn.

'Blackie!' She beams, despite the disarray, and comes forward as if to lift me. Neat as a dancer, I slip by her, perching instead on the back of the sofa. This is what she had been moving – or righting, perhaps – the cushions I once shredded now look far worse used, the cotton batting leaking out like the innards of a beast.

'Bushwick's people gave this place a good going over, didn't they?' She kneels before me and I see what she has been after. The papers she did not remove are scattered now across the floor, muddied with the prints of boots and other marks. 'I don't know what they were after, though. I doubt those oafs could even read.'

She gathers up the pages, bouncing them on the floor to straighten them and returns them to the desk. That piece, I see, has also been moved, and its drawers lie now on the floor.

'I told him I had the ledger.' She looks around and blinks, lost in her thoughts. 'I'd think this was a message, only he did come here seeking something, before . . .' She shakes her head. 'I don't know what it is.'

Food is not the answer, but I don't refuse when she fishes a last piece of that cheese out of a corner, cutting off a slice. She sniffs the bread carefully when she finds it on the floor, but she eats that too, knowing better than to offer me such poor stuff. She has propped the door shut with the desk chair and relaxes now, lying back on the couch. There is no hearth here, no fire, but it is shelter of a sort. Her breathing settles into an easy rhythm, and my own eyes begin to close when we hear it: a scraping too big to be a mouse. A rattle of a knob. The door.

She is on her feet in a moment, her eyes darting from the door over to the window. I am on the ledge but I cannot see her take this route, this high and the perch so narrow. Panic passes over her face – the realization that she is trapped – and then she grabs the board that once framed the door in one hand and, in the other, the small knife she has used on the cheese.

The door rattles and the chair scrapes inward. She raises the board as a hand reaches in. And drops it. 'Tick!' She pulls the door open to embrace the boy who is, I am relieved to see, alone. 'Thank God.'

I do not know if her relief is because the intruder is this boy or because the boy is safe. I keep my distance as she embraces the dirty child and pulls him over to the sofa. The bread is gone, but she hands him the cheese and a jar with some kind of paste. As she does, he reaches into his thin jacket and pulls out a cloth-wrapped package that he presents with both hands, as he would a prize.

'The book.' She looks up, his impromptu meal forgotten as she takes it and then embraces him once more.

'I thought, well, if you want to take it to AD . . .'

'No, no, I don't.' She sits back, unwrapping the ledger and opening it. 'Thank you, Tick.'

'I was thinking.' The boy studies her, ignoring the food. 'If you give it to him, maybe he'll forgive you, Care. Maybe he'll let you come back.'

'I'm not going back, Tick.' She speaks casually. Concentrating on the ledger, she does not see the distress her words cause. 'I meant what I said. I'm going to take over the old man's business. I can stay here. *We* can stay here, Tick. The old man paid the rent in advance, by mail. I just have to make this one case and we can keep this place. A place of our own, Tick. And a job – a real job.'

She turns a page, shaking her head slowly, squinting in the fading light. 'If only I could figure this out,' she says. But then she closes it, looking up, at last, at the boy. 'It doesn't matter. I have enough. I'm going to Diamond Jim in the morning, Tick. I can tell him who stole his necklace – and then got rid of Fat Peter to hide his trail. He'll take care of the rest and we won't have to worry anymore.'

She turns back to the book, too distracted to notice that the boy does not share her enthusiasm. That his head hangs down and he doesn't eat. That his hands play nervously in his pocket as we sit in the growing dark.

TWENTY-SEVEN

The boy doesn't want to go. That much is clear by the way he fusses, curling up in his makeshift nest – those slashed pillows – as Care tries to rouse him in the morning.

'Please, Care . . .' His words are muffled as he rolls over, pulling the old quilt above his head. She had found that quilt in the wreckage last night, its lining torn open, and given it to the boy. Although I bristled at this, in truth she didn't need it. I slept by her, stretched out by her side on what remained of the sofa's frame, both to lend her my warmth and as a safeguard, should that boy – or any other – make threatening moves in the night.

'Let me stay here.'

'Tick, I need you.' She shakes the boy, more gently than I would have advised. 'Get up.'

He's still grumbling as she reaches for his clothes, shed overnight.

'What's this?' She lifts his trousers, more patch than whole cloth at this point. She reaches into a pocket and pulls out the brass weight.

'I found it, when I went back for the book.' The boy sits up and rubs his eyes. 'You threw it.'

'So I did.' She tucks the boy's keepsake back into the trousers before handing them over. His complaints spent, he begins to dress.

'Where are we going?' He takes the mug she has handed him. Although she's been wisely wary of electric light, she has risked a plug-in kettle that screeches like a trapped rabbit when it boils.

'Not *we*, Tick.' She fills a second mug, stirring in a spoonful of powder. Curious, I leap to the tabletop and sniff, recoiling at the bitterness of the brown grains swirling. 'I'm going to talk to Diamond Jim.' She smiles at my discomfort and strokes my back. 'Present my evidence.'

'Your evidence?' The boy is fully awake.

'Don't you worry.' She raises her mug, hiding the grin that has widened as the boy mouthed the unfamiliar word. 'I have an errand for you, if you don't mind.'

He shrugs. This, after all, is what he does.

'I know he startled you, but I want you to find Jonah Silver for me.' She has clearly thought this out. 'He's down on his luck, Tick, but he's a good man. I want you to tell him he can stay here, with us. I may have work for him, even. He doesn't have to—' She pauses. This part isn't clear – at least, its presentation to the boy. 'He doesn't have to work for anyone he doesn't want to.'

The boy's brow knits, confused by the double negative perhaps. 'That bum? But you can't trust him.'

'Why?' She leans in, suddenly serious. 'What do you know, Tick?'

'He didn't like the old man.'

The girl shakes her head, her confusion apparent.

'He wouldn't recommend him, he said.'

'But that—' She pauses, pained. 'No, we did good work for him. He thanked me.'

Another shrug. 'That's not what Diamond Jim said. I heard him talking to his boys.'

She ponders this as she drinks, but says no more as she takes the mugs down the hall. While she's gone, I watch the boy, who has more in common with a magpie than he does with the girl who has taken him in. The brass weight, for example: it is useless out of context. A shiny, small thing, but it means something to him. He takes it out of his pants and looks at it, rolling it around in his hands, even as his eyes dart around, seeking other small items to pocket. He watches me, too. Sees how my eyes narrow as he rifles through the papers Care has piled so neatly. He picks up a pen and I stand, stretching. My arched back makes him pause, and in that moment, she returns, mugs in hand.

'Let's get moving,' she says, stacking the mugs on a shelf.

'What about him?' The boy nods toward me. I am sitting, my front paws together, as demure as a debutante now that he has put the pen down.

'You're right,' she responds. For a moment, I am concerned. I turn, ready to jump off the windowsill. Ready to make a dash for the door. But she only reaches past me to open the window. The air outside is damp and cool, rich with information. She shivers and draws back but I stick my nose outside, reading the air. 'You see? He can come and go now.'

The boy mutters. I do not believe this is what he intended, but I have other concerns to occupy me now. I have heard their plans, and so I do not wait, and as Care ushers the boy toward the front door I make my own descent – window to ledge to the alley below. The night's shelter has done me good. I leap and land with a grace I'd not remembered, and my satisfaction is deeper than vanity. I am on a hunt, and I cannot afford to fail.

TWENTY-EIGHT

My goal is simple: I seek to understand what happened to me. How I came to be in that culvert as the rainwater rushed into flood. This is not an idle question, nor one I can easily answer with carelessness or age. I have observed myself, as I do others. I prefer high places to low, dry to damp. And I do not trust easily, when I trust at all. How, then, I came to near drowning in a roadside ditch, I do not understand. Nor what those two goons – the thugs who haunt the girl's life – and their sinister colleague have to do with my near demise.

I am not given to introspection. We beasts live in a continuous present – we eat and mate, fight when we must and rest as we can. However, that image – that dream – haunts me. And although I acknowledge that its latest iteration, with the boy Tick as the central figure, makes no obvious sense, I cannot escape its implications. If I could remember, I would not spend time on such useless research. But I cannot. I am missing some part – some crucial element – of my past, and I fear that with it I have mislaid a clue that could serve me – could serve the girl – in our present straits.

Those brutes, they are key. They and that culvert with its overwhelming flood. I have no desire to revisit that scene – even the thought makes my skin prickle and crawl like a case of mites. But I have picked up a scent, faint as a new leaf, which gives me hope. It is different from the others I have come across recently and yet somehow familiar. More to the point, it is mixed, ever so slightly, with other scents I recognize. The bite of chemicals. The mud of the river and the sour sweat of those two ruffians. The only factor missing is that of fear – human fear – so notable in its absence on this damp spring morning. It is the scent of an alpha male, a hunter like myself. Only one I do not recall, at least not outside my dreams. No matter, I am on the trail.

This isn't a simple task, a case of tracking a scent to its source. This figure is not only potent, he is accompanied by his crew. Three times those villains have surprised me. By the culvert, by the tracks, and then again as Care and the boy waited across the street from Diamond Jim's. I will not let them do so again.

It is with extra caution, then, that I take to the fog-slick streets, stretching my body to run low and sleek along the gutter and then up along a fence top. It should not surprise me, perhaps, when I see the girl turning into a passage before me. She has taken her own, more open path, but I could have predicted that our trails would cross if they be not one and the same. I pause, hanging back atop a marquee, as she turns down one particularly familiar street. Of course, she is approaching the jewelry shop, only this time she is coming via a back way, careful and alert. Crossing the roof, I see her as she makes her approach. Diamond Jim's. I remember it well, the smug proprietor handling a female not much older than Care.

Although I cannot make myself invisible, I slink down a drainpipe to where a ventilation shaft has been left uncared for and rotting. The vermin who have discovered this make themselves scarce at my approach; their sense of smell is finer even than mine. But I am not concerned today with fat grey rats or their nesting young. I creep inside the tight and fetid space, making my way into the building unnoticed by any human. I am not hunting now. I want only to listen and to watch.

'It's some girl!' A female voice, young but harsh with wear. The same female, I see a moment later, Diamond Jim had been fondling in the alley. Unsure, perhaps, how well her voice carries, she has come into the back room and stands, blinking, her eyes heavy with mascara. I am looking down on her through the vent. I am in the inner sanctum of the greasy entrepreneur known as Diamond Jim.

'Says she wants to see you.' Her voice lacks affect despite its volume. Her face is likewise impassive, the movement of her irritated eyes the only sign of life.

'Well, send her in.' A deep voice, full of itself. Male.

As the click-click-click of heels retreat, I realize the second speaker is not alone. Ribald comments remark on the departing woman's skirt, her hair, her body, and I begin to understand the deadpan delivery. The armor-like cosmetics. Cats may be equally direct about their appetites, but we never belittle the ones we desire.

Another entry, and although I cannot see her from my grate, I can tell by her footsteps, by the way she breathes as well as her scent, that the newcomer is Care. I can sense, as well, the male reaction – an intake of breath. Of appraisal, and I bristle in anticipation. These men are a type foreign to me, but I see in them the behavior of predators, the kind who hunt in packs. My antipathy is total, and I feel the fur along my spine spiking in disgust.

'I have what you've been looking for.' The girl begins to talk as soon as she enters. She has pitched her voice low and she has chosen her words carefully. It's smart, giving the appearance of strength. Although I am still alert, I begin to relax. 'I've finished the old man's job.'

'You have, have you?' The boss – Diamond Jim. Only there's an uncertainty beneath his casual query. She has started this conversation. She is in control of this, and he is feeling around for a way to take it back. To reclaim his standing before his colleagues. 'You're on the job now?'

Chuckles, the coarse double entendre a cue for their support. The girl, wisely, does not react. 'You contracted him to do a job for you. To retrieve the stolen necklace or to provide information that would result in its retrieval.' She speaks coolly, her voice direct. 'I have done that.'

'Open your collar, sweetheart.' The voice has become teasing, a slight lisp softening the final word. 'Let's see how it looks on you.'

More laughs. Two men, situated to either side.

'I don't have the necklace.' A slight wobble; she is feeling the strain. 'What I do have is information that you can use, either for the retrieval of the missing jewels or . . .' She leaves the sentence unfinished, although I suspect she concludes with a flourish of her hands. It's a dramatic gesture, designed to turn her lack into a positive. Better than the stolen goods, her phrasing says, she has given him options.

'Or what, babe?' He sounds short-tempered now. The tactic hasn't worked. 'You got something for me? Some kind of trinket? A keepsake you want to trade?'

'I have information for you.' She is repeating herself. I can hear the strain as she tries to regroup. 'I have followed up on all the leads and I know who stole the necklace.'

'What do you think, guys?' He's playing to his henchmen, enlisting them in some game I do not understand. 'Do we believe her?'

'I don't know, boss.' A low rumble, part growl, part laugh. 'What's she got to show for it?'

'I said—' Care again, a little louder.

He cuts her off. 'Exactly. Now, if you had something to give us . . . A little token of your esteem?'

Footsteps. The men have advanced. It takes all of my will not to snarl and leap, assuming I could force my way past the metal grid of the vent. I suspect the girl is expending a similar effort, willing herself not to run.

'Wait.' A command, firm and clear. The men stop. 'You hired the old man, my mentor, to uncover who had stolen your necklace. I have completed the job. George Bushwick has your necklace. I suspect he employed others to do the actual theft, but that shouldn't matter to you. He is the one behind the theft.'

A moment of silence. I can hear her breathe, a little shaky, and I hope that none of the men below share my aural sensitivity. This is not what she expected. Nor Diamond Jim, either, I believe. The silence is one of reckoning and recalculation. I examine the grill and consider my options.

And then it happens. A bark like thunder, breaking loud. A laugh. Diamond Jim is laughing, and then his two henchmen are laughing with him, big, meaty laughs forced from the belly to support their leader's mood. I strain my ears to hear what else is going on as the humorless thunder fills the room. I do not hear any major movements. The girl has not run, nor has she been attacked.

'Oh, that's rich,' the big man says at last. He sniffs back tears and I picture him wiping his eyes with a be-ringed hand. 'That's good, sweetheart. Real good.'

'Mr Jim?' She sounds like a child again, her voice high-pitched with confusion.

'Go on. Run along.' Those big hands, those rings. Light footsteps as she stumbles back toward the door. 'Don't waste any more of my time. Unless—' I hear her stop and turn. 'Unless you do find something for me. You hear me, sweetheart? Come back with something real.'

A second wave of laughter accompanies her footsteps as she turns and leaves, walking as quickly as her injured dignity will allow. I long to follow, to find her on the street. To press my own small body against her in solidarity and comfort. Instead, I make myself wait. As quickly as it rose, the laughter dies down, the two taking their cue from their boss.

'She's been checking up on Bushwick, boss,' one of the men offers. 'Watching him, maybe.'

'So she has,' says their leader. 'Hey, maybe she will come up with something. She's a sharp one, that girl. Almost makes me sad.'

TWENTY-NINE

Care is fuming when I find her on the street. She's too preoccupied to question my appearance here, downtown. Her fear – the shredded remnants of her courage – has turned to anger. 'I don't get it,' she spits the words out, as much to the pavement as to me. 'I don't get that jerk at all. He paid for information. That was the deal. The old man never said he'd get the necklace back. Right from the start, he was clear – odds were the piece was already broken up. That's what the pros do, and whoever took that necklace was clearly a professional.'

She's walking fast, shoulders hunched, working off the scare as nervous energy. 'I know I'm right. The old man knew, too. "Fat Peter's not on the level," he said. Diamond Jim just wants to cheat me. And he did. I gave him the info. For free. I told him.'

I have been trotting to keep up. She's moving quickly, hurt and angry, but one word stops me. I freeze as she pounds ahead. She has been venting, the useless, necessary spewing of the young, and I have not focused on her rant until now, convinced that as she calms she will regain mastery of her emotions. Of her mind. But in her mood, she's missed a beat – a crucial fact – and I have too. She feels cheated and devalued. Granted, their comments would do that. But their forced humor – that bark of relief – was telling. After she left, the men discussed what she had done. They praised her work. They understood its value, their admiration in inverse proportion to their insults, and it hits me: they knew. Before she told them, they were aware of Bushwick and his perfidy. They were seeking something else.

In her anger, she is unlikely to realize this. I struggle for a way to tell her.

'I told him,' she says, her muttered words reach back to me. I bound ahead to reach her and then stop before her, staring up at her.

'What?' A hint of a smile plays around her mouth. The energetic walk has relieved some of the tension, and, as loath as I am to admit it, I have amused her, confronting her like this. 'I swear you're trying to tell me something. You think I'm wrong?'

If only I could talk, could communicate with simpler language than my staring eyes, my lashing tale. This semaphore is inadequate when I would have her re-examine her own words. Rethink her overhasty conclusion.

I stare at her with all the intensity that I can muster. I know what my eyes appear like to her. Green and cold. Unearthly and unreal, kind of like the emeralds in that missing necklace. And in that moment, I find myself remembering my dream. Those men who stared at me – they saw something in me. Something of value. An awareness – a consciousness. They knew that I understood their role, grasped their culpability and intent. For all that I am a furred beast, those three men, name-less and cruel, perceived me as a sentient being. I saw them, and they knew it.

This does not help me now. To the girl before me, I am a distraction, if a welcome one, and I must scurry as she reaches out her arms. No, I do not wish to be held or carried. And it is with growing confusion that I trot alongside her as we return to the office with its broken door. How did those men see the awareness in me that this girl cannot? We pass through the lobby, skirting with unspoken agreement the ripe squatter who now snores beneath the stairs. The door she has propped behind her little more than an hour before has remained closed but she is hesitant, leaning on it as if to hear what may wait inside.

It's the smart move, utilizing the survival skills that someone – her mentor, the old man – has had her hone. I am bothered, however. I need peace. Time to think. I rub against the door frame, the beetle-rich scent of broken wood still fresh. I hear no other human inside; smell nothing beyond the girl, the boy and the unfortunate downstairs. And so I lean against the broken portal, the meager pressure enough to start its swing.

'Blackie!' She ducks as she whispers as if to stop a heedless act. But unlike her, I do not have to augment imperfect senses. I do not hesitate and, small and sleek, I find it easy to elude her hands. As our interaction has made me once again aware, I am a cat.

Emboldened by my move, she pushes the door further. Even her dull senses let her know the room is undisturbed. Closing the door behind her, she looks about, then makes a beeline for the desk.

I leap to the window. The alley below is quiet; its smaller inhabitants seek the dwindling shadows. I track a sparrow as it flutters, awkward with the debris it carries for its nest. I note its single-minded focus. This small creature would make easy prey, distracted as it is by thoughts of family and home. Yet its very vulnerability brings me back to my own thoughts, the questions I settled here to mull. The idea of home and family disturbs me and is easy to dismiss. No, I do not believe I was ever a domestic beast, nor would I want to be. But to be recognized – as those three killers did – that is something odd. Something I do not understand.

'Here it is.' The girl's voice breaks into my reverie and I blink over at her, aware that time has passed. She is sitting in the desk chair, the papers she had sorted now spread before her. Leaning forward, she resembles a small bird herself, her crest of hair falling in her eyes. 'I knew it.' She brushes the hair back with one hand while the other flattens out the page before her. It must have been one that was discarded, left crumpled on the floor by Bushwick's men. I jump down, curious to examine such a document – something of importance to this girl and yet so easily overlooked by the crew who came to search.

She is lost in thought, biting at her lip as I gain the desktop. She strokes my back, an automatic move, as I step forward to sniff the page. The girl, yes, she is everywhere. The old man, too. I have come to recognize the scent of ash and woolens, a dry and woody scent. Other males – those thugs, the big ones. They were here. They may have handled this paper, even, though in truth their scent is strong enough that I cannot distinguish hand from boot in this context, nor do I know if they can read. And something else, as well – fainter and yet

– yes, the slightly rank perfume of the warehouse. What I thought was the stench of droppings, of dampness and of rot, is something different. Sweeter, artificial and not quite capable of masking the decay underneath.

I close my eyes and open my mouth, the better to take in the scent. But the gentle pressure of her hand has increased. She is moving me. Sliding me over to focus her own face on the paper.

'Sorry, Blackie.' I cannot help my disgruntled mew. 'I've got to read this. It's the contract. Clear as day – recovery or information, which he knew. In fact, he said . . .'

Her mouth goes slack, as if she's been struck. She looks at me. 'I was wrong. I didn't give him anything he didn't know, Blackie. I didn't give him information. He knew. Diamond Jim knew – he knew about Bushwick before I told him. That's why he didn't react. But he didn't care.'

There is little I can add to this, although the involuntary purr that rushes through me must seem a poor response to the confusion on her face. 'What?' She shakes her head but I hang back. She is asking the right questions now. Better ones than I have, and more likely to be answered. But before she can go further, I hear a noise outside and my response – I stand on guard, my whiskers alert and bristling – causes her to gasp.

'Who's there?' She pushes back and I see her reaching for a book or board. I hop down to let her know she need not fear.

'It's me.' The dirty face appears as the door cracks open. 'Care?'

'Tick!' She rushes to the door and pulls the chair before it back. He steps in and looks around, panting. He has run. 'I'm so glad. You wouldn't believe what I found. What I figured out. Did you find Jonah?'

She's talking quickly, unaware that the boy has been running, not seeing how his thin chest heaves. But with her last question his face pinches and she stops.

'What is it, Tick?' She bends to face him, wiping away the marks of dirt and sweat with her thumb. 'Could you not find him?'

He shakes his head and blinks. Tears, not just sweat, have

made those marks. 'I found him, Care. Down by the loading dock, just like you said. Only—' He stops. Swallows. Tries again. 'They said he made a run for it. That he was trying to jump a train. Only he didn't make it, Care. He's dead.'

THIRTY

Any response she might have made is interrupted as the boy bursts into tears. He quiets almost before she can comfort him, though, pulling away from her embrace to wipe his face roughly with the sleeve of his jacket.

'Sorry, Care.' He sniffs, his face unreadable. 'I don't mean to be such a baby.'

'You are—' She stops herself in time. 'You've had a shock. It's understandable.'

'It's not like I haven't seen a stiff before.' Another sniff as, chin up, he assumes a tough-guy pose. 'It's just – it – he was really messed up.'

'I'm sorry.' Care withdraws to the sofa, her eyes still on the boy. 'Poor Jonah. You saw it – saw what happened?'

The boy shakes his head. Swallows. 'No, but they – they had him there.'

'Nobody tried to help?' She answers herself. 'No, not that crew. They wouldn't.'

'They were all saying how it was his own damned fault.' The boy is talking, seems to want to talk. The girl doesn't respond but he keeps going. 'How he got what was coming, him not holding up his end and all.'

'Not holding up his end.' Her voice is soft. She shakes her head, then turns again to address the boy. 'He was an old man, Tick. He shouldn't have been doing that kind of work anyway. Not anymore.'

'It wasn't the work,' says the boy. 'It's that he was always talking. The other guys on the dock said he couldn't keep his mouth shut.'

'He couldn't . . .' She stops herself. 'Who said that, Tick?'

A shrug. The boy is himself again, the shock of what he has seen dulled by the retelling. 'The lugs on the dock. The guys who unload the trucks. You know.'

'And did any of them see what happened?'

Another shrug, eloquent in its lack of commitment. 'They were all talking like they knew, and, Care, it must have just happened. I mean, they brought him back and he was just lying there, like . . .' Another swallow. 'It was pretty gross.'

'And they just kept him there, laid out.'

The boy nods. He is looking queasy again, looking the child he is. But she's not seeing how his face has gone soft and bunched up. She's staring into the middle distance, biting her lip as she thinks.

A minute passes, maybe two, and then she turns toward him again. 'I don't think it was an accident, Tick.' I cannot see her face from where I sit, but her voice has grown hard. 'I don't think, if he was hit by a train, there'd have been anything much left to lay out. I think they killed him – and they killed him because of me.'

I jump down from the sill. This is an interesting development, and I follow the girl to the desk to examine for myself the papers to which she has returned. I make my next leap with care. She is hunched over the cluttered surface and will not want to be disturbed. It does not matter. She barely acknowledges me as she scans the document before her. 'The question,' she says, running her finger down a piece of paper, 'is why.'

'I don't understand.' The boy steps up to the desk and tilts his head. It is clear he can read no more than I, but I at least content myself with watching the girl. Waiting to see if she pulls any new pages from the pile.

'I didn't get a chance to tell you,' she says without looking up. 'I met with Diamond Jim. He was there, in his shop with his muscle, and I told him that I'd solved the case. That Bushwick was behind the robbery. That he probably still has the jewels, though I'm betting the necklace has been broken up by now. And, Tick.' Here she looks up. I can see that she wants the boy to understand. I can see also that he's trying, mouth slightly agape as he listens. 'He didn't care. I think he already knew. It was the weirdest thing.'

She bends back over the paper. 'I found the contract. He was promised either info or the jewels. Paid half upfront too, but he didn't care.'

'Maybe he heard already?' The boy's voice is tentative. He's trying out a theory without realizing his own process. 'I mean, if his guys roughed up Fat Peter before they offed him, maybe they already knew about Bushwick?'

She shakes her head, still reading. 'Bushwick should be toast. He should be as dead as Fat Peter if he stole from Diamond Jim and was found out. And he's not – he's not even scared. When I realized how odd it all is, I remembered something Jonah told me. About how Bushwick is the big boss now. It made sense, 'cause that's how he was acting, and I was wondering . . .'

She breaks off. 'You heard them say it was because he was talking too much, right?' The boy nods. 'You're sure of that?'

'Yeah.' The word comes out like a croak.

She nods to herself. 'Jonah wasn't supposed to tell me that. That's why they killed him, Tick.'

The boy is silent. This is not an unusual development, I sense. These children live in a world of casual violence and retribution.

'But why would that be a capital offense?' She is asking herself, thinking, no longer reading. I sit up to watch her. Her pale face is smutty, streaked with dust and grime; these children seem to attract filth, no matter how often the girl washes herself or washes her friend. The finger she rubs absently over her chapped lip is frayed as well, the nail chewed down to the cuticle. And yet, there is something feline about her. The movement of her eyes, perhaps. The way her brow knits, as if she would bring her ears up, keen and alert, scanning for the slightest sound.

'The answer is here, Tick. I know it.' She looks at me and I blink, slowly, to encourage her. I too know the frustration of feeling a solution to be ever so slightly out of reach. I sense a kinship with this girl, despite her youth, her inexperience, her inability to see . . .

'If Diamond Jim knew that Bushwick was behind the robbery but didn't do anything . . .' Her voice startles me, and the train of thought is lost. 'Could it be because Bushwick is his boss? You know how AD is about tribute.'

She barely acknowledges the boy's enthusiastic nod. She is

thinking aloud, and so I fold my paws beneath me and close my eyes, the better to hear her reasoning through.

'If Diamond Jim wanted to give – *had* to give – the necklace to Bushwick, maybe it made sense to pretend it was a robbery. To hire someone to hunt for it, knowing . . .' She laughs softly. 'I bet he had insurance on the thing. I bet he made sure of it, and now he's going to collect. No wonder everyone is so happy.' Her voice has turned bitter. Turned cold. 'Everybody makes out. Only the old man was too good at his job. He came around asking questions and Fat Peter must have said something – given something away. The old man said he wasn't on the level, right?'

'Not on the same level,' Tick mutters. 'It might have been that.'

'Either way,' the girl adds, 'he said – or they thought he said – too much. The ledger . . .' She looks around before she remembers. 'No, they don't care. But the marker . . . What is that about, and why do they need it?'

She reaches into her pocket, retrieving the pawn ticket, and stares at it for the longest time. As she does, the boy settles on the couch. He is bored – the shock of what he has seen has passed, leaving him tired and drained. He sticks his hand into his own pocket, pulling out the brass weight. I watch him as he tosses it from hand to hand, and then turn back to observe the girl, her pale face a mask, now, hiding thoughts I cannot read.

THIRTY-ONE

The room is quiet. I drift, as is my wont, toward sleep, settling into the drowsy dream-like state that allows me to better review my thoughts. I twitch at a touch. A fly or – no – a hand.

'He's so soft.' It's the boy, his voice quiet. 'He looks so beaten up, but his fur is really soft.'

'Let him sleep, Tick.' The girl now, her voice gentle. 'He's not a young cat anymore and he walked all over the city with me today.'

The hand withdraws and I shift, tucking my nose beneath my tail. I will not argue with her assessment, though I reject the implication that I am exhausted or unwell. No, I have lived, even if I retain little memory of times past. What I do have is a sense of proportion, of timing, that a younger mind lacks, and which at this point alerts me that something is amiss. The girl – we – have missed a beat, and I would like to pick it up.

It is not simply that the girl cannot quite make sense of the killing of Jonah Silver. As I slip into semi-consciousness, I find myself pondering what I have heard, and an unaccountable sadness washes over me. Grief, perhaps, albeit trimmed with a sense of culpability. Of responsibility or guilt, saturated by an overwhelming melancholy. Were I human, I could weep.

It cannot be for that scarecrow of a man. I did not know him, having no recollection of him before the day's introduction beyond the merest flicker of recognition, one I can trace to the girl having mentioned his name. Besides, death is part of my routine, dealt by me as often as not, and not anything to be laid so low by. My own death, yes, I have tasted it. Fought it, too, and will continue to do so. But that is our nature, which we beasts do not question. The death of others? It is of little account.

No, it must be for the girl that I am sad. This girl whom the man would have protected. Tried to shelter – as others have—

I wake with a start, having fallen more deeply asleep than I'd intended, having dreamed of concealment and betrayal. The boy is dozing beside me, stretched out on the sofa. The girl is gone. I yawn, back arching and tail outstretched to fling off any vestige of stiffness, and as I do, the inchoate impressions of my dream come back to me, coalescing into a sense of urgency. Of dread.

The girl has missed a cue. This I had known, I had sensed while she dredged over the papers, over the events of the last few days. What has come to me now is not what has been overlooked – not exactly – but a sense of its importance, not only to her queries but to her more essential being as well. Her freedom – possibly her life – is mixed up with this quest of hers; the threats that poor man would have sheltered her from are lurking. And my role? Cats are not reflective. We do not pause to consider our place in this world. We simply are. We do. We act. With that in mind, I turn once more to appraise the room behind me. The boy asleep, the jumble of papers on the table. No, I will not find my answer here. Turning once more to the window, I ready for the leap and exit, silent as a ghost into the city beyond.

The sun is setting. I slept longer than I had intended, and while time has little meaning in any abstract sense, I am aware of the shadows stretching across the alley. Dusk brings good hunting, the first waking of night creatures, the sleepy fumbling of daytime dwellers. For me, however, my search this time is of a different kind, and while I would prefer the clarity of daylight or the cloaking of night, I am committed to this errand regardless.

At the alley's end I pause to sniff the air. Spring is growing stronger, the warmth of the season bringing forth a flowering of scents. Young birds, newly fledged, the ripening of what fauna can survive among these stones. And – yes – the river, its nearness clear to me in this damp and warming air. Despite a shiver of apprehension – a chill as if a hawk had just passed overhead – I head toward that scent. I do not know what answers I will find, if any. I do know that I must try.

There are advantages to being a cat. A cat alone, that is, and not burdened by the presence of a young girl, no matter how well meaning. As an unaccompanied feline, I am free to find my own way through the city, and as the day's shadows lengthen, I move quickly, my jet-black fur giving me a freedom that no human could ever know.

Unencumbered by the girl, who needs must travel by the surface routes, I make my own way. Time slips away as I glide through dark alleys and over fences. The day darkens and the moon rises as I leap and run, a dark streak in the glowing night. Night is my element, and I take strength from the scents and sounds. Prey scatters before me, but I have another pursuit on this night. I am seeking the truth.

I am headed back to where this adventure began. I am headed for the river.

THIRTY-TWO

B eing feline has many advantages, as I have said. One of them is that we do not force ourselves to follow straight lines. Over a fence, along a roof, I make my way toward the fetid artery that pumps life into this city. As I clear a trash heap – the vermin within squawking in terror – I muse on what that means, and what I can do that the girl I have aligned myself with cannot.

The girl has her strengths. Brave and loyal, she has stood by me as she has her younger friend. Smart, as I have said, in that way of humans, and determined, working hard to understand that which she has gathered before her. That, alas, is also her weakness. Seeking a linear cause, a single meaning in what she has heard and what she has learned, she has over-looked the slantwise meaning – the implication behind the remarks. The casual comment that could unravel it all.

'They need it for the deal.' The dead man, Jonah, had told her this, but so preoccupied was she with the thing itself – the 'it' – she had forgotten. 'I tried to save him,' he also said. The deal and his death, it is clear to both of us, are related. Only as bright a child as she may be, she has not had my experi-ence following a trail. Piecing together the clues that will lead, ultimately, to the reward. In this case, the trail begins with a common thread. The scent of the river, rich and full. The place where, but for her intervention, my carcass would have ended. The site, I have reason to believe, where all these disparate elements may yet come together.

Or may not.

By the time the moon has begun to set, I am within hailing distance of the river. The ancient warehouses, most as hollow as the water-rotted piers, loom ghostlike over the pockmarked streets, their missing cobbles filled with rainwater too foul to drink. The train tracks, with their scent of cinder and oil, pass by here, too, cold now and silent.

Closer to the water, human activity picks up. Although it is past the hour when daylight creatures should be asleep, I hear voices inside the shuttered buildings, muffled by the night. I skirt the light that leaks out of their windows, ducking into an alley as a door opens, spilling out two men, wobbly with drink. I shelter by a wall, the refuse shielding me as they get their bearings. Make their plans. Spring is spring, even for humans, and although the night is chill and damp, in the dark behind me I hear the sounds of rutting, furtive and rough.

'Hey, you owe me.' The act is finished while I wait for the drunkards to be gone. The commercial nature of the transaction clear.

'You smoked so much scat you should pay me, darling.' My ears prick up. The voice. It is the girl's former comrade, her leader – I hesitate to use the word benefactor – AD. 'But you knew I'm going to be flush. Didn't you, darling?'

Movement, and the intake of breath as in pain or surprise. Then he laughs, and she murmurs an apology. Soft words, the hint of an endearment delivered in fear rather than affection.

The flash of a lighter – the click and the blue spark – and that now-familiar acrid pungency wafts toward me. The couple, silhouetted against the brief glow, separate, the woman leaning back against the filthy wall. I watch, waiting, as AD leaves her and comes toward me, stopping at the alley's mouth to light a cigarette. It was his lighter I heard, although the chemical glow remains behind, with his temporary mate. Illuminated by the red glow, he looks both more gaunt and taller in the flame light, and I take the time to examine him. To weigh whether his appearance, if not his words, have any relevance to me or to the children. I do not expect him to see me, sheltered here by the trash. I am small and dark, and humans, I have found, rarely see what they are not expecting. Perhaps I move; my tail does have the habit of expressing that which I would keep hidden. Perhaps my eyes, as smooth as glass, reflect the glowing ember of his smoke. For a moment, he looks at me and I experience the oddest emotion. I feel he sees me, as humans so rarely see others. More than that, I believe he recognizes me in some way.

I back away, the only prudent path for a smaller creature

on a night like this. He watches, for a moment, then shakes his head and walks on, tracing the path those drunkards have taken. Back to the building with its noise and light.

'Yo, you know who I just thought of?' His voice booms out as he pulls the door open. 'You must remember—' And it closes, muting the words that follow.

They are of no concern. I deal in reality – the fact of his presence, more than his thoughts or memories, are what matter to me. I have come here seeking convergences. Explanations. A reason why two powerful men should seek to harm one girl. I have found a third, less powerful, perhaps, by the brute measure of their world, and yet certainly a master of his turf.

Behind me, the woman coughs as she stumbles. I wrap my tail around my feet, having no desire to be trod upon. This sad soul presents no other threat to me. Barely able to walk, she teeters toward the same door that AD entered, only to pause in the shadows as the cough takes her.

'Damn,' she says in a breathy voice and reaches for the wall. Leaning forward, she vomits, her head hanging low. It's anyone's guess at this point whether she will fall or right herself, but something other than sickness is driving her, and with an effort she pulls herself upright, staggers back a few steps and then stops. She wipes her mouth and pulls down a top that does little to shield her from the night chill. Then she, too, opens the door.

'Well, look who's back—' Again, the words are cut off as she slips inside. The last thing I hear is laughter.

Curious about AD and the transaction I have just witnessed, I retrace her steps down the alley. It is a blighted place, littered with refuse and waste. This close to the water, much of the garbage is organic – the carcass of a gull, gnawed to the bone, briefly takes my interest. The droppings of the river rats, glossy with fish, and a moldering pile of vegetable peelings – the bar must have a kitchen – make the pavement slick, and I chose my path with care.

What draws me are not these leavings, however. Nor the traces of blood and sex left by the wall. No, as distasteful as I find it, I follow the trail of that caustic stench, that strange burning, to its source. It is easy to find, still warm from that flame. A glass tube, a vial or pipe of some sort, its odor most intense at its open end from which the foul smoke must have emanated. I sniff it gingerly and draw back with a start. It is sharp, like the jagged edges of its fellow vials, several of which lie scattered around, and bitter, with a bite that makes me lick my poor nose for relief. A horrible substance, yes, and instantly recognizable, at least to one such as I. This is what AD offered Care that day when I accompanied her to their lair. This is what I have smelled on the boy. Suddenly, the marks on his hands – burn marks – make sense, as does the girl's concern. I have seen the whore stumbling out of the alley. Have seen her sickness and her craving for more. This is not a life I would wish for any living thing. In this light the girl's desire for independence – for a life separate from that room full of AD's acolytes – becomes distressingly clear.

Such insight does not, however, answer the more pressing questions on my mind. And so, taking a moment for the burnt scent to clear my passages, I contemplate my next move. A 'deal,' the scarecrow Jonah had said. Quite possibly the same deal that the old man had been inquiring about when he met his end. Unlike a human I do not jump at conclusions, finding them as elusive as a centipede in the dirt. I seek patterns, that is all, and from them I trace and track and hunt.

A burst of laughter – the bar-room door has opened again, expelling two more men – interrupts my thoughts. And as I step back, more careful now, into the shadows, and they pass, I detect a familiar odor. Looking up, I find myself surprised for the first time this night. It is the brute, Brian, the one who has pursued Care. The one from my dream. Although his red face is now more the product of drink than of my brief mauling, I would know him anywhere. His companion, though, is not his fellow thug – the one with a face like a rat. He is walking with AD and they are heading toward the buildings.

I am momentarily torn. I came here with the intent of studying the docks. That is where this deal would supposedly happen. It is also where Care's friend and mentor met his end. But I am intrigued by this odd pairing and, with an instinct that I hope is informed by experience, I decide to follow.

Soon we are walking down a broken road, its pavement

crumbling. And then I know where we are. To my left, as the pavement falls away, lies a culvert. Here is where I first met that choleric savage. Here, where I nearly died.

They are talking, laughing as they walk, seemingly oblivious to their nearness to this small and squalid stream. I cannot be. Perhaps their senses have been dulled by habit. By the drink and drugs that they consume. Perhaps they simply do not care, the rivulet one more feature of the crumbling cityscape that they call home.

I cannot be so blasé. I smell the water, low now and poisoned with waste. Smell, too, the rats and other living things that use this unclean source. Scavengers, all. Had I been slightly less strong – had the girl not ventured in – I would have made a meal for such as them.

These men, too, are scavengers. Having witnessed AD with that woman, I perceive the same instincts driving him that I would in a rat. The weak, the young – I remember the girl's cohort in the abandoned building – are fodder in his desperate battle for survival, nothing more. He is no mastermind, but rather the tool of someone. Someone like Bushwick? Care thinks so, I know that, but I remember the stink of fear on him and I wonder. As I follow, making my way from the shadow of one pile of rubbish to the next, I bide my time. I will wait and watch before I make up my mind.

'What's that?' I freeze. AD is not as impaired as he might seem, not as drunk as his red-faced colleague, and I have been distracted by my thoughts.

'What's what?' His bearish companion spins around, his booted feet sending fragments of asphalt bouncing down into the shallow stream.

'I thought I saw something.' AD cranes around, tall and looming. I flatten, slowly and, I hope, imperceptibly, willing his human-dull gaze to skim over my midnight fur. 'Like, someone following us.'

'You're drunk.' The big ruffian claps a hand to his companion's back, but AD waves him off then steps forward, toward the culvert. 'It's nothing. Maybe a rat.'

AD holds up his hand for silence and looks around. I see his eyes, reflecting light from some distant building, the grime rimming his broken nails. I press my belly into the cold dirt. I know he cannot smell me. He lacks the senses, lacks the skills. But still the fur along my spine begins to rise. I consider where I will bolt if he makes a move.

'Come on, AD.' The big one's voice has taken on a whiny quality despite its depth. He shifts from one foot to another, cold or bored. 'It's all in your head. Or maybe it's one of those brats you use as runners.'

'No.' AD shakes his head, scans the road back toward the bar and then the empty street ahead. 'I told them to all get lost until tomorrow. That I wouldn't need them until then.'

'Maybe it's a ghost then.' With a shrug, the big man kicks the dirt. Pebbles roll by me, splashing into the oily water. 'There's got to be some of them around here, for sure.'

'Maybe.' AD doesn't seem convinced and turns toward his colleague. Back up the deserted road. 'Wouldn't that be just my luck? The old man haunting me the night before the big deal?'

'Ha,' his companion barks. 'If he were that smart he'd still be alive, wouldn't he?'

'Maybe.' One last craning, checking to the right and left, and AD starts walking again. The fur along my spine settles. They are heading toward the buildings, empty shells whose windows look blacker even than the pockmarked road. I give them a good head start before I follow, darting sideways to a pile of rubbish and then to a dislodged curbstone. AD is on high alert, I gather, no matter what his extracurricular pleasures may be.

I consider the implications of this, of his comments about a deal, as they turn a corner ahead. I had known the old man's death had taken place down by the water. The girl had said as much. It should not surprise that her onetime leader, AD, would have some knowledge of – if not involvement in – his murder. To have this brought home, though, so close to where I nearly met my end, is chilling. I do not consider myself an imaginative type. I trade in facts, as all beasts do. We eat, we mate, we live. But for a moment, I find myself wondering about Care's previous companion, the mentor to whom she feels such loyalty.

Did he recognize the moment of his death as it came upon him? Did he see the perpetrators who were cutting his time short? It is fruitless musing, of course, as all such thoughts are, but it distracts me for a moment as I let the two men move ahead. And then I look, and they are gone.

I freeze. I stand in the lee of a rusted-out car, its tires, doors and anything else removable long since stripped from its metal hull. The wreck obscures my vision, but as a cat I prefer my other senses. My guard hairs, erect, pick up the breeze and vibrations of the street. My whiskers tingle at movement around the way. My ears – yes, I hear them. No longer talking, but their breathing, the big man's congested and loud. While I was distracted they turned inward toward a sunken doorway. Its stairs are obscured by rubbish of a more organic kind.

Slowly, as if I were stalking prey, I approach. The two men disappear inside but a broken window provides access and prime viewing. It's the building where the girl had been sheltering, where she had found the boy. Only now the group that had called it home – the six or seven youths who had laughed at her – has dispersed. Something else is different as well. The smell of burning has not dissipated. I suspect it will not be gone from this place until the last of the brick has crumbled into mud and the wooden laths of the exposed wall have burnt to ash. But it is much diminished. These two changes are enough to make the place seem both larger and colder.

The big thug senses it too. 'Lonely, ain't it?' He shoves his hands in his pockets as he looks around. 'Hey, if none of your brats are here . . .'

He looks toward AD. In the light from the street I can see a yearning, hungry look on his fat face.

'I'm out.' AD doesn't even look up. He's gone over to the corner where he fiddles with a cabinet – could it be a safe? – and withdraws an object, wrapped in rags.

'You gave the last of it to that skank?' The big man steps up to him. Stops and steps back. 'Whoa, sorry, man. I was out of line.'

'Yeah, you were.' AD turns, a gun in his hand. 'You know better, man. Just wait until the deal goes down. We'll have everything we need. Everything you could ever want.'

'Yeah, yeah.' Brian licks his lips. 'So, everything's set?'

'Uh huh.' AD holds the gun up. Turns it over. In the weak light, it reflects blue. 'We've got to get the marker back, and that's it. But I have a good idea where it is. Where she is, I should say.'

THIRTY-THREE

There comes a time to acknowledge one's limitations. Deficits of strength or wit, perhaps. At times, even of will. This is not one of them. Although I, as a furred creature, lack many abilities – the most frustrating at this point in time being my inability to either confront these criminals directly or, at the very least, specifically and clearly warn the girl – I do have other capabilities which more than make up for their lack.

In brief, I turn. I am faster and stealthier than these men. I can find Care and will figure out a way of warning her. In addition to my small size and dark color, I have another advantage: I now know what they seek.

Quick as a water bug across a kitchen counter, I slip out of the building and up to the street. The moon is gone, the sky not yet hazy with the mottled dawn. But it's not the darkness that holds me up. No. I pause for thought. I am quicker and, I dare say, smarter than these lumbering men with their cruel ways. But I do not have much slack for error here. I will have difficulty enough once I find her.

Diamond Jim. He and that necklace are at the center of her quest. He was the one who hired her mentor, and yet he is the one who seems to have no further interest in recovering the materials that were apparently lost. However, she has already attempted to pry information out of the stout, self-satisfied businessman and failed. That he is part of this I have no doubt. My acute sense of smell has already alerted me that the class distinctions among humans are thinner and more malleable than they would let on.

I cannot see her returning to Bushwick's, and for that small mercy I am grateful. That leaves – no . . .

I stop so quickly my paws cannot take hold and I slide to the lip of a puddle. Coming up the street, I see an unmistakable silhouette: the girl, and this time she has Tick in tow.

Mrow! With a howl like a beast possessed, I throw myself in front of them, puffing my fur up for emphasis.

'Blackie?' She stops. I hiss.

The boy steps back. 'I told you,' he says. 'That cat's nuts.'

'No.' She extends one hand, motioning him back. The other is clasped beneath her coat, holding something. The ledger. 'Something's spooked him. What is it, Blackie?'

She steps forward and I stare up at her eyes. She is trying, her brow knitted as she concentrates, and I am reminded of another time. Those same eyes, filled with tears and sadness. Green with flecks of gold, brighter than in daylight. Brighter, despite the storm, despite my own fading. I could not cry out, then. I could only stare as they receded. As I receded. Only, she saved me.

'Care, it's really late.' The boy's whine breaks into my reverie and the image is gone. In this dim light, the gemstone colors of her eyes are as murky as a roadside puddle. 'I'm tired.'

'Yeah, me too.' She's whispering. They both are. This part of town is quiet for a city. But it's more than that. What had AD said about ghosts? There are too many memories here. Too many people have died.

'You coming?' She looks over at me and I realize my fur has flattened. My back settled down. My warning has gone unheeded and I have no other tool to deploy. I brush against her to signal my assent.

'It's the ditch, isn't it?' She reaches down to pet me; her hand is cool on my back. The boy turns to her but she ignores him. This is private, between us, and my purr, faint though it may be, acknowledges this.

Without another word, the three of us walk on – back to AD's lair, where he and that savage wait. As we make our way, I formulate a plan. I cannot tell her, not precisely, what she faces. I can, however, give her warning.

When we reach the building, I make my move. I wait until Care and the boy are on their way down the broken stairs and slip in through the window. AD and Brian are sitting on some makeshift bedding, the flickering gas flame of a small lantern glinting off the brown bottle they pass back and forth.

'What's this?' AD calls out as the girl descends, blinking. The light isn't much, but it stands in stark contrast to the dark outside. 'Care?'

The brute beside him lumbers to his feet. This is my moment. I jump.

I am too far away to reach his face. Even his hands, scarred and calloused as they are, would be more vulnerable than his legs. But my purpose is not to disable him, merely to make the big man call out – to buy the girl a moment's notice and deprive him of the element of surprise.

'What?' I have landed on his thigh and with all my claws extended manage to pierce the thick and greasy cloth to scratch the skin inside. 'Get off!'

I am pulled back, the hand closing on the looser skin of my neck. I release him and close my eyes, waiting for the final blow. The shock of pain. I am lucky. He merely throws me and I collide with the far wall, shaking loose the last of the plaster that sticks to these laths before I fall to the floor.

The girl gasps. She turns to stare at me, and so I make myself stand despite a stabbing pain. My effort will have been in vain if it only distracts her further.

'Hey, darling.' AD is on his feet now, smiling. 'Just the girl I was hoping to see.' He steps toward her, the gun by his side.

'I want to talk to you,' she says. She holds her ground, although I can hear the minute tremble in her voice. 'I want to make a deal.'

That stops him. His smile turns quizzical and he tilts his head. When the ruffian by his side starts to move, he puts his hand out to stop him. 'A deal?'

She nods. 'You want the marker. I want some information.' I am the one who is panting, but it is she who licks her lips before continuing. 'Why did Diamond Jim hire the old man? Was it all a scam – insurance fraud or a payoff?'

She's offering too much. We all see it, and AD's smile widens, the flickering light showing off his canine teeth. 'Insurance fraud?'

'Reporting something stolen that you've really given away.' She swallows. 'Or traded.'

'Traded is right, darling. Only you have no idea how much

insurance a pretty bauble like that can buy.' He steps forward, holding the gun. His other hand outstretched. 'The marker?'

She pulls out the ledger. 'Here.'

He doesn't even take it. 'I have no use for that.'

'Here then.' She hands the ticket to him.

He takes it and, with a last glare, tucks the gun in the back of his pants so he can better examine the slip of paper, turning it over between his long fingers. Bent like this, his face is obscured. 'This? But all it says is . . .' He frowns, the dirt accentuating the wrinkles in his face. 'No, my girl. Hand it over.'

'I don't . . .' She pauses, shifts. Chin up and defiant. 'Tell me why.'

'You aren't as smart as you think you are, darling.' He shakes his head. 'I already did. Now, give it here.'

She shifts slightly, unsure of what is coming. But I am not surprised when the boy steps up and then steps past her, with sad eyes that are both apology and explanation for everything that has gone down.

'Tick?' AD once again extends his hand. He is waiting. 'Give it here.'

The boy reaches into his pocket, eyes downcast. When he pulls out the brass weight, Care starts forward as if she is going to say something. As if she is going to reach for him. Instead, she holds herself back. The boy hands the heavy trinket to AD and steps back, his hand returning to his pocket.

'*That's* the marker?' Care's eyes swivel from the boy to the men.

'Didn't know how to read this, did you, darling?' AD examines the bottom of the weight with its incised markings. 'Didn't know what it signaled.'

'Tick, did you know?' She turns to the boy, breathless and confused.

He shrugs.

'Our little magpie doesn't want to sing,' AD growls. 'No matter, it all worked out just fine once I realized what the boy had nicked. Once I groked its worth. He picks up everything. Don't you, Tick? Even things you're supposed to pass along. Some message boy you turned out to be.'

A harsh intake of breath, almost a sob. 'Fat Peter – you thought he'd gotten it, that he was holding out . . . The emeralds,' Care gasps out the words. 'Oh, Tick.'

Another shrug. The boy stares at the floor as if he can see something in the dim light. Care watches him as if she can do the same.

'Well, you've got your marker now.' She's speaking carefully, her voice modulated to be even and calm. 'Though why you still need it . . .'

A humorless laugh. 'Wants her little friend to keep his toy, does she?' AD turns to his colleague. 'But the boss almost got caught out when he didn't get the heads-up and he doesn't like leaving loose ends.' The red-faced man beside him tries for his own laugh and barks instead, rough and hollow.

'It's a token, too, darling. *His* token.' AD leans in. '*The* token, you might say. For the best deal old Jim ever made.'

'He's getting something in return – from Bushwick?' The girl is thinking aloud, piecing together the few fragments she's uncovered. AD squints at her. He doesn't like it.

'We're all getting something, darling. You, too, if you want to come back. I'm going to need every one of you street rats in a few days.' He leans back and picks his teeth. 'I'm going to get fat as old Fat Peter. Get myself a proper place, like he had. Wear some fine clothes. Dress you up, too, my girl. If you want.'

'No.' Care takes a step back, then another. This far from the lantern, her face is in shadow, but I can see the sudden tightness around her eyes and mouth. The worry as she processes what she is hearing. 'No. Thanks anyway, AD. Tick?'

She reaches out her hand. In the dark room it catches the light, casting a shadow that dances over the brick wall. Another shadow stretches to meet it, dark and clawlike. Closer to the lantern, it looms much larger as it settles on the boy's thin shoulder. The faint light picks out the dirt outlining the broken nails.

'Tick's staying with me,' AD says, his voice full of certainty. 'He's done pretty good, keeping me up with goings-on around this town, and I'm willing to forgive him a certain lightness in his fingers. Besides, he's got a taste for the life, now. Don't you, Tick?'

The boy doesn't respond. His head hangs in shadow, his dark hair obscuring his features.

'Tick.' Care's voice breaks. She swallows and licks her lips. 'Tick, you don't have to stay with him. I don't care if you – that you . . .' She stops. He hasn't looked up. 'He's a boy, AD. He's just a child. He and I – he's like my brother. I'm going to take care of him.'

'How you going to do that, darling?' AD's voice has relaxed into a drawl. He's enjoying this – playing with her as I might a resilient rodent. 'You still intent on setting up shop like your old man?'

'Why not?' She steels herself. 'He taught me things. I have skills.'

'Taught you how to get yourself offed, most likely.' He's drawn the boy back. He's bored and ready to move on. 'Poking about in other's affairs. But Tick stays with me.'

'Tick—' A last appeal to the child. He looks up, but he is so far in the shadows now, I do not think she can see this.

'He doesn't want your mothering, girl,' AD growls again and steps in front of the lantern so his shadow falls before him. 'He wants what I can give him. What I'll have for him in plenty, now that he's given his little plaything back. You'll pay for that, won't you, Tick?' He turns, his shadow a grotesque giant looming large. 'But I'll still have a place for him once we're through.'

The boy yelps as AD's companion grabs his arm and Care starts forward. I will leap, if I have to. Will attack, with tooth and claw, although I already know I have met my match. The confrontation does not happen.

'Leave it, girl.' AD steps toward us. Behind him I can see the brute as he ushers the boy into a farther room. 'Go while you can.' His voice has grown softer again and Care looks up at his face. To me, the deep grooves appear the same as before. The ingrained dirt, the stubble. She blinks, though, as if someone else has appeared. She opens her mouth and reaches out.

'Go.' AD shakes his head, his voice sad now. 'Just . . . go.'

I look up in alarm as Care makes a strangled sound and see the light reflecting off the tears on her cheek. Without another word, she turns and runs out to the street, and I am close behind.

THIRTY-FOUR

'It's not fair.' The girl has recovered by the time we return to the office. Although I am exhausted by the night's adventures, spent and sore, she paces around the small room. Heedless now of danger, she has switched on the bright electric light and casts shadows as she walks. 'AD has plenty of runners. Tick was never a regular. And he's not – he doesn't need the scat, Blackie. Not yet. Though if AD keeps giving it to him, giving it to him when he's hungry or cold . . .'

She leaves the thought unfinished. I am watching her from the windowsill, washing my haunch, pressing my tongue against the bruised and swollen flesh. I find no blood. My hide is too thick to be easily broken and my fur seems to have insulated me from any worse injury. But I will feel this night and the accumulation of insults to my body.

'The weight.' She stops, shaking her head, then starts pacing again. 'As a marker, but why? Marker for what?'

I pause, leg askew, and look at her. Of course, she does not know the details of the deal pending in a day's time. I blink, unsure how to tell her. But she has heard enough.

'He's not cooking anymore, that's clear. So he must be getting it – bringing some in. But why . . .' She sighs and collapses on the couch. I leave my perch on the windowsill to lie beside her. She is tired, overwrought. If I can relax her and get her to rest, she will – we both will – be the better for it. I stretch out and, without thinking, she strokes me, the rhythmic pressure warm and comforting. The pain in my side dulls. Under her touch I feel my body stretch, the muscles relax and lengthen. With my eyes closed, I feel I could extend to fill this sofa, my feet up on the arm rest, my arms behind my head. It's an odd illusion, but lying here, the girl by my side, I find it strangely comforting as I drift off to sleep.

It is that smell. That pungent, bitter smell that hits me first. The drug – the one AD manufactures. The one Tick, apparently, has developed a fondness for, although he is not yet as addicted as that poor woman in the alley. I am in the dark, the cold dark, but I would recognize that stink anywhere.

The laughter, however, is less familiar.

'Relax,' says a voice, male and heavy with authority. 'You're not giving anything away. You're building your base. Everyone here will be clamoring for the re-up, and you'll be the one with the source.'

'I guess.'

I turn and see I am not in complete darkness. Rather, I am hidden. Crouched behind a stack of flimsy platforms – pallets, the word comes to me. In the spaces between their wooden slats I can see two figures. No, three, and the flickering glow of a fire. I see no faces, only bodies. Men, standing, dressed for the weather – the cold that has me shivering in my hiding space. But just from those two words, I identify one of the speakers. AD, only less sure of himself than I've ever seen him. Now that I have identified his voice, I can make out his scrawny form standing a few feet away, hands in his pockets. Like Tick, only bigger. I cannot remember the gang leader looking so vulnerable or unsure. 'Only . . .'

He doesn't finish. He actually scuffs his feet, and I see that they are standing in a wide, open room. A warehouse space. Despite his height, he looks small to me. Insignificant in this setting.

'It's not a waste, it's an investment.' The speaker accents the last word in a way that's familiar to me, and I strain to see. Only, I am not as flexible as usual, for some reason. I feel ungainly. Stiff. In my dream state, I am more aware of my age, of the wear I have subjected this old body to. 'Come on, don't hold out.'

A hand extends toward AD. It reaches out of a coat sleeve trimmed with fur. I start and almost waken. I recall that fur. The stench of death, of fear, although the reek of the drug masks it. I shiver in my sleep. I need to readjust, to see more. But as I do, I knock against the pallet, my old limbs too clumsy with the cold. And suddenly the voices change to shouts. Commands. I am surrounded. Grabbed and dragged from my hiding place, thrown at the feet of the men standing there. I know this warehouse. I know these men. This deal. They see this knowledge in my face, and reach for me—

'Ow.' I open my eyes to find the girl looking down at me. Her hand is in her mouth but even so I can see the line of red where I have scratched her. I look up in mute apology, unable to express my dismay.

'Just as well.' She pulls herself off the sofa and makes for the desk. 'I really need to figure this out.'

Forlorn, but also preoccupied by my strange dream, I follow, brushing against her ankles as a gesture of peace. She sits at the desk and when I jump up to join her she doesn't protest. One advantage of being a dumb animal: we are not held unduly responsible for our actions.

'What gets me is that AD wasn't cooking.' She's talking to herself, but I listen. She is an observant one, and I am interested in her process. 'He's always cooking, at least small batches for the crew and all.' She's staring at a piece of paper – the original contract – but I do not think she sees it. 'And the crew was scattered, as if he didn't need them.'

I want to tell her about what I have witnessed. About AD giving out the drugs he made. About my dream. I simply sit and lash my tail. I am listening. Aware.

'But he wanted Tick – that much was clear. I don't think . . .' She bites her lip, looks at me. 'Tick's in trouble because of me, Blackie. Because I've asked too many questions. Because—'

She stops. I too have heard the echo in her words. 'Damn it. This is what poor old Jonah was talking about, only I was too set on finding the necklace to hear him. It's not about the necklace – it's about this deal, whatever this deal is. It's big. Bigger than the usual, and it was true about Fat Peter, he was just small potatoes – not on the same level. I should have listened when Tick tried to get it right. That's what the old man was trying to tell me. That's what got him killed. And now AD's got Tick.'

She stops, staring into space. I watch her and wait. She is

putting together what she has learned. She sees that there is a deal going down, something that involves that awful drug. Something that she has inserted herself into.

Only she has given up the marker. She has been warned off. She will be safe now, if she lets this go. The old man is dead. Tick may be a hostage, but the boy has been complicit in these dealings. Has made some choices that she may consider unwise but were his to make. I think of the fur. Of the stench of death and fear. I think of that awful moment of discovery. Of being trapped. I will her to be smart. To make the right choice. To live.

'I don't believe it, Blackie.' The sun is barely up. It rakes through the room, highlighting the shadows beneath her eyes as she pushes back from the desk and reaches for her coat. 'I know Tick hasn't made the best choices, but he's a kid and I . . .' She pauses and I can see the tears glittering in her eyes. 'This is my fault, Blackie. He may hate me for it, but it's what I've got to do.'

I stretch, the stiffness of my nightmare not entirely imagined. She is talking to herself more than to me, but I know if I wait she will explain herself. It is a failing of sorts. A weakness that could make her vulnerable to another with less charitable motives. I have come to find it pleasant, as if we were conversing. Not that she is capable of understanding the subtleties of my mind or my various modes of communication.

As I listen she rattles on, gathering the last of her foodstuffs in her bag as she talks. She seems uncertain about what to take, and I see that she is thinking she may not return.

'The old man always used to tell me to think for myself, Blackie.' She picks up the short knife she has used for the cheese. Wipes it off and puts it in her pocket. 'That those in authority are as likely to be hindered by their position as empowered by them. And Tick and I, well, we were lucky to get out of the system when we did.'

She has taken the contract and the other papers. The ledger and, after a moment's consideration, a piece of the door frame that has lain splintered on the floor since we returned. 'But I don't have the leverage to stand up to AD and his new buddies. Not yet.' Now she stands by the door, giving the room a last once-over. 'And I need something heavy to use if I'm going to spring a trap.'

THIRTY-FIVE

'm not a fan of cages of any sort, and I know too well how traps can backfire. And so it is with deep unease that I accompany her to a section of the city as yet unknown to me, to an area of bare sidewalks and buildings that smell of rot.

Part of it is that the aftermath of the nightmare has stayed with me. The feeling of vulnerability as I watch something horrible take place. The sense memory of being grabbed, of being taken, is too close to my own experience, and while I cannot recall the actual moment of immersion – whether I was caught unawares by the flood while sleeping in a low place or captured and thrown in with malicious intent – I value my freedom too much to like these cold stone walls, so high they would shut out the weak morning sun.

Even Care seems to have second thoughts now that we're down here. She pauses in front of one building's grimy steps. A puddle has formed in the worn spot and I sniff it, hoping for a clue as to the occupants who trudge past here, but I get little. Sweat and worn leather, the threadbare ends of clothing worn for too long. This is a place of drudgery rather than cruelty, though, and that perks me up. And the foul smell of the drug – that, at least, is absent.

'Carrie? Is that you?' The girl jumps and I slink back, squeezing myself into the shadow of the stairs. A dull lump of a woman approaches. Not much taller than the girl, she appears several times as wide, a hillock rather than a human, an illusion aided by her mushroom-colored wool coat. An oversized purse of the same nondescript beige hangs over one arm, while in the other she holds a paper bag already stained with grease and a paper mug. 'Carrie Wright,' says the hillock, small brown eyes blinking under a frazzle of rusty curls. Her voice is warmer than I had expected. 'As I live and breathe.'

The girl straightens and stands her ground. We are out in the open here, as open as this claustrophobic street can be, and so I sit up to watch. If the girl does not deem this creature a threat, perhaps she is the reason we came here.

'Miss Adele.' The girl's voice trembles, though with fear or something else, I cannot tell. 'I was hoping to see you here.'

'Of course, of course. You always could come by.' She shifts the mug and bag to her left hand, hiking the purse up her shoulder as she does so – a movement both cumbersome and familiar, the daily burden no longer noticed. I am mistaken, she is not a hillock. She is a bear, emerging clumsy from its winter rest. This done, she reaches out as if to touch Care – or to grab her. 'Let's go inside.'

'No.' Care steps back, just out of range. The bear blinks then lets her arm drop. 'I'm sorry.' Care's voice softens. 'I just came because I need your help.'

'Of course, anything.' The bear nods, making her rusty curls bounce. 'I'm afraid the investigation into your parents' accident has been suspended, but—'

'It's about Tick.' Care doesn't let her finish. 'Thomas. I've done what I can. Tried to keep him with me, take care of him, but he's gotten . . . he may have gotten involved in something too big, and I might need help.'

'You could bring him in.' She stops. Care is shaking her head. 'You want protective services? An emergency intervention?'

'If I have to.' Care's voice breaks a bit. 'I'm not sure, but I may— Is there a number? Somebody I can call?'

'I have a card.' With her free hand the bearish woman starts to rifle through her purse, which begins to slide off her shoulder. She grabs it and kneels, depositing the paper bag on the steps. I step forward. It smells interesting, and it is warm.

'What?' She jerks the bag back and hands it, with the mug, to Care before returning to her purse. After a moment's furious digging, she pulls out a card. 'Here. This is the hotline. If a child is in danger, we will come. In force.'

Care appears thoughtful as she looks at the card.

The woman, in turn, is reading her face. 'I'm sorry I didn't give you that before, Carrie. It wasn't that I didn't believe you or Thomas. It was the system. We thought it was a good place-ment for him. For you. This city . . .' She stops. Care keeps staring at the card. 'I'm sorry.'

Care tucks the card in her jeans with a nod. 'Thanks,' she says as she hands back the bag and the mug.

'Keep it,' says the woman. 'It's the least I can do.'

We share the donut in an alley about a quarter mile away. Despite the relative quiet of the street and the departure of the woman into the building, Care is eager to get away and doesn't even stop to examine her bounty at first. She walks quickly, her head bowed, but we are not interrupted, and when she finally slows we are back in familiar territory, the buildings more rundown but the streets less populous, even now as the morning sun begins to dry the puddles.

The pastry is cold by then; its creamy topping thick. I lick it for the richness of that greasy coating but leave the doughy part untouched. Care looks longingly at the wet bit I have discarded but contents herself with the remainder, dipping it in the even milkier contents of the paper mug.

'You want some coffee?' She sees my nose twitch as I take in the scent of warm and sweet, then holds the mug down for me to taste and laughs as I recoil at the bitterness beneath the cream. Her response warms me, more than that foul beverage could, and I find myself purring. We are on the sunny side of the alley and I have begun to feel better about this day. Better about everything, except the idea of a trap.

'I can't really do it,' she says and I look up. She has the same concerns as I do, I see. It is these concerns she addresses, rather than any query of mine. 'I mean, I won't call protective services. They're just for leverage with AD. They know him. He's done some time for using kids and I've got to get Tick out of there.'

I do not understand what she's saying, though I can feel the thread of uncertainty that runs beneath it. Still, we are warm and have eaten. I am drifting toward sleep when she stands and wipes her hands free of crumbs. 'Freddie will know how to reach him. Freddie or Junebug.'

She turns to look at me. 'Sorry, Blackie. I should let you sleep, right? It's just . . . I've begun to feel like I can bounce things off you. I can't talk to Tick like this, even when he's here. When I was working with the old man I got used to it. Got used to putting my thoughts into words. Sometimes it helped.' She shrugs. 'I guess cats are good listeners.'

I don't disagree. Instead I yawn and stretch. If she's heading out, I will accompany her. My dreams have been too disconcerting of late for me to crave sleep like some heedless kitten anyway.

'If AD kicked everyone out, they'll be at the club.' She stops and looks at the sky. 'If it's not too early.'

She takes off at a determined pace and we fall into a companionable rhythm. Like me, she pauses before crossing a street. Like me, she moves quickly through open space, looking for movement and other signs of life as we proceed. We have both learned caution on these streets, and although her instincts may lack the acuity of mine, she has been trained and trained well.

It is therefore with some trepidation that I follow her down a narrow passage that does not have an outlet at its end. For me, this is less of an issue – its brick borders are porous and I see at least one space where I can squeeze in if need be. For the girl, however, the alley is a dead end. The walls of the decrepit buildings are stories high and the fire escape hanging above is rusty.

No matter, she reaches for it. And when she can't grab it, searches in the alley. Sure enough, a wooden cane – its rubber tip half torn off – is lying against the wall. Using its rounded grip, she pulls at the fire escape ladder until it slides down with a clang. It's still ringing as she grabs its rusty side rail and steps onto the first rung.

'Blackie?' She looks around for me. I skittered back at the clamor, and watch now, wary, from halfway down the passage. 'It's OK?'

She smiles and extends an arm. I remember my dream.

The feeling of being caught, of being dragged into danger –
hauled to my death. I recall all too well drowning. The eyes
of those watching. I look up at her eyes – the girl's – green
as mine and nearly as fearless. I remember the feeling of hands
taking me against my will.

    I jump.

THIRTY-SIX

We are in a low space but warm. The girl crouches as she advances, standing slowly as she approaches the center where the angled roof is at its peak. We have climbed to the top of the building. Or she has, to clarify. Once I landed in her arms, I accepted the berth of her bag as she ascended the ladder and entered an open window three stories up.

'Freddie?' Her voice is quiet. There are others here. Along the sides of the garret, bodies lie under their makeshift blankets. My nose identifies them as human but gives me no more, and I assume, from the trepidation in her tone, the girl can do no better. 'Junebug?'

'Care?' One of the bundles stirs. A head appears and then the top of a torso – female. Nude. Through the worn cloth of the bag I make out the dark-haired girl from AD's basement. She leans on her forearm, unconcerned about her nakedness and blinking. 'You need a place to crash?'

'No.' Care starts to make her way over, careful not to step on any of the other sleepers. 'Thanks,' she adds belatedly.

'Watch it.' She jumps to the left as a hand reaches out from under a moth-eaten overcoat. 'Hey, come here, girl.'

'Over here.' Freddie is sitting up now and gestures for Care to come and sit by her side. 'Don't mind Zeno. He won't tax you just for visiting, and if he does, I'll pay up.'

As Care settles, leaning in against the low wall, I examine this Freddie. Older than Care, I judge by her heavy breasts and her scent, though by how much I could not say. She is undressed, save for a scarf in her hair, and as she begins to sort through a pile of clothes beside her a hand – male – reaches for her. She pushes it away. Its owner grumbles and then falls back asleep.

'Freddie, I was wondering if you could help me find someone.'

The girl fishes out a worn tank top and, pulling it over her head, keeps looking. 'Uh huh?' Her voice is noncommittal, her attention given instead to a green sweater. She turns it back and forth in the faint light, no doubt noting the holes in the hem and the sleeve, and then pulls that on too.

'Someone big.' Care looks at her, willing her to pay attention.

'Big?' The other girl smiles and removes her scarf to finger-comb her curly brown hair. 'You looking for an arrangement?'

'No, no.' Care shakes her head. 'Not like that. I want to report—' She stops herself and swallows. 'I have something to sell,' she says.

'Like, to AD?' Freddie reties the scarf.

Care shakes her head. 'Bigger.' I watch, unsure of her plan. I have my suspicions, but they hint at a dangerous game. 'Too big for AD. I was thinking of going higher.'

'Mister?' Freddie's voice drops to a whisper.

'Mister – like, Mr Bushwick?' Care keeps her own voice low.

Freddie pauses and I see her chewing on that name. Then she shrugs. 'Maybe. I just know him as Mister.'

I close my eyes, a strange calm flowing through me. Perhaps it is the warmth. The bodies in this garret, the commercial enterprise that must still take place below, have heated this enclosed space more than any room I have inhabited in recent memory. Perhaps it is the pouch I still rest in. It is comforting to be held in this way, the scent of the girl dominating the rank sweat of the others. But it is also, I know through means that I cannot explain, because this girl is following a trail that has been long laid out.

Yes, I think to myself, the low rumble of a purr beginning. This is what must happen. She must seek out Mister. We must . . .

'Is that a cat?' My eyes pop open to see Freddie beaming down at me, the wear in her face eased by her wide-eyed smile. 'How cute!'

'Careful.' Care draws back even as her friend reaches for me. But she need not fear my claws, not today. Instead, I allow the blowsy brunette to pull me from the bag and haul me into her blanket-covered lap. She has offered shelter, of a sort, to the girl and seems likely to provide information as well. Besides, she is warm.

'So,' the brunette says after an appropriate amount of cooing. The two females are leaning together against the wall, the blankets pulled up over their shoulders. 'What are you looking to sell?' She is stroking me as she speaks. But although I am purring and my eyes have closed, I listen carefully, curious to hear how Care will answer.

'Just info,' she says. My ears perk up. This woman is her friend but she does not trust her – not entirely. 'It's possible that someone is ripping him off.'

Freddie nods, her hand resting on my back. 'That would be worth something.' She sounds thoughtful. 'It's not – not someone here, is it?' Her body shifts as she looks around.

The girl doesn't bother to look. 'No,' she says. 'They're not the type.'

'You'd be surprised.' There's a sharpness in her tone but Care does not respond and the brunette returns to stroking me. The two sit in silence for a moment, and I feel myself start to drift.

'It wouldn't be that goon he's always traveling with. What's his name, Brian?' This close, I can feel Care shake her head. 'Or his scrawny buddy?'

'Please, Freddie.' The girl's voice is low, barely more than a whisper. 'It's better that you don't know.'

The bigger girl shifts but keeps petting me. She is waiting, possibly, hoping that Care will break – will share something. Possibly she is thinking, running through what she knows. Who she knows. How. It is my job to stay still, to encourage the sharing of information, the cozy confidentiality between Care and this source.

It has its challenges. Combined with the warmth, the constant stroking is hypnotic. I am listening, collecting impressions and already planning how to share what I may gather with the girl. Already, I am envisioning those two hoodlums, strong-arm men of the crudest sort. They are flanking their master, the brains of the operation. Care is waiting. They are waiting.

'Well, I hope you know what you're doing.' Freddie breaks

first, frustrated at being left out. Her tone is peevish and her hand has become heavy. I look up at her, noting how her full lips pout. 'Whoever it is, Mister is not going to be pleased.'

'I know.' Care's tone is serious and I wonder if she is having second thoughts. She is not the killer that I am, and the news she carries may well bring a sentence of death. 'But I need this.'

The brunette shifts and I resist the urge to sink my claws into her soft thighs. She's curious, waiting to be entertained. With a sigh, Care obliges.

'Someone – well, it was a cheat that hurt a friend of mine. Hurt him bad. And now, well, if I can do him a good turn, maybe he'll sponsor me. Use me.'

'*Use* you?' Freddie looks her friend up and down, her body shaking with barely concealed laughter.

'My services,' Care clarifies. 'I mean, if he'll spread the word that I can find things out. That I—'

'That you're a rat?' The brunette has stopped laughing.

'That I can find things out,' Care repeats. 'Find people, things. Figure out what has happened.' She pauses but the silence is no longer companionable. 'It's not like I'd go to the cops.'

I ride up and down as the big girl sighs. 'Well, it's your funeral,' she says at last. 'Just don't bother him before tonight.'

'What's tonight?' Care sounds like herself again. Girlish, but it's an effort.

'You're kidding me, right?' So does the brunette, though I can hear the boredom creeping in. She shifts, and I stretch out along her thigh once more as she renews her ministrations. 'That's all anyone has been talking about. The big deal. They're bringing in a load. They're going to light this town up.'

'With what?' Care has been out of the loop too long. Away from AD too long.

'Scat, silly.' Pleasure has replaced boredom in Freddie's voice. The pleasure of being the one who knows.

'But AD is the cook around here.' Care is talking to herself. Piecing together what she's heard. I think of an alley at night. 'Or he was . . .'

'He isn't anymore.' The hand stops and settles on my back.

Freddie is done. 'He's moving up. He's going to handle distribution, at least for the waterfront. You can ask him yourself.'

'AD? I don't think so.'

'Well, if you want to see Mister, that's who you're going to have to go through. Him or Diamond Jim. They're going to be down on the docks tomorrow night. They're managing the whole thing.'

'Wait.' Care sits up with a start. Freddie pulls back and I tumble from her lap. 'Diamond Jim?'

'Yeah, That's why he's getting to play. I heard he bought in with something big.'

Care walks more slowly after we leave. She stops at a cart that smells deliciously of meat and, a half a block later, settles against a building to share her purchase. Chicken, I think, though rat is a possibility – it has roasted so long it is both the color and consistency of leather. We eat in silence, both of us licking up any traces of the salty sauce.

The silence suits me. I am musing over my dream, the echoes of that half-waking memory taking on the names and faces of those we seek. They are monsters, I know for sure. As I scour the leather bottom of my toes, I remember how I batted furiously against the water. How I gained no purchase against the flood. How it pulled me under. How I sank. Yet there is some part of this that eludes me still, something I do not understand.

'I don't get it, Blackie.' Care has been sucking on the skewer that held the meat. Now she taps it against her teeth, considering. 'I mean, I get Diamond Jim wanting in. A deal that big could finance him for a long time. And I figure he's fronted before. AD wouldn't know a swell like him otherwise. But why hire the old man? He gave him a deposit and everything – for information. That was specially agreed to. It's in the contract. And why kill Fat Peter?'

She pauses, the stick resting against her lower lip. 'That might be unrelated. Fat Peter was greedy. Greedy and stupid, everyone said. But Jonah, too? He was just a poor old man.'

The sun is high and I have fed. Her voice is low and soft,

blending with my memories of the waking dream. The old man . . .

'The answer has to be in something he said. But what . . .'

My eyes closed, I can visualize the older man. Gaunt and scared, Jonah started at every shadow, yet he had risked his life to tell this girl something.

'The marker? No, they took that. Took Tick, too.' She sighs and shakes her head.

He had shaken his head, too. Hung it as if weighed down by grief or a memory. What had he said?

'I kept it straight.' The words come from the girl's mouth as she, too, remembers. 'He refused. He thought he could—'

She jumps up so quickly I mew in protest, but she does not apologize. Rips her bag open and pulls out a handful of papers, half of which she drops on the broken pavement. One she grabs, holding it in both hands. It's the contract, which she has already read so many times that I recognize its scent – the markings on its surface. 'Rivers.' She says the name out loud. 'The reference. The blank in the ledger – and the ticket that had no name. The whole thing was a set-up, Tick. The whole job. There never was any robbery. That was never what this was about. They just hired the old man to make it look real, and when he found out the truth they had to shut him up.'

THIRTY-SEVEN

As a cat, I have little sense of time. For me and my kind, life flows in an uninterrupted stream, from dreaming to waking and meal to meal. We do not bother ourselves with deadlines or watches, and our sense of the passage of the hours comes only from such concrete issues as a certain stiffness in one's hindquarters, the yearning for food or the comfort of another.

Therefore, it would be foolish of me to venture how long we remain on that street. How long I do, at any rate, soaking up the weak early spring sun. Although the girl doesn't go anywhere, she is in constant motion, pacing and cursing, grabbing at the papers from her bag and shoving them back in again. I can tell she's bothered by the way she murmurs, her voice almost a growl. I wake and stir as she kicks a paving stone. I cannot but feel calm, however. The news of a double cross, of a trap set for one of her own seems inevitable to me in this world of predators and prey.

'It was the downtown office as much as any reference,' she says out loud. I sit up and yawn, taking the morning air into my mouth, showing my fangs to the world. 'That was why the old man trusted Diamond Jim – why we both did.' She shakes her head and collapses on the broken pavement beside me.

'I wonder if he knew. If he suspected who Diamond Jim was really working with.' She pauses, mouth slightly open. It seems, for a moment, as if she can taste the air. Can read it, like I do. She seems to be gathering information. Putting the pieces in place in her mind. 'He liked to know things. "Knowledge is power," he always said. He wouldn't have interfered, though . . .'

She stops. I have seen her bite her lip before. She is lucky her teeth are not like mine. In so many ways, she is unlike me. For all her apparent independence, she is not that tough. She is, in many ways, a child.

'No, he might have, Blackie. If he thought that they were dragging in Tick or me . . .' Again her voice breaks off. She pulls the card from her pocket and stares at it like it will tell her something, but then she puts it away.

'He and I used to talk about this. About my education. About Tick's. He used to say Tick didn't have enough of a base. I always thought he meant that Tick wasn't smart enough. Wasn't as quick as I am, but maybe that wasn't it, or not entirely. Tick was really young when his mother gave him up. He'd been in the home for a few years when I got there, after my parents . . . after the crash. He took to me. He was such a sweet kid. If you knew him then . . .'

She stops. Her lip is beginning to bleed where she has worked it raw.

'I don't believe he would betray me, Blackie. Anything he did he did either because he thought it was what I wanted or because he had to. I mean, he's a kid. Small for his size, and he gets hungry. Gets picked on. And after our foster father . . .' She stares at the card again. And again she shakes her head. There's a battle going on inside her, and it has made her as itchy as if she had fleas.

I shiver, my coat twitching all over at the thought. But that is all. Maybe it is the cold. The nights still have frost in them. Maybe it was that dunking. I've not been bothered by vermin, I realize. I have not thought about such things as fleas or ticks. Nor, really, about any other hungers beyond my belly. Maybe this is the natural outgrowth of that constant dream state. Maybe it is age or the wear and tear of injury and the streets. It occurs to me now, though, that all I have thought about since the culvert – the vision – is this girl. This girl and that one strange image of three men with cold eyes.

'They're monsters, Blackie. The lot of them. AD's the most obvious, but that Fat Peter worked the trade, too. And if Diamond Jim and Bushwick are in league? No, Tick's not safe with them, and I bet the old man knew it. I bet he thought he was protecting me too.' She looks at me, her green eyes sad. 'I bet he would have tried to stop them. Maybe he did.'

She rests her chin on her arms, staring into the street. From the side, I can see the tears welling up in those eyes, the way her lips tremble. She is sorrowful, as lost as any creature I can recall. I lean toward her, pushing the flat of my head against her elbow in a clumsy imitation of a head butt. I am a denizen of the streets, and the gesture is somewhat foreign to me, despite this day of purring and being stroked. She sniffs and looks over at me, momentarily distracted. So I repeat the motion, rolling my eyes up to look at her as she reaches over to massage the base of my ears. I add a purr, knowing it is a poor offering in the face of so much loss, and rub my cheek against her. And when her lip stops trembling, when the ghost of a smile begins to play at its corners, I do it again, pushing my head hard into her arm. It works. She smiles.

I am a cat, but I am not a brute.

'Thanks, Blackie,' she says. She is running her hand over my back and I do not have to fake my pleasure. I stretch as her warm hand soothes me, smoothing my fur and my tired spine. It is always a matter of small gestures, minor movements, adding up. Building. 'Sometimes I think you know what I'm feeling,' she says, her voice once again calm. I lean into the pet. I listen. 'The old man always said cats could communicate. Maybe he was right. Maybe you can read me – you just don't know how to tell me—'

She stops. Her hand stops, right by the base of my tail. I look up, my reverie broken by the abrupt cessation of pleasure.

'What if he wanted to tell me something but didn't have the time?' She looks at me as if I can answer. I blink. It encourages her. 'He must have found something. He was the best, Blackie. He really was. He could look at a scrap of cloth and tell you about the person whose coat it came from. He could tell you how it got torn off and by whom, too. And, I mean, it took me long enough, but even I figured out that the theft wasn't real – that it was a front for something.

'Diamond Jim might have hired the old man to make the set-up look good, but I bet he got more than he planned. The old man found out what was going on – found out about this deal, about the scat coming in or whatever – only he didn't get a chance to stop it. But he left word for me, Blackie. He left that message with Tick and he left me the blank pawn ticket, too, knowing that I'd figure out it meant that there was no product. No necklace to redeem. But I don't know if he figured out what that meant for the job. For him. If he knew what was coming.' She pauses and I wait for the return of the tears, of the trembling. She shakes them off. 'He always left signs for me, Blackie. Tracks that I could follow – that he trained me to follow. He always left clues.'

THIRTY-EIGHT

This girl has potential. I have long thought that. But she does not understand the hunt. 'Search for clues,' she has said, and I envision an act both careful and quiet, like the long wait for a small head to emerge. Not this hurried march back to the office, back to a place her foes have discovered.

She clearly has other thoughts about the process as she bustles about the old man's office. 'That must be what Bushwick's men were looking for,' she says as she pushes the desk away from the wall. It moves with a rumble and growl that's a bit loud for my taste, and I retreat to the windowsill to watch as she runs her hands along its back. 'Clues. I mean, I know about the marker. But a weight? Really?'

She has flopped on her back to peer under the desk, and her next words are muffled. In part, I confess, because I am bathing. Such activity makes me nervous. But when she emerges she is shaking her head. Her hands are empty. Whatever she has hoped to find is not there.

'I don't get it, Blackie.' She leans back on the desk and looks at me. If I could advise her, I would. Calm down. Be quiet. Let the prey reveal itself. Since I have failed thus far at transmitting any of my knowledge to her or her kind, I fold my front paws beneath me and sit in my most tranquil pose. At the very least, she is being quiet now, and I appreciate the cessation of noise.

'The old man knew about the weight – about the marker.' She's talking to herself more than to me, but I blink again to urge her on. 'That's why he told Tick to tell me about Fat Peter, about the measure being off. About it being bigger than Fat Peter. Much bigger. He knew something else was going on, something besides that necklace. He had to.'

She slumps down on the floor with a sigh. 'Or maybe he was killed before he could find out more. Or before he could find a way to get a message to me.'

We sit there in silence and I start to drift. I think of waters, rising, and open my eyes with a start.

'Of course.' Care is pulling herself to her feet. I do not know if my movement has wakened her or hers me. I stretch and watch as she once again pulls the papers from her bag. 'Rivers. This contract. That's why he let Diamond Jim fill it out, why he left it here for me. It's all here. Everything. The old man would have known that was a fake business, a fake reference. He must have suspected something was wrong with the case. But why . . .'

She stands there staring at the paper. I do not think she is reading it again. Her eyes are focused on the middle distance, and the light off the alley has begun to fade, the shadows of the building across the way already creeping through the room.

'He knew something was up, I'm sure of it. He took the case so he could find out what. He took their bait but he left the contract, like he left word about the weight. Just in case. He must have suspected a trap, but he couldn't have known . . .'

She wipes her eyes and reaches for the light. Now she is reading again, examining the contract as if she had never read it before. 'Rivers Imports on Dock Street, of course.' She looks up and there's a light in her eye. A reflection of tears. Or a spark. 'The old man was killed down by the river, Blackie. Not far from where I found you. And that deal Freddie told us about? The one Diamond Jim was so eager to buy into? That's happening down by the docks too. We're going down there and we're going to find out what's going on. I'm going to finish what the old man started, Blackie.'

I jump down to stand by the girl, my tail erect, whiskers bristling and alert. We are going on the hunt.

The girl is growing smarter. Rather than just rush out, she prepares herself. For starters, she goes through what remains in the old man's closet. A long overcoat in a nubby tweed comes out first. She buries her face in it and I know even her inferior senses are picking up the fruity fragrance of pipe tobacco that lingers around the worn collar. She tries it on and I wonder at her planning. Although it is thick and doubtless warm, a benefit for a skinny creature such as she is, it falls to her ankles. Although I have seen her shiver, wrapping her arms around herself when she is not holding me, this coat is not a very practical garment for someone who might need mobility or stealth. But when she pairs it with a cap of the same fabric, I begin to understand. By donning her mentor's clothing, she seeks not only to emulate but to evoke him. To create an illusion and possibly force her opponents to act in a way that will betray them – or betray their colleagues.

To this she adds the cheese knife, poor thing that it is, and that board she has been carrying, the piece from the busted door. She opens the coat and slides it in a tear in the lining, a hole, I surmise, that has been used before for just such a purpose. She takes a few more items as well from within the desk, shoving them into her jeans and the deep pockets of the coat. Lastly, she reaches for her bag.

I look up at her. I have been standing, watching her preparation, my tail beginning to lash as the excitement mounts. Now I meet her eyes, green on green. As green as any emeralds. I wait.

'Blackie?' She holds the bag open. Crouches down on the floor, and with a leap I am inside, the worn cloth shifting beneath my feet. I stick my head out to retain my bearings and to signify that she should not close the flap. I do not know what her plans are or how we will proceed. I do know that I will need to be able to move, to jump and to strike. This is more than a hunt: we are going to war.

THIRTY-NINE

I t is an odd thing to be bounced along like a kitten in a hammock. I find my claws flexing for balance as the bag sways against the thick tweed. Care is moving fast, running as often as she walks and making the most of the twilight and her street savvy as she darts from shadow to shadow. Almost, I feel, she could be a cat with her swift, silent moves. Almost, I feel at one with her, as if I too had a death to avenge.

She has made her plans before we set out. Consulted those papers from the desk and others that she had unfolded on its surface. Although I do not read – neither those letters that mean so much to her nor the so-called map she has found, with its shadings and lines like so many mouse trails – I am confident about where we are heading. We cats do not need such tools for orientation, not when our other senses are engaged. Besides, I know the waterfront. Its smells, its features, its capacity for danger. I may not have the exact bearing that Care is heading for – as I have said, I do not deal with such trivia as addresses or signposts – but I am confident we are heading to the right place. That we are heading to where it all began.

Perhaps it is that confidence that makes me feel I am drifting. That or the rocking motion of the bag as the girl enters the city's less populated quarter and maintains a steady pace. At some level, I am aware that I will need to be alert – alert and strong – once we arrive at our destination. On another, I am marshaling my reserves. I have been run ragged recently, bruised and beaten. I am not, as I have noted, a kitten anymore. I am a mature feline, and as we cats will do, given the opportunity, I find myself drifting once again into that dream state of half waking where we spend so much of our time.

I am sinking. I am always sinking, even as I extend my claws into the worn denim. Even as I shift and readjust in the bag, more awake than not. I stick my head out, curious about our progress. The girl is making her way between high rises. Across a vacant lot now filled with rubble and past a crane, silent against the sky. The shadows fall across her, across us, longer now that the day is ending. I see them, even as my eyes close again, as I slide back into the recesses. Bars against the light, moving as we move. Moving closer.

I squirm slightly and readjust, dreading what I know I will see next. Three faces, cold and blank. Three sets of eyes, impassive. Cruel. They stare as they have always stared, and I roll onto my side. My ribs are still sore and my hind leg twinges as I kick myself over. I need to stretch, to lie in the sun and sleep, but this half-drowse, neither restful nor productive, must make do. I flip, pushing myself off, and hear the girl grunt as my claws slip through the thin cloth and deep into the tweed. I cannot have punctured her, not with that thick coat, but the movement has thrown her and she shifts, resting her arm against the bag. Holding me, briefly, against her.

Holding me against my will. I am in the warehouse again. Behind the stacked pallets, watching and waiting. Only, I am not the one watching – I have been watched. Been seen, and now I am surrounded. My arms are pinned to my side. I feel the heavy cloth press against me, restricting my movement as I would kick, as I would jump. Against my will, I am dragged from behind the sheltering stack and held as the leader – the tall man with the dead eyes – comes forward. I know those eyes. That face. I know what happens next.

'Kill him,' he says.

'Whoa!' The girl is standing over me, her hand in her mouth. I have clawed her. Torn through the bag to the hand holding me to her side and made her bleed, and now she sucks the sore, eyeing me with a wounded look.

I jump from the bag onto the pavement. The perfume of opossum situates me but it is faint. We are nearer to the river now, that locating scent overrun with fish and rot. I long to investigate – to round the stone around us and seek out the wooden wharfs, the teeming waterside. The mix of aromas is intoxicating, rich with life even this early in the season. With death too, I realize.

And I remember. This building, this street – they are not

far from where the girl rescued me – from where the old man must have met his end. And that thought brings me back to myself, to my companion. Belatedly, I blink up at her. I did not mean to draw her blood. I would not hurt her for all the world.

'Mew,' I say, looking up at her shadowed eyes. It is a poor attempt at an apology, this sad, soft syllable. For once, I am ashamed of myself. Of being a beast, so easily manipulated by my own fancies, by my dreams. By my overladen senses, here where it all began.

'It's OK, Blackie.' She removes her hand from her mouth and looks at it. I can see where the blood is welling up, slowly, in bright red beads. 'You must have been having a nightmare.'

She fishes a handkerchief from the depths of the pocket. A scrap of cloth that is somehow familiar to me, that I knew would be there, and wraps it around her hand, tying the makeshift bandage in place. 'Anyway,' she says – to herself, I believe. 'We're here. He was found somewhere around here.'

We are sitting, I now realize, in the shadow of a stoop. A niche between a building and its grand entrance stairs. Stairs I have circumvented before, and with reason. For now, this space is safe. In the twilight, where we sit is shadowed. I am as good as invisible by virtue of my coat. The girl is more visible than usual in that oversized brown tweed, but the waterfront seems to have died down for the night. It is cold, the wind off the river damp and chill, and for a moment I wonder whether it is too late in the season for snow. No matter. I shiver and move closer to the girl, glad of that thick coat, as I am of my fur. This wind, which sneaks around the stairway to find us here, will drive others inside. They will be seeking the warmth of the bars, of the alley. Of their drugs.

'They dumped him in that ditch, Blackie. Did you know that?' She is talking to herself, for sure. To build her courage for what she will do next, and that is why my ears prick up, why I feel my guard hairs bristle at her tone. 'Farther down than where you were – down by the tracks. Another hour and there wouldn't have been much left to ID, but . . . I don't know why they didn't throw him in the river. I mean, I'm glad. Nobody would have ever found his body if they had.'

She flexes her hand and I wonder what she is thinking. I do not believe I injured her that deeply. No, she is preparing, rehearsing some scenario in her mind, some scene that I cannot imagine.

'That was three days before I found you, Blackie. It was almost like . . .' She shakes her head, dismissing whatever thought has crossed it. 'No, but he liked cats, Blackie. The old man always said we could learn a lot from cats.'

I am listening. Alert and suddenly aware . . . Footsteps, soft and obscured by the wind. Someone is approaching the building. I stiffen, straining to make out anything that will give me – give us – an edge.

'What is it?' the girl whispers but has the sense to duck down, crouching in the lee of the steps. She is safe there, hidden, and I am freed to leap onto the stairs. From here I see two men approaching, collars turned up against the cold. One of those collars is fur. Not fox, I think, with a shiver. One hand reaches up to adjust it, to turn it further against the wind, against any who might be watching from the blank, black windows as they pass me and pass inside. Bushwick.

'Was that? Never mind.' The girl's face peeks up beside me as the door slams shut. 'I wish you could talk, Blackie. I swear you'd be a good partner. But I should do my own groundwork. That's what the old man always said. "Do your groundwork. Know what you're getting into, and who was there first."'

I do what I can, perusing the worn steps for any unusual scents. The men who passed have left little trace beyond their leather and tobacco. The river scent is strong here, obscuring all else at first sniff, and when I close my eyes to concentrate I find myself caught up in its complexity. Fish and flesh, fresh and less so, the spring melt releasing odors that have been caged all winter, that have been carried from far away. I catch the faint tang of the drug, of scat, though it is not, I think, from the men who have passed. I get, as well, another familiar scent – sweet and slightly putrid. The smell of death.

Approaching footsteps, louder this time, make me jump back down to where the girl waits. I burrow into the folds of her coat and let her warm her hands on me, both of us silent as the newcomers approach. Folded into the warm tweed, I

am enveloped as well in the now-familiar smells of tobacco
and sweat. Friendly smells which contribute to the sleepiness
that creeps over me. Only when the footsteps pass do I catch
a whiff of something else. Cigar smoke. A harsh laugh as the
men push inside the heavy door.

'Diamond Jim,' says the girl. 'Time to move,' she adds, to
shore up her own courage, I suspect. She begins to sit up,
despite her nervousness. Despite, I suspect, her reluctance to
unseat me. And so, to relieve her of the latter, I jump up, once
again, to the stairwell – and leap immediately down again.

'What is it?' She has the sense to cower, covering me with
her own body. I would squirm free. The coat, hanging over
me, muffles both sounds and scent, only I do not want her to
respond. Do not want her to move.

Still, even within her coat, I can make out that two more
men have arrived. The one in front is tall and lean. He walks
quietly. I might not have heard his footsteps at all, his shoes
good leather and his movement careful with grace. It is the
other, two steps behind, who has given them away. Thick and
heavy, he rolls with his bulk, and I sense he does not care
who sees it. This is a man whose poundage is his asset, a
muscle man in every sense. A guard.

But it is not the guard who alarms me, though he is big.
Powerful in the flesh. It is his companion – his boss – who
sends a chill down my spine. Whose presence cuts through
the wool of the girl's coat and touches my every scar and
bruise. He stands, still, by the door as the heavier man holds
it open. Scans the street, turning without a word from the city
proper down to the waterfront and back again.

Peering out from the girl's coat, I catch the movement, the
glint of light on watchful eyes. He seems to sense that they
are not alone, and I see him frown in concentration as he turns
our way.

The girl holds still. Holds her breath, even, her hands on
my back and belly, as if afraid I will reveal our position. I
freeze as well, conscious of his silent gaze, the way he looms
above us, tall and lean, silhouetted in the dim light.

I wait for him to look down at us. I anticipate his face. His
eyes.

'Boss?' The guard's voice is soft. He holds the door ajar with his leg but one arm reaches out. The other – I sense the movement as much as see it – disappears inside his jacket, waiting for the command.

He doesn't get it. Without a word, the man turns and disappears inside the door. The guard waits a moment, looks around at the still streetscape then follows him inside.

'That was something.' The girl beside me exhales. Her voice is light, almost laughing. She has been scared, I can tell, and now seeks to rebalance herself – regain her nerve. 'I wonder if he's the dealer. He seemed pretty posh.'

That wasn't the word that came to my mind, but I cannot offer another. Instead, I clamber from her lap as she shifts and then stands. I do not feel good about this, about her plan to confront these men – to turn them on each other. But the die is cast.

We wait for another dozen heartbeats. I watch the moon break through the clouds, sketching out silhouettes that stretch along the iron-grey street. I think about the man who has arrived, about his silent appraisal. The face I couldn't see. There is something on the tip of my consciousness, an impression as fleeting as one of those moon shadows. A faint memory. This place, that man . . .

I'm on the tip of recovering it – the thought, the image – when the girl stands up.

'I'm going in,' she says. She has steeled herself, her declaration a final push. With footsteps not much lighter than the strange, tall man, she jogs up the stairs and – taking a deep breath – pulls the latch. The door opens easily, silently, and, my own courage faltering, I dash by her ankles into the dark antechamber of Bushwick's riverside warehouse.

'Blackie?' Her voice trembles and I press against her, reassuring her of my presence. Although I can make out the details of the empty space – the discarded papers in the corner, the rodents exploring the garbage by the stairs – I can tell she is hindered by the dark. She waits a minute, letting her eyes adjust, and when she proceeds she does so carefully, feeling the floor with each step before committing her weight. It is a slow process but I respect her caution and stay with her as she moves toward the stairwell. Surely she must see the glow from above. The meeting, for surely those men have come to talk, to seal their deal, on a floor above.

Yes! She has, and now she moves like a cat, taking the last few feet toward the stairwell so quietly the rats barely pause. Then she hugs the banister, working her way up. Her face slants upward, toward the light, and I see once again how young she is. How frail. A growl begins deep within me. This girl should not have to be here. She should not be on the street alone. I take the steps ahead of her, trusting that she knows I am here, with her, as she climbs.

I pause before the landing, my size giving me the advantage of stealth as I peer over the last step. To my left, a door, outlined in light, must be where the meeting is taking place. Two men stand guard outside. But before I can explore – before I have a chance to warn the girl – she is behind me. She crouches behind the banister and puts her hand on my back. She shivers slightly – nerves or the chill night – but her breathing is quiet and deep. She is acknowledging me, seeing what I have seen, and is readying herself for what lies ahead. Once again, I think that someone has trained this girl well.

But where is the other guard?

She takes one more deep breath and starts to stand. She will go in that door. She will brazen this out, despite a fear that has made my fur stand on end. She stands – and whips around as footsteps approach from down the hall.

'What's this?' AD appears, a cigarette hanging from his long, filthy fingers. 'Care? My darling, your timing couldn't be better.' He flicks the ash on the floor. 'You want to join the meeting, don't you?'

'I'm here to talk to Bushwick,' she says. Pulling herself to her full height, she faces the gang leader, chin up. Her voice is steady. 'I have intel for him. Something he can use.'

AD smiles and takes a drag. 'Good thing I came by to escort you in then, isn't it? 'Cause this is an invitation-only event.'

He reaches out, as if to take her arm, but she turns and starts to walk. Keeping one step ahead of him, she marches toward the office. The guards are smiling, more relaxed than earlier, and one of them knocks on the door and pushes it open without waiting for a response. Not hidden in the carryall this time, I have stayed behind, but I can see Bushwick as well as Diamond Jim inside the cavernous room. It's luxuriously appointed in a masculine way – and in stark contrast to the rest of the building, brass nail heads glinting out of leather furniture and a freestanding humidor of some exotic hide.

Both Diamond Jim and Bushwick are seated as the door opens. The jewelry dealer is slouched in a leather-backed chair, angled toward a desk and, beyond it, a grimed-over window that reflects the room's harsh light. His posture, if not his belly, makes him look like a deflated balloon. To his right sits the importer. Not behind the desk, which is the centerpiece of the office, large and dark and substantial, as if it itself were in charge. Instead he reclines on a small sofa, his legs extended over the worn carpet. The desk they both face is empty. The third man, I realize, has left. I do not know if this is his office or by what authority he assumed the central position. I only know that the meeting has already taken place.

Care looks from one man to another. Surely she notices the absence of the third man. Surely, she understands its import. Then I realize, for her purposes, it does not matter. She is not concerned about that other boss, anonymous to her. A businessman. What she has been pushing for is to get Diamond Jim and Bushwick in the same room. She seeks to expose Diamond Jim's hypocrisy, to avenge her mentor's death. But something is amiss. Something I cannot explain.

'Look who I found poking about.' AD has come in behind her, and with a moment to decide I barely slip in before he closes the door. 'Little hood rat, she is.'

He reaches for her. To claim ownership, rather than to move her, here in this room of leather furniture and big men, but she pulls her arm away in a brisk motion. Pulls herself up to stand as tall as she can. She inhales and nods at Diamond Jim. It's a warning, one the fat jeweler doesn't understand. He merely chuckles as she turns to address his partner.

'Mr Bushwick.' She starts to lick her lip – I can see her tongue dart out between the chapped lips – but she catches herself. Stops before she gives herself away. 'I've been wanting to speak to you again. I know you doubted me before, when

I came to visit. But now that you have Diamond Jim here, you can ask him yourself. You see, I know about the deal. About the marker, which AD here has reclaimed for you.' She nods toward her former gang leader. I know she is wondering about Tick, wondering if he is on the premises, but she keeps her focus.

'I know that the price of admission was the necklace.' She stops, this time for effect. 'But what I know, and what you don't, is that Diamond Jim was the one who reported it stolen. He was the one who called the old man in, to make it look legit – to get his money back. He cheated you, wanting to play it both ways to get in on the deal, and then, when the old man figured it out, he had him killed. Either way, you're both responsible for his murder, and all for some stupid necklace.'

The room is silent. The men all stare at Care, and from my vantage point, behind the edge of the sofa, I cannot tell if their faces are angry or surprised, or some combination of the two. I hear a sharp intake of breath and I prepare to leap. Humans tend to lash out when they are in a rage, and they do not always attack those who most deserve it.

What I do not expect is the hiss as AD lunges forward. This time he succeeds in grabbing Care's arm and dragging her back toward him.

'The necklace? Stupid girl.' AD is spitting, he's so angry. 'The fee wasn't the necklace. It never was.'

'Shut up.' Bushwick sits up, struggling with the soft sofa before he can stand. He turns toward AD, his voice curt and tight. 'We got the marker. The ship's mate has it, so we don't need this one anymore.'

'She's one of mine.' AD pulls Care closer. She stumbles against his body and looks around, confused. 'She's been getting above herself for a while now. Just like the old man, but I can use her.'

'I told you we should have taken better care.' Diamond Jim is on his feet now too, moving quickly for such a fat man. 'They're still unloading—'

'Shut up!' Bushwick's voice ratchets up as he steps forward, one arm out as if to block the jeweler from advancing. It's plain to see he's scared, and, turning from him to AD, Care suddenly grows pale.

'He wasn't just cover. For the necklace,' she says, her voice soft but clear enough to carry as she turns from Diamond Jim toward Bushwick. 'You hired him – and you vouched for him. The two of you together. It was a plan . . . You set him up. You set him up to be killed.' She swallows and licks her lips, no longer caring who sees the emotions plain on her face. 'You were afraid he would interrupt this – interrupt your deal.'

The two men turn toward each other. One quick glance, but it's enough. The girl doesn't have it right, not quite. But AD isn't giving her a chance to catch on. He's dragging her toward the door.

'Come on, darling. You've had enough for tonight.'

'Wait.' Bushwick raises his hand. 'We can't – don't make it messy.'

'I know better than to draw the heat,' AD calls over his shoulder. He pulls his gun from under his shirttail and places it on the desk. 'Besides, she's still good for some coin.'

He has her arms behind her now and frogmarches her out of the office. I am torn. These men – the bond between them means something. Something that Care has missed. Something I dearly want to know. And yet . . . As the door swings shut, I dart through, startling the guard who has begun to close it.

'What the—' He kicks and misses.

His companion laughs. 'Bad luck for you, Randy!'

It's a bad place for me to stop, out in the open, and AD is already pulling the girl down the hall. I've heard this lackey speak before, never laugh, but as I whip around he falls silent, his mouth hanging open.

'Hey, maybe it's you he's after.' His companion snorts. It's bluster, not a real laugh. His friend can't stop staring at me. 'The way he's looking at you. It's like he knows you.'

He's right. I'm staring. That laugh. These two, here, now. I feel on the tip of a breakthrough – on the edge of making sense of all this – when a scream interrupts me. Care. In danger. I turn as the two men behind me laugh once more. The larger one has a particularly nasty chuckle, his words making the situation clear.

'About time he broke that one in,' he says. 'Make her earn her keep.'

I race down the hallway to their echoing laughter, the sounds of a struggle somewhere up ahead.

'No!' I hear her voice, loud and clear, followed by a grunt. Shock or – no – pain, and I leap the last few feet to find a door closed against me. I remember the room inside. A show-room of dead pelts. A couch.

'Bitch!' AD, angry now. The sound of a slap clear even through the barrier, as is the thud of something heavy falling to the floor. A body, I think, as I throw myself at the door. It does not budge. I howl. I am howling. My heart is breaking. Behind me I hear the humorless laughter of evil men.

And then, suddenly, a different sound. Different footsteps, fast and light, from the far dark recesses of the hallway. Tick, breathless, looks at me. Looks at the door.

'AD, you in there?' he calls. His voice is reedy and he reeks. Scat. Too much. More than any one boy could smoke and still live. 'AD?' He bangs on the door and calls again, his voice breathy and nervous. But not, I think, high. 'You there? We have a problem.'

'What?' The door opens and AD leans out. His cheek is bleeding, and I recognize scratch marks. The hand on the door frame is bleeding too, the mark of teeth clear along the inside of his thumb.

'One of the pallets broke and we're not sure what to do.' The boy shifts from one foot to another, uncomfortable with bearing bad news. 'I mean, nobody wants the product to get wet and the ground out there, well, you know . . .'

As he speaks, my ears pick up movement. Behind AD, the girl is stirring. She is standing.

'Hell.' AD runs his bloody hand over his face, leaving a trail like warpaint on his filthy cheek. Tick sees it and stares. Even for this world, the look is dramatic. 'AD . . .' he starts to ask, then stops. I hear more movement. A step. She is up. She is approaching, but slowly. I hear hesitation – perhaps a limp.

She needs my help.

I look up at the boy. He is staring nervously at AD, trying

to see beyond him. He has picked up something – a shift in the light, a shadow, a sound – and in a moment he will alert the gang leader.

I consider my options. Time is short, but . . . I think of the girl. Of what she has done. Of who her allies are. My allies. I throw myself at the boy, rubbing my body against his thin legs. It works. He looks at me in surprise and makes a sound of pleasure. A hand reaches toward me. A boy's hand, looking to pet the kitty.

'For pity's sake.' AD glances down, distracted. And in that moment, stumbles forward into the hall, Care's small knife in his back.

'Tick.' She's blinking, tears on her face. She reaches for the boy but AD grabs him first, pulling him backward like a ragdoll. With his other hand he pulls the small knife from his flesh, barely wounded by the makeshift weapon. It clatters to the floor as he lunges for the girl.

He hasn't figured on me. I leap and bite, latching onto that outstretched hand with my fangs and two front claws, an unholy growl whining from my throat.

'Blackie?' Care steps back then stops as AD shakes his arm – shakes me – loose. I hit the floor awkwardly. My left hind leg is numb and I scramble to position myself, to attack again.

'You need some help?' The men on guard seem amused by the proceedings. A girl, a child and a cat. They are reluctant to leave their post. One of them, laughing, tosses AD his pistol.

'Nah, I've got this.' AD catches it and scowls, his face dark. He holds Tick close with one wiry arm as he tucks the gun back into his pants and eyes the girl. 'You really want to do this the hard way, Care? After all we've meant to each other?'

'Let Tick go, AD.' Her voice cracks. She steels herself, says it again. 'Let him go.'

'And?' That greasy smile. He thinks he's tamed her. He's got the boy. He's got the gun. I see it, and my fur stands on end.

'Let him go.' She steps forward.

The boy is staring at her, shaking his head. 'I belong here, Care. I stole the marker. It's my fault Fat Peter was offed.'

'Your fault?' She pauses, confused.

'I was supposed to bring it here. It was the signal.' Tick is pleading. Willing her to understand. 'I knew they'd blame him – blame Fat Peter. I knew when the old man showed up. But he was awful. He was . . .' He hangs his head.

She mouths the words. 'Oh, Tick,' she says. 'No.'

And AD makes his move. He grabs for her, one hand still on the boy. It's an awkward lunge and he misses. Care seizes the boy's hand and pulls him free.

'Run, Tick!' She sets off, still holding his hand. 'Run!'

It's too much. The boy is not as agile as she is, not as fast. He stumbles and AD snatches at him as Care whirls around – only I am there. I am between them. Fur extended, tail aloft, a growl like a demon wind filling the hallway. I wait for the shot. For the pain, the noise. But AD has halted, transfixed. Even Care freezes.

'Run!' I don't know whose voice it is. Mine. Tick's. The voice of a ghost long gone. It breaks the silence and Care takes off down the hall as the impact catches me squarely in the ribs. I am flying, I am falling, but it is a boot, not a bullet, and with a ragged, painful breath I manage to right myself and run after her, blinded by pain into the dark, down a long passage, the back stairs and into my own version of a nightmare. Into a room that I know all too well.

FORTY

We are in a large space, unheated and noisy with motion. It's a storage bay off a loading dock, the roll-up door open to the cold wet night and to the train tracks beyond. The pallets are no longer piled high. Instead, they sit on the floor, as children – AD's gang – labor over them, carrying crates from the back of a truck to stack them against the wall.

Care has stopped short at the sight of this industry. At the sight of her former comrades. But they don't notice. They're too busy, and the men watching over them stand and smoke and watch.

I catch up to her, my sides heaving. I taste blood in my mouth. She feels my warmth and lifts me, and I try not to whimper in pain. She steps backward, slowly, and I remember my dream. Hiding here was easy when the pallets were piled. Easy until it wasn't. Those men, dragging me out.

Care is small, though, and the bay is dark, the headlights of the truck only illuminating the constant chain of carrying and stacking.

'So much,' Care says, more to herself than to me. 'I've never seen so much.'

She has inched back to the wall and begins to move sideways. Just then AD breaks in, tumbling out of the stairwell.

'Where is she?' he yells. He is dragging Tick by his collar. 'Where's the girl?'

'You having problems with your crew?' One of the guards drops his cigarette. He grinds it into the pavement as he takes a step forward, his tread heavy.

'No.' AD shakes his head. I can hear his voice tremble, his tone change. 'No problems. Here.' He throws Tick forward. The boy stumbles but catches himself. 'You sent this slacker to find me?'

'Those pieces of crap.' The guard gestures with his chin to

a pallet, its slats splintered as he lights up another cigarette. 'They're breaking.'

'I've got more.' AD steps forward, eager to please. 'Hang on.'

Beside me, Care flattens herself against the wall, sidling deeper into the shadows. Her breathing is shallow, quiet. If she could become part of the wall, she would. But AD is occupied and doesn't even notice as I limp forward to examine the wood risers. I do not remember this smell, raw wood mixed with damp, which puzzles me. Curious, as well, is my perspective. Despite my pain I reach up, standing on my hind legs to examine the stack. The structure is haphazard, these rough constructs thrown on top of each other with little thought for balance or stability. And yet the pile appears so much larger than in my dream. More formidable, if not more solid. But there is something else. Something beyond the scent, the size . . .

'Blackie!' The girl's whisper breaks my train of thought and I turn to see her crouching, a look of panic in her eyes. Following her gaze, I understand. AD is returning, shepherding two of his crew before him toward the pile of pallets. I watch for a moment as the three approach. They seem bigger than the figures in my dream and yet less intimidating.

'Blackie!' Her voice, a hiss of breath, brings me back, and I follow, slowly, as she creeps off toward a corner. When I catch up, she reaches for me and I pull back. There's too much to observe here, and besides, I am hurting. Each breath brings a stabbing pang. But when I see her pain, I relent. She is shaking, frightened more than actually wounded, I believe. My presence – the warmth of my fur, ragged as it may be – seems to comfort her, and her hand on my back is light and kind.

Still, this is no place to wait. The presence of the pallets may mean nothing but the memory of my nightmare lingers and I dare not risk exposure. As AD turns, directing his crew, I slip away. The girl's eyes are not as keen as mine, her sense of smell useless when it comes to discerning differences in air currents. Off to our left, farther along the dark wall, I sense an opening, and in it I see a possibility of escape.

It will be a tight fit, but luckily the girl is slim. Half bricked over, forgotten, perhaps in some earlier renovation, the doorway leads to a narrow stairway – broken linoleum worn thin in patches. I peer up to see if it is passable – it seems to be, although this flight is cramped further by an inner wall and by decay that has eaten into the risers, crumbling some steps down to a toehold. Switching back on itself, the stairway ascends into a darkness even I cannot see. They seem to lead away from the interior wall, though there may be another, narrowing them to uselessness. They may be blocked above, the air an illusion, a draft from some rotted crack, the confined passage a trap.

Even if it offers escape, I know that is not what the girl wants. She had hoped to turn the two men on each other. To make the jeweler pay for betraying her mentor by exposing his ruse to the importer and, in their confusion, rescue the boy. But that did not work, for reasons I still can barely grasp. And with that option ruined, we should exit. At any rate, we need to leave this busy bay – she needs safety, to be away from AD and his cruelty, and I would like time to rest and to mull over the odd convergence of dream and waking life.

This doorway, I am relieved to note, is not familiar. Although I sense neither danger nor any human presence in the narrow stairwell, I pause, half in, to gauge the distance to its zenith. Air flows down – not fresh but moving freely. Still, I wait. My mind is less clear than I would like. I feel my tail lashing, as it does when I think, but in this dark corner I do not think even its motion will draw undo attention.

The girl sees it, though. I hear her come up behind me and gasp as she realizes what I have found. 'Good, Blackie.' She reaches to pet me, as if I had performed at her command. The contact does us both good. It is never bad to feel that one's talents are valued, and I start up the stairs with more bounce in my step than I had previously thought possible.

But the girl does not follow. I realize this as I reach the first landing. I turn and see her, looking back out at the room. Her hands grip the brick that frames the narrow doorway, her fingers turning white from the pressure. Beyond her, in the bay, I hear yelling. One voice – AD, I believe – shouts the others down and is followed by a sharp slap and the sound of someone falling. A cry, cut short. Care leans forward, and I fear she is about to head back out.

'Tick,' she says, her voice too soft to carry. Besides, the room is now filled with the sound of movements. Voices call out orders – 'Hey, grab this!' and 'Over here' – as they run across the concrete floor.

I watch, unsure of what to do, of how to urge her to save herself. The boy has made his choices and they are bad. But I cannot in good conscience wish the girl away. The air from above is not as fresh as I had thought. There is something putrid up there that makes me draw back. I bare my teeth, unsure of what lies ahead. For the first time in a long time, I am unsure what to do. I consider retreat.

'Come on,' the girl decides, stepping by me as she makes her way up the stairs. She is angry – I can see it in her stride. Hear it in the way her worn sneakers pound the broken stairs, and I am seized by fear. She is not thinking clearly, in this state, as she charges up these dark and secret stairs. And while I once hoped this hidden passage would lead us both to safety, I now hang back. That odor is vile. It fills my mouth and would choke me. Like the blood I taste. Like water, like the flood.

No! Whatever lies ahead, I cannot let her face it by herself. Already she has passed from my sight, her footsteps fading as the narrow stairs turn once again. I cannot . . .

Summoning my last reserves, I race ahead, leaping from stair to stair. The broken lino is slick and on one step I slip, my bruised belly hitting the edge hard enough to make me gasp. I pull myself up and dash ahead, pausing only when I realize the footsteps have stopped. Care has stopped – or left the stairwell. I cannot lose her. Not now. A final burst of speed and I have reached the top – an open door, and Care nowhere in sight.

FORTY-ONE

I am drowning. My mouth fills and my heart will burst with the strain. But no, I blink away the vision and realize that it is scent, not water, choking me. For a moment, it is as if I were not a cat, a creature of heightened senses. As if this outpouring of odor was foreign – was, in fact, a substance that could overwhelm me.

It is a room – one I had missed in my earlier visit, though I had theorized its presence. Guessed at it. A storeroom, the source of the coats I had seen in that tawdry showroom. Large and dark and full of furs badly cured. Of the smell of decay, of death. The scent is stronger here than in that shabby lounge. High square windows, begrimed and fogged by time, let in some light – outside, the moon must be at its zenith – but their few broken panes are not enough to release the corruption. Indeed, what air there is, and a chill breeze does send a scrap of rag flapping, must draft directly to that back passage, for the air in the stairwell gave little hint of the depth of foulness here.

And then I see her, pale in that faint light. She is stumbling toward the far wall. A fixture, a box. No, to a phone, and as she pulls a card out of her pocket I make my way to her. I am moving slowly. The climb has taken its toll, my injured side heaving, and the smell – the overwhelming scent of death . . .

'Child in danger,' I hear her say, her words calling me back through a dark fog, through the water. 'Please, come soon.'

What happens next is confusing, the more so because my head has begun to throb. The girl begins to race around. She pushes aside the coats, releasing more of that fetid reek, and dives between them. I want to chase her, to pull her out. This is bad. This is danger, but I cannot. The glow from above grows and pulsates, blinding me. By the time she emerges I am in despair, but although I am howling now, my wail a seemingly distant thing, she does not return to me. Instead, she makes her way around the perimeter – her movements desperate and more hurried. I sense her flailing, even as I cower and cry. Only when she finds something – a door – does she return.

'It's OK, Blackie. We're getting out of here, I promise,' she says. She does not understand – this is not my fear. This room is not merely a cage, not a trap. It is infinitely worse – a room of death.

'Only I've got to get Tick.' She is still talking. 'No matter what. I promised him, you see.'

I do not. I see only the light, pulsing in time with my throbbing head. When she reaches for me, I pull away. It is not Care, the girl I have come to trust – to love – whose hand comes toward me. It is another's – rougher, larger – and I lash out in agony and fear.

'OK.' She pulls back and I glimpse her shock. Her pain. 'I'm sorry.'

With a worried look at me, she heads back toward the stairwell. It would be difficult to see from here, even were my vision clear. The doorway was designed to be hidden from the uninitiated, and as I watch the girl steps into it sideways and seems to disappear.

I howl. I cannot stand it. Being here is terrible. Losing her, worse, and so I quiet myself. I force myself to follow. Panting from the pain, I slink into the stairwell. She has already begun to descend back to the loading bay, but I catch up with her. She has paused, alerted by the noises below.

'I didn't think . . .' She stops and draws back. The air here is clearer and I feel more myself again. Peeking through the hidden entrance, I see why she has stopped.

The truck outside has gone. The bay, however, is still open. Only now the light is changing, flashing in time with sirens as cars race up and brakes squeal. In a moment, spotlights flood the interior of the bay, illuminating every crate and pallet. In front of them a line of uniformed men advances, their shadows long before them. The crew stands there, as if transfixed, as another uniformed newcomer emerges from the depth of the bay. He propels AD before him, holding the gang leader's long arms secured behind his back, over the filthy shirt that hangs loose over his jeans.

'This one made a break for it,' he yells to his colleagues. AD turns wistfully toward the open bay. In the distance, a whistle blows.

Beside me, I sense Care craning her neck. We are in the shadows here, the entrance to the stairwell hidden in the stark black. Still, she is careful, keeping inside the dark. Trying to see without being seen. Looking, I realize, for Tick.

'Guess who was in the office.' Another uniform, a woman, appears, stepping in front of the bay. She has Diamond Jim in front of her. The fat man looks deflated, like a sad toad blinking in the glare of the spotlights. 'Says he's not the boss. That he's just an investor here.'

'Investor.' The other cop laughs as he hands AD off to a colleague, an officer with a baton. 'Hang on to him.' They are rounding up the rest of the crew. They are putting them in restraints, working their way down the line. Care is standing on her toes, holding on to the door frame. Looking.

'Tick!' she calls out, her voice too loud. People turn, but as they do a scuffle breaks out.

'Watch out!' AD has pulled his gun. The cop in charge drops his baton and raises his hands. But as he begins to back up, to back away, a shot rings out and AD falls forward with a cry.

Care gasps – they all do – but she is forgotten in the turmoil. The police have found Bushwick. He has been hiding behind a stack of crates. A stack of crates on one of the pallets. I begin to see double and blink to clear my vision. More noise. Bushwick is on the ground. He is cursing. Struggling. His imprecations take in Diamond Jim – 'You coward, you fool!' – and then everyone in the room, which is odd. He does not seem in a position to threaten. The two cops who stand over him look ready to beat him back down again. Still, his voice is a rumble. A curse.

'You don't know what you're doing.' He pushes himself up and gets onto his knees. 'You can't do this. You can't be here.'

He is angry. Undefeated, it would seem, but once again, even through my haze, I get something else – bitter, acid. He is afraid. There is something driving him that scares him more than these cops. There is someone.

'Tick!' Care cries out again, and this time I see why. The shadows from the spotlights are dark and defined, but the edges of one have started to move. It is the boy, behind a crate. He is taking advantage of the confusion. He is trying to sneak past the cops, out to the bay. To the train track beyond and the freedom of the night.

In the distance, that whistle again. Metal growling, thundering closer. Closer still. Another wail. It can't be Care's voice. It's not possible. Her second cry is softer than her first, and with all the hubbub it would not be audible across the open room. But for a moment, Tick pauses. He looks up.

And in that moment, it happens. Bushwick lunges. Pulls away from the officer who holds him and grabs the boy, lifting him off his feet. With one arm around Tick's waist, he has drawn a blade – a box cutter – and holds it to the boy's throat.

'Just leave. Leave. All of you.' He holds the boy close and looks around. The open bay yawns behind him. 'You can't be here. You can't—'

It happens that fast. A second shot, the sound a thunderclap in the open space, and he is down. Care gasps and would leap forward, only I am there, underfoot, and she trips, stumbling out of the passage.

It does not matter. The cops are focused on the man, who has fallen backward, and then on the boy. A cheer goes up. One officer has hoisted Tick up for all to see. He has blood on him but he appears more stunned than injured. In fact, as the cheers die down, we hear him.

'Put me down!' He kicks and writhes as the police laugh. Behind them, Bushwick stirs.

'Not just yet, little man.' A woman in an overcoat – a woman with a large purse and rusty curls – emerges. She nods at the cop and takes Tick firmly by the hand. The cop steps back, but as he does so the impossible happens. The prone Bushwick rises, bleeding but alive. Stumbling, he breaks for the dock and, as the cry goes up, jumps to the ground, running. The track is lit by the oncoming train, silhouetting the big man and the three officers in pursuit.

'He's going to make it!' One of the cops – the one with the gun – stops still, drops to one knee and draws. The train does not slow, its whistle warning all in its path. Bushwick staggers up the embankment, the rock and cinder spewing out from beneath his feet. Another of the cops – younger, leaner – sprints toward him, reaching for his collar, for his leg.

Bushwick jumps – and misses. An agonized shriek cut short. The lead cop stumbles backward in horror. The others stop running and lower their weapons. Inside the bay, the sound of vomiting.

The woman has Tick's hand in hers. He pulls back but the fight is gone. He looks over at us – at Care – but he goes with the big woman. Beside me, Care sobs – once, with a heave of breath that I think will break her heart. But as the rest of the crew is rounded up and herded past the spotlights, their fight gone, she crawls backward, broken into the stairwell.

'That your big boss out there?' One of the cops is looking at Diamond Jim. It's not a question, though, and the jeweler doesn't answer. 'That's who you invested with, huh?'

I retreat to where Care is sitting, hands on her knees on one of the broken stairs. I lean against her, exhausted and confused, but I can share my warmth, and for a minute or two we sit there silently, taking in what has happened. But as the cleanup continues she rouses and starts back up the stairs, climbing as quietly as she can. I follow, my head once more pounding as we near the hidden storeroom. The smell of death thick in the air; the stench making it hard to breathe.

'Well, at least Bushwick got what was coming to him,' she says when we get there. She has collapsed against the wall but I cannot join her. I stand, staring at the coats. Trying to understand. 'I should have known he was the boss, that the marker was going to him. Known that he . . .'

She stops, a look of horror on her face. 'The marker – that was the signal that the old man was on his way. The old man – *he* was the price. He wasn't killed only to get him out of the way – his death was what Diamond Jim brought to the deal.'

My head explodes in light and noise. The door bursts open. Men are yelling. Running. I am in pain and I howl. I cry with a voice not my own. A desperate cry. A man's scream.

Too late, too late. I see this room and I know. I see the thugs.

Their master staring as they throw me down. I see the gun. The
noise. The pain. The three men watching as I fade. I see my
death. I *smell* my death. Have smelled it all along. That stench.
The furs. I was killed here. I was killed. I was . . .

'What's that?' A voice breaks through. 'Someone's there.'
A flashlight runs along the floor. It leaps over the narrow
entrance to the stairwell, my sharp eyes catching the shadow
as Care disappears inside. 'Who's there?'

I launch myself with a caterwaul, ready to face them down.
To buy her time. To die again.

'What the—?' The light blinds me once more. And then
– a laugh.

'It's just a cat, Rico.' Another laugh. The men were scared
as well, unsure of what they'd find. 'Some mangy old stray
they must have let in to keep down the rats. Kind of like the
ones that old man used to feed.'

'Well, shit.' The flashlight swings instead to the coats and
up the walls. The men retreat. Another room searched. More
inventory to log.

I find her in the stairwell, sobbing quietly with fear and
loss. I am still stunned, taking in what I have learned. Absorbing
what I now know. I lean against her with my cat body, giving
her what comfort I can. This girl is my charge now. My protégé.
My child. I feel her calm and settle as the noises outside begin
to disperse. By the time we descend, the bay is dark and
locked. Yellow tape festoons the doorway and the empty
pallets; the smell of blood and vomit.

Care has a bad moment when she tries the door. It is
padlocked and will not budge. But now that I remember, I am
able to lead her to a secret entrance, the remainder of the
smugglers' passage, and onto the street. I am bone tired, sore
and aching from the night's event, and I do not object when
she lifts me up. She is trembling, not entirely from the cold,
as we make our way through the city.

By the time we return to the office – my office – the sky
has brightened, a harsh grey light showing me the toll this
night has taken on her. She is too young for this life. Too
young for such dangers, but she has not had many options.
Besides, she is smart, this girl. And I have trained her well.

'I'm glad they got Diamond Jim,' she says as we settle into the couch. I curl up beside her, purring from the sheer pleasure of being still. Remembering that other time, that other life. 'He deserves to go to prison for life. Actually, he deserves worse.' We are quiet for a bit, and I wonder what she is thinking of. Of the old man, who loved her so. Or of Tick, whom she could not save.

'At least Bushwick got what he deserves,' she says again, her voice growing sleepy. 'That bastard.' She is fading. 'I never knew he had it in him to be so cruel. To demand . . .' She falls silent and I know what she is thinking. To demand a death. A tribute. A blood price. 'I'm going to keep after Tick, though. I'm going to find . . .' Her breathing becomes even and slow and I begin to drowse. We are at peace. We are safe. Now, perhaps, I can let go. To surrender to the pain, the fatigue. To the wear of an age and a battle that is now finally done.

Done. I wake with a start, jumping to all four feet, my fur on end and new energy coursing through me. An impression of drowning has come to me. Of sinking into deep waters, into death, as three men look on. Two goons, yes, but a third man – cold-eyed and silent. A man who inspired fear – fear unto death – and who was not there to be taken, to be killed. A master whose mark made all happen. Who will, as Bushwick knew, be angry. Who will be looking for the one who alerted the authorities. For a girl and a little boy.

I am not done here, not yet, and I will stay. I am a cat, and I have one life left.